WAVES
ALIGNING

WAVES
ALIGNING

Dear Anna,
I hope all your
Waves keep Aligning for a
Smooth Sail

By Adaora O

Matador
9 Priory Business Park,
Wistow Road, Kibworth Beauchamp,
Leicestershire. LE8 0RX
Tel: 0116 279 2299
Email: books@troubador.co.uk
Web: www.troubador.co.uk/matador
Twitter: @matadorbooks

ISBN 978 1789018 714

British Library Cataloguing in Publication Data.
A catalogue record for this book is available from the British Library.

Printed and bound in Great Britain by 4edge Limited
Typeset in 11pt Sabon MT by Troubador Publishing Ltd, Leicester, UK

Matador is an imprint of Troubador Publishing Ltd

To every human swimming against the tides.

1

H ALF AWAKE, CHINNY FROWNED AT THE FIRST CROW THAT always heralded the start of her day. Since she turned seven years old, she had always dreamt about a day when she would be able to sleep for as long as she liked. In her opinion, the cry of the supercilious cock always telling her it was time to pull her frame off the bed and begin her day did not signal a happy life. Her discomfort with life as she knew it grew progressively and today, ten-year-old Chinny not only wished she slept longer, but also looked forward to when she would go to the city and become one of those sophisticated ladies in the magazines which Ejiofor, her friend of eight years, brought back home at Easter and Christmas.

She cried so hard on the 4th of January as she watched Ejiofor go after his mother and sister into his father's car, on their way back to the city after the Christmas holidays. For days, the tightness in her chest and the lump in her throat refused to go away as she recalled her friend, waving through the window, saying, "Clean your eyes o? We will come back at Easter o?" For some inexplicable reason, Ejiofor believed adding 'o?', a local variant of 'okay?', at the end of every statement provided the warm blanket of comfort needed for any situation. This often confused Chinny because, on most occasions, it only made the warm blanket feel wet and heavy.

Chinny almost jumped out of her skin as the second crow rang through the air. She had to wake up. The cock, as usual, did not show any signs of getting off her case anytime soon. So, although every cell in her body shrank in protest, she hauled her frame out of bed. Her father Dede had cleared his throat once and his next reaction would be to reward her with an incentive for having second thoughts about their early morning devotion. It often came wrapped in a curt slap on her back or a nearly hard knock on her head. However, once Chinny made it to her parents' room for the morning prayers, she seldom remembered the sting of the light slap or knock recently served her, since prayer time for Chinny only provided a change in location for courting the concluding part of her sleep time. 'Sleep courting time' served as a psychological cocoon that spared Chinny the agony of sacrificing precious sleep time on the altar of morning prayers. But the lifespan of her cocoon suffered an unforeseen end, many thanks to her mother's bright idea of alternating who led the songs often sung in worship before the Bible reading and prayers. To say that this turn of events did not go down well with Chinny would barely scratch the surface of the depth of her torture. In her opinion, her brother's more than occasional absence from home blessed him with the evasion of this painful morning drill.

With the prayers over, Chinny wore her ankle-length kaftan, picked up her chewing stick from the cup on the stool beside her six-spring bed and headed out. It was time for the first of her four trips to Mr Oko's house. He installed a brand-new borehole two days ago, which meant clean water just came closer to home but at a price. As soon as she opened the door, the eastern early morning harmattan chill, typical of the month of January, slapped hard across her face.

"Chimoooooo!" Chinny exclaimed dramatically, calling out on God for help in the eastern Nigerian dialect – Igbo – in the way she always did when met with anything shocking. Stepping back and quickly shutting the door, she went to her room to pick up a wrapper from beneath her pillow. Now snugly wrapped, she headed out again, took a bucket from the side of the house and walked off to fetch her first bucket of water for the day. As she chewed vigorously on her stick, she thought, *Next week, I will buy myself a toothbrush and toothpaste. Ejiofor says they are better for cleaning the teeth.* She trod along but this time with a determined bounce, forgetting the harmattan chill that was still very present.

"Chi," as her mother called her, "is this your third bucket?" Chinny poured out the bucket of water into the drum beside the kitchen door.

"Fourth Nne'm," she responded. Chinny always referred to her parents or anyone she held dear as 'Nne'm' or 'Nna'm', depending on their gender, meaning 'my mother' or 'my father' respectively.

"You must stop before you pull out your arm from its socket. I have told you to always carry this bucket on your head. It is a lot easier," her mother chided.

Chinny gave an over-emphasised nod and with a playful glare said, "Thank you! You want my head to fall into my body, so I can look like Sempe the village clown's twin? The heavens forbid!" Ama smiled fondly at her daughter's awareness of beauty. Chinny typified beauty by all standards. More refreshing to Ama was the almost equal allotment of time her daughter gave to her quest to enhance her beauty and her pursuit for an enriched mind. She wondered if fate would be more kindly to her daughter than it had been to her.

As the weeks went by, the evening breeze became less brutal than its morning counterpart. The shadows came out to play and Ama dished the okra soup she just prepared with the antelope meat Dede bought on his way back from work. Tonight, his favourite soup would go with cornmeal. Before now, cassava meal always accompanied soups in the Onas' residence. But since Chinny came across a piece of information in one of Ejiofor's books, she took to opting for soup alone for dinner. The book claimed that cassava meals contained four times the starch found in cornmeal dishes. It took weeks of Chinny's near starvation for Ama to find out the reason behind her child's behaviour. Today, her parents thanked her for this enlightenment. It was now clear why the entire Ona household bid farewell to cassava meals. They since observed that getting out of bed in the mornings following a dinner of cassava meal always required considerable physical, emotional and mental effort, compared to the mornings after cornmeal and soup.

Ama secretly admired her daughter's interest in the nicer things of life. She set the plate of cornmeal and okra soup on the tray and called out, "Chi! Ask your father if he would prefer eating inside or outside."

"Inside," Chinny shouted after a couple of seconds and went to take in the tray to the dining room where they all settled for dinner. Dede did not say much as he ate. He could be described as a man of deep introspection, but today's silence indicated that something worried him. Ama suspected her husband now considered himself a failure as the head of the home and his steady withdrawal confirmed her suspicion.

They ate in silence, relishing Ama's good cooking. Brooding mind or not, Dede's taste buds were in excellent working condition.

"Nna'm?" Chinny ruffled the silence.

"Yes, my child," said Dede while chewing with relish on a piece of meat.

"Remember you told me I would go back to secondary school this year?" Her voice bubbled with excitement.

"Mmhh." Dede nodded, grating the meat between his molars. There were soft tendons in this piece of meat and Dede liked tendon-wired meat in particular. Ama guessed that the reason for her husband's meat preference might be economically motivated. Tendon-wired meat cost soothingly less than lean meat. Chinny reminded her father that school resumed two weeks ago and told him of the soon-closing payment window. She wanted to return to school to begin class two.

Mrs Johnson, the school principal, had told Chinny to stay home and promised to reserve a spot for her until her father paid her school fees. This was after Chinny showed up at the school gate for five consecutive days following her unceremonious withdrawal from school, only a couple of days before her class one third-term examinations. When Dede informed Mrs Johnson of his decision to withdraw his daughter from school, as her elder brother Dubem had finally passed his secondary school entrance examination, the school principal became confused and emotional. She argued that Chinny, being the brighter of his two children, stood a better chance at education. But Dede's decision was final and the fact that Chinny passed the entrance at one sitting while Dubem passed the same examination only after his third attempt did nothing to sway him.

"What do you want me to do?" he asked her, not really expecting an answer. "I can afford to send only one child to school. Knowing that formal education is the only way to succeed in life, would you consider my picking the female over the male a wise choice? There is a high probability of her leaving to start her own home as a woman soon, married to a man who may someday tell her to remain at home and care for his children irrespective of how much money her father has spent sending her to school."

Mrs Johnson had no defence but tried a final shot. "But there have been male children who turned out to be irresponsible men, refusing to be useful to themselves, their families or society. Their level of education or the lack of it regardless," she said. That was it! He was pitching his tent in his son's favour.

How dare this woman imply that my son would be a failure? Dede thought as he stormed out of the principal's office.

With the nagging issue of which child to send to school put to rest, Dede went home happy, not realising that while his day had just turned cheery, the rest of Mrs Johnson's was spent in depression. Chinny was a special child, being a girl notwithstanding. If her hands were not spilling with the responsibility of caring for her own children after her husband decided to live out the rest of his days with her former housemaid, abdicating the responsibility of caring for their four children, she would have taken Chinny under her own wings.

"Eeh? Nna'm?" Chinny shook Dede out of his reverie, her face aglow with dreams and hopes of fulfilling them. Her often boisterous disposition made it difficult for Dede and Ama to feel the absence of their son Dubem, who had just started his secondary education in Udu town.

Dede's next words were as sharp as a million needles, descending in savage brutality on his daughter's heart which, before now, was a brightly coloured balloon, inflated to its maximum capacity and content to float over the sunny field of life. She looked on with sad eyes as her father told her he still did not have the funds to send her back to school. "The money I make from the sawdust factory is not enough to cater for you and your brother. I do not want to bite more than I can chew," said Dede in a choked and resigned voice.

"But Nn... nna'm... nna'm, I... I... I got the admission first. I was already in class one before... before Dubem passed his own exams," Chinny stuttered. Her sockets gave way to her emotions as the tears began to pour unrestrained. Ama's eyes brimmed over while she cleared their dinner dishes. "Nne'm, please explain to Father. I will not need to pay boarding fees!" Chinny implored her mother's retreating figure, her cracking voice echoing in the quiet living room. When her mother looked back with a tear-stained face at her daughter and continued to the kitchen in quick steps, Chinny's eyes became like those of a kitten in the sudden company of many poodles. She turned back to her father and began in a rushed voice to explain. "Mrs Johnson. Mrs J… Johnson, she said I can go to school from her house. Nna'm, please understand. I really want to go to school." She paused, her eyes wide with expectation as her father's head hung in thought. But a while later, he shook his head and mumbled that even the tuition without the boarding fees would be the last straw to break the proverbial camel's back. Chinny cried out in exasperation and ran off to her bedroom to cry some more.

Angry sobs escaped her clenched mouth. With her face buried in her pillow to muffle the sound, Chinny slid between emotions. Hatred. Pity. Anger. She tried the blame game. Why did her brother take up her slot? But try as she did, Chinny could not invite Dubem into her 'blame-party'. She remembered he seemed reluctant to go to school. He took it a notch higher and begged their father to allow her to remain in school while he found a way to defer his admission. Dede's response to his son's suggestion was a resounding slap across the face.

It was unfair for her parents to decide who went to school based on the size of their pockets. They should create bigger pockets. "If Father had a decent job like Ejiofor's, he would not have been in this dilemma," she moaned.

Thinking about her mother made Chinny more frustrated. Better formal education thrown in the mix of her mother's life experiences would certainly make a difference. Without a certificate of any form, Chinny thought it impracticable for her mother to get a job that did not require her sitting at a stall for hours, beckoning on disinterested people to buy fast-wilting vegetables. Why in the world didn't she go to school? Desperate for answers, Chinny grasped at straws of logic before she turned the blame on herself. Her unreasonable ambition stared her in the face. She would concentrate on constructive ways to increase the extra income she already added to that of the family and, if fate smiled on them, there would be enough funds for her schooling. But until then, the song about going to school would become one to be hummed to herself alone. Her decision brought more pain to her chest and drew fresh and fast-flowing tears from her eyes. Defeat hung over Chinny's entire being like an imposed oversized cloak.

Stopping herself from drowning in her own thoughts, Chinny suddenly sat up and, with the back of her hands, wiped the tears away from her eyes. She began to tap the pad of her right foot in that fast and animated rhythm always indicative of a bright idea lurking in the corner of her mind. Rubbing off the last trace of tears from her face, she broke into a half-smile as she got up and took out a box of books from under her bed.

Ama walked into her daughter's room just as she sat back in her bed and a startled Chinny shifted and threw her cover cloth over the box.

"Are you still crying?" Ama asked her favourite little girl.

"No Nne'm." Chinny braved a smile.

Ama moved the poorly concealed box of books away to sit beside her daughter. Putting her arms around her she said, "I know how you feel child. I felt the same way a long time ago. You know, my father was wealthy in his day and as the only girl among his three children, he doted on me. He belonged to the unpopular few who believed all children were created equal by God. This made him decide to give me as many opportunities as my brothers got. Through him, I understood the true value of being a child and learnt to pay no heed to anyone or anything suggesting otherwise. This stance did not afford my father many faithful friends. And like my mother said, even though they hated and jeered at the values he stood for, calling him a fool behind his back, they presented themselves as friends for the gains they could get from associating with him. Of course, he was not foolish enough to believe everyone loved him. But being human, how few his true friends were, remained unclear to him.

"In due course, he sent me to his brother, four towns away from home to get a secondary education in a school considered the best school at the time. To cut the long story short, without telling my father, my uncle turned me into a food vendor at a construction site. He lied to my folks about what I was doing, while collecting funds from my father for my supposed education. He took all the money I made at the construction site. But that did not deter me. I read every educational book that I set my eyes on, hoping I would soon be sent to school. Four months after I left home for school, or so my family thought, my father set out to visit me, in spite of all the messages I sent home. In the letters

I sent, I told them of the wonderful progress I was making in school and asked my parents not to bother making the long journey as I lacked nothing in my uncle's house. Unknown to them, I never sent home any messages. My uncle made sure of that. All the letters my folks received were sent by him and his wicked wife. Sadly, my father did not get to his destination. He died in a car accident. It was during my unavoidable visit home for his burial that my uncle's mischief shone through his haze of deception. One puzzle yet to be solved to this day is that two days before the burial, my elder brother disappeared without a trace, leaving my mother, my younger brother and I to face my father's family alone. This left my mother shattered. She developed a stroke which she never recovered from and died three years later."

"Nne'm, you have never told me about this part of your life. I always wondered how you could talk a little like Ejiofor's mother even though you did not go to school. But why did your uncle do such a thing?" Chinny asked, sniffing back a sob.

"I realised years later that my uncle had always been envious of my father and actively sought ways to clip our wings and keep us in obscurity. His plan was to waste my time to such an extent that I would have no other option than to succumb to my fate and get married. Oh, he was almost successful!"

"Almost?" Chinny asked.

"Yes. My uncle got his way in part because we not only ran short of funds after my father's death, but I became too old to go back to school. To escape poverty, I got married to the first man that sought my hand – your father. But my uncle failed because I married the kindest man alive. Your father promised I would go back to school no matter my age, but you know life and its penchant for making puppets of man's plans. Chi, please do not hold any grudge. Your father is only making this choice because his hands are tied. He is afraid of taking a chance on you because he thinks the world is tipped in favour of the male child and may still push you around even if you are educated. Make no mistake – if the funds show up tomorrow, he will not hesitate to give you the best. He has my father's steel resolve but not his funds. At least not yet. His recent communication style is only a reflection of his frustrations. We are crushed that we cannot show you how much we care about you. Chi, please do not hate us. I promise you, we are thinking of ways to make it better. Believe me, we are."

Chinny looked at her mother with eyes that reflected wisdom beyond her years and nodded. "Yes Mother, I know Father loves me and is doing his best, but I also know something else… no matter what, I will be somebody important one day." Ama wiped away the two tear drops that stole down her daughter's right cheek and smiled her admiration. She held Chinny in a hug for a seemingly endless moment. Afterwards, Ama headed for the door but paused. She wanted to know how or where Chinny got all those books from. Disappointed in herself for doing such a poor job at hiding her box, Chinny told her mother that the books belonged to Ejiofor. He gave her all his school books at the end of every session.

Regardless of the odds standing before her, Chinny made up her mind to aim for the stars. She settled in bed on her belly and began to read one of the many books in the box – *English Made Fun Book Two*. With Easter just a few weeks away, a spark lit her gloomy sky. Ejiofor and his family always came back to Abotiti village four days before Easter Sunday. So, Chinny not only slept like a well-fed and dry baby that night, but carried on sleeping through all the nights preceding Easter like the entire universe had not a single worry to offer her.

As soon as Kika saw Dede heading towards him, he tucked the Naira notes he was counting into his pocket with the stealth of a trained sniper. If there was something Kika could not share, it was his money. Not even with his younger brother Dede.

When Dede got to his brother's mini courtyard, he greeted him with the customary half hug and pretended he did not notice his mid-morning accounting. Kika smiled from ear to ear at Dede, for even though he could not share his notes with anyone, he loved his younger brother almost with the love of a father. Offering Dede a seat, he asked what he could serve him with an even bigger smile. Kika prided himself on the completion of his beautiful three-bedroom bungalow. The sitting room was always locked with a key, which he kept in his bedside cabinet. His wife, Violet, shared a room with their daughter Adaiba, while their two sons stayed in a second room when they were around. They managed their father's spare-parts business in the next town. The third room served as Kika's own mini palace. The only time Dede challenged his brother about his style of home governance proved to be a huge mistake – they kept malice for two weeks.

"What can we offer you?" Kika asked again when his brother seemed not to have heard him the first time. Dede shook his head and informed his brother that he came to discuss something of great concern. "What is it brother?" Kika asked, consternation etched all over him. Dede confided in his brother about the dilemma he found himself in, regarding his daughter's education.

"She is quite intelligent. You know she passed the secondary entrance at one sitting? Looking at her daily has been extreme torture for me since I withdrew her from school. It is almost as though I am limiting her because she is a girl. Ever since I told her that she would still not be able to resume school this session, I have died of guilt a little more each day. If only my resources were enough for the two of them, I—"

Kika interjected, "But you are only being wise. Nobody will expect you to invest in a girl's education and leave the boy, when we all know that in no time she would end up in a man's house. A man that can even order her not to care for her own parents. Besides that, a female is what she is – a female who is weak. How much can she achieve with an education? A boy on the other hand can stretch his ambitions and with an education, his possibilities are limitless. Since you can only afford to send one child to school, I say choose Dubem and let Chinny do something else like restaurant business, hairdressing or tailoring."

Dede sighed. "Honestly, the child who will care for me in my old age is the last thing on my mind. What I want is a legacy for my two children regardless of their gender and the best legacy any father can give his children is the exposure and empowerment an education provides. I think I am failing Chinny because she is my second child, a girl child who will not carry my name forever. What is in a name or gender anyway? Look at me... the only reason I lost my job as supervisor at the Southern Railway Line is because Papa believed I could still manage with a pass in mathematics. Had he given me the money to re-sit just that one subject, I would not have been among those selected to be relieved of their duties when the railway line experienced financial challenges. Now, here I am in the village, cutting trees and sawing wood to make sawdust for poultry farmers. Meanwhile some of my female co-workers retained their jobs because they passed mathematics with credits." The emphasis Dede placed on 'female' drew a sheepish smile from his brother.

Still not swayed by Dede's reasoning, Kika said, "The issue here is that you do not have the money to send two children to school, simple! Do you want to kill yourself? I find it tough, scraping around to send Adaiba my daughter to school, and between you and me, when it becomes too hard to bear, she will go and marry like her other mates. By the way, you talk about returning to the village as if it is such a terrible thing. What about those of us who never left and consolidated here? I did not do too badly as a village champion, did I?" The two men burst into hearty laughter as Kika called out to his wife to get them some refreshments. Violet had been hovering indoors, making herself scarce. She sensed the men were discussing something of extreme importance.

2

A FEW HARMATTAN SEASONS LATER AND WITH CHANGE BEING AN unavoidable part of time, trips to Mr Oko's house for water no longer featured in Chinny's early morning routine. Clean water now flowed through the taps in the Onas' home. Chinny counted the money in her piggy bank made from an empty milk can; 35,700 Naira. Looking just like a cat who drank all the warm milk, she put away her money but not before Ama came in.

"You should open a bank account soon. It is not safe to keep this amount of money in the house. Anything can happen – thieves, flood, fire…"

Before her mother could go on in her wild journey down doom's lane, Chinny raised her right hand, making an exaggerated circle over and around her head in a superstitious motion to push away ill luck and said, "God forbid! It is not my portion." The dread of losing her money filled Chinny each time she thought about how much sweat trickled down her nape as she earned it. Chinny learnt to make soap, which she supplied to her customers. Though she always told them her product could be used to wash clothes and dishes, never to be trusted for their skins, they bought large quantities anyway. This, in addition to a few other odd jobs she did, fetched her substantial money. Ama found her daughter's gesture comical and told her to think seriously about that bank account as she left for the monthly market meeting. About to float away in her world of novels, Chinny made a mental note to open a bank account as soon as possible. She knew it was no use wishing ill luck away without a commensurate effort on one's part. The words she always threw at Adaiba, her cousin, echoed in her head, 'The reason God put a brain and not custard in the human skull is not to occupy space, but to promote thinking.'

With the Clarkes' home-coming to Abotiti to mark the yearly celebrations now a tradition, Chinny could bet all the money in her piggy bank on Ejiofor's bear hug on her birthday, which often fell around Easter. Only once, and a long time ago too, did the Clarkes pass on spending Christmas in the village. The usual wit and cordial banter Chinny enjoyed with her best friend only came in the letter he sent through Adaiba on her way back from the city, after her vacation at her aunt's. The letter said the Clarkes were going to England for Christmas. She took out the five-year-old letter from underneath her mattress to read again and recalled how her disappointment gradually slid into acceptance, then elation at the prospect of Ejiofor going to the place they both had only read about and seen on the television. The smile that began to form around her mouth faded a fraction when she got to the part where Ejiofor wrote about hoping to study in a university in Europe. Here she was, still grasping for a secondary education while her friend's wishful thought of many years ago seemed to be turning into a reality. Ejiofor had plans of not only going to university, but to one miles away from her. Not wanting a dampener on her mood, she tucked the letter away. She had a seventeenth birthday get-together to plan, and Easter was in a week.

"Chinny!!!" Dede's voice rang through the calm of noon.

"Yes Father!" She skipped out in response.

"Your mother has gone to her stall, so you need to clean the fish I bought. Make peppered fish soup for dinner."

Chinny headed for the kitchen instantly but stopped mid-way. "Nna'm, maybe I can make it after I return from work since it is for dinner."

"Okay my child." Dede seldom disagreed with his daughter's line of thought and he tried his best not to make it obvious this time. So he added, "But hurry back so we do not have a late dinner. Remember you told us that if we eat our dinner late, we will all die. I am going back to the shop." Chinny laughed long and hard at her father's comical interpretation of her advice that eating dinner too late into the night

13

caused a gathering of stomach fat, which a team of researchers claimed to be a contributing factor to certain diseases. She went back to her room to get dressed and missed the look of admiration in her father's eyes.

Dede's heart welled up with sheer pride at who his daughter had grown to become. He drew inspiration from the way she handled the disappointments in her life. Rather than moan over his unfulfilled promises, by age eleven Chinny began taking jobs to gather funds for herself, her lively spirit undeterred. She reflected the true image of what any human being should be, taking huge obstacles as mere blocks to be removed, walked over or walked around. As he drove back to his shop, Dede made a decision. He had a plan for his daughter and would discuss it with Ama later in the evening.

Decked in a pair of boot-legged denim trousers and a halter-necked African print top, Chinny looked amazingly beautiful for a seventeen-year-old young lady. Her mother's good genes could take credit for Chinny's smooth matte-black skin, but the extra glow could only be explained by her unrepentant love for fruits and nuts. Chinny appreciated healthy eating but did not mind at all if she went to bed on a stomach full of almond nuts and oranges. She spent hours picking the fruits that fell from the many almond trees in her father's compound. Once done eating the succulent fruits, she sun-dried the large seeds to crack them open afterwards for their delicious nuts. For a long time, Chinny referred to the large fruits by their popular name – 'fruit' – until Ejiofor not only told her they were called almonds but showed her a picture of one in his *Science Is Discovery Book One*. Only then did she re-christen her dear 'fruit'.

Ready for her day's activity, Chinny pulled out her wooden truck. This truck radiated class. It wore a multi-coloured duvet fabric, which made it not only appealing, but comfortable to sit on. Strips of coloured ribbons also dangled on its two handles. A small rubber ball attached to the right handle let out a chime whenever pressure was applied. As she pushed the truck out of the gate, Chinny moved with the grace of a queen. The lovely flat shoes Ejiofor's mother gave to her last Christmas took credit for the extra bounce in her steps this hot afternoon. She paused for a moment to reach for some mint drops from her back pocket and, popping one disc of coolness into her mouth, she wheeled away in rebellion against the menacing sun.

At ten minutes past two o'clock in the afternoon, Chinny arrived at the Future Bright Primary School. She sighted Rufus, the school's security guard, from a distance and even though she considered him a bit of a chatterbox, his conversations in Nigerian pidgin always left her thoroughly amused. She greeted him with a warm "Good afternoon Mr Rufus."

Rufus looked up from the paper in his hands and beamed. *"My friend how naa?"*

"Fine oo!" Chinny replied, in a gallant attempt to match her friend's speaking style. Rufus' face showed his delight on seeing Chinny, but she noticed how fast he went back to poring over the paper in his hand and decided to be a bother. With a naughty glint in her eyes, she chided, "Ha Rufus! Did I not see you betting last week? What happened? Did you not win any money?" She was referring to Rufus' favourite pastime of playing the local lottery, called 'pool betting'. Rufus replied in the negative but soon had an ear-to-ear grin as he informed Chinny of the breakthrough permutation technique he learnt the day before, from a fellow player who won last week's jackpot. Rufus was doubly sure the technique – if applied properly – would make all the difference in his life. He believed that this time, he would 'hit it big'.

He tilted the paper towards Chinny, pointing to a group of numbers on it, and continued, his eyes alight with excitement. *"You see this one eeh? I don pam am. In fact, the money wey I go drop for this game na times three of the money wey I drop last week. This one na sure banker."* By now, Chinny reeled with laughter at the lack of wisdom reflected by her friend's plan to bet three times the amount he bet on the lottery the week before.

"RUFUS! You will finish your last month's salary! How much did you bet last week?"

Rufus hesitated before deciding that telling her posed a risk to his peace of mind. *"I no go tell you. You go tell my wife,"* he said.

Chinny shook her head in denial and assured him of her silence on the matter. "Never! I will not tell her. After all you did not win and besides, last week has passed." He regarded her for a while and with a lame grin, Rufus informed her that he placed a bet of 1,200 Naira last week. Chinny shook her head in pity at the unassuming soul called Rufus. Her next words took Rufus by surprise. "Mr Rufus, have you wondered why that man who won the bet last week does not want to win again this week since he knows the '*pam*' to *combine*?"

It took moments for Rufus to digest her words before in a moment of epiphany he opened his mouth in realisation. "*Na true you talk oo! E be like say this thing na luck oo!*"

The school bell went off and Chinny cast a quick glance at one of the school's blocks, then returned her attention to Rufus. "Yes, I speak the truth and if you have good plans for your two beautiful children, you will put an end to your get-rich-quick schemes and try saving up." Just then, amidst the children milling out of their classes, four children spanning ages three to five spotted Chinny and ran towards her with unmistakable glee. "Easy, no running, be careful," Chinny called out as she attempted to steady them. She reeled out the questions. "Did you enjoy school? Did you finish all your snacks? Who got everything in class today?" She picked each one of them up and sat them on the truck. Chinny feigned a tantrum when they informed her that they ate up all their snacks. Rufus looked on with a smile. Now comfortable with the children's sitting positions, Chinny made to wheel away, but paused and turning to Rufus said, "You know you are a very rich man?"

He denied it very quickly. "*Me? Nooooo! I be poor man oo.*"

Chinny laughed ever so softly and continued, "You are rich because only a rich man can bring out 3,600 Naira to make better the course of another man's life all in the name of playing pool." With that, Chinny wheeled away.

A shocked and speechless Rufus neither heard nor acknowledged the chants of "Goodbye Mr Rufus" ringing out from the children. He suddenly snapped out and called out to Chinny's retreating figure, "*Wait! How you take know how much I go bet this week?*"

Without as much as a backward glance, she waved. "Bye bye Mr Rufus."

Hands akimbo, Rufus kept his eyes on her and shaking his head, muttered in complete wonder and admiration, "*Chaiii brain, brain, brain!!!*"

"'A' is for antelope, 'B' is for basket, 'C' is for coconut, 'D' is for donkey..." Chinny sang while Eniola repeated after her. As the only child left on the truck, Eniola, or Eni as she was called by those charmed by her disposition, now looked like a little princess being transported in her own carriage. She reminded Chinny of another Eniola, a little girl she ferried a few years ago, but unlike Eni she had been nicknamed Nini by those who were fond of her. Now in primary four, Eniola Okoye or Nini remained an absolute charmer. With the sun's unbearable wrath descending on her, Chinny made a note to pay Nini a visit one of these days and started a trot on the dirt road leading to Eni's house. Eni was in her second term in primary one and as each day slid by, Chinny feared that a separation lurked in the corners, since at the end of the third term in primary one, every child would have assumed a considerable level of independence and would no longer need to be ferried to and from school by her. This served as another source of funds for the education Chinny so pined for. She identified parents who did not have the time or who were reluctant to take their children to school every day and sold a service to them. She would pick their children up in her fancy truck, take them to school and when school was over, bring them back to their parents' home, store or restaurant at a fee of 25 Naira daily. Some parents owed her occasionally, but they always paid their debts. Though keen on the money she made, Chinny experienced more fulfilment knowing she featured in another child's fighting chance at education.

"Miss Chinny, Miss Chinny! Why am I always the last one to get home?" the little girl asked. Chinny rolled her eyes in exaggerated exasperation and dug into her reserves for an *acceptable* answer.

"Well Eni, it is because I like to stay with you the longest."

"Why?" Eni pressed. Chinny laughed because she expected the 'why' question. The little princess on her afternoon cruise seemed quite pleased when she learnt that she always got home last because she was not just beautiful but also special, and Chinny liked to show her off to many more people. The rest of the trip went on in relaxed silence with

Chinny lost in thought and Eni, who now tired of sightseeing, nestled to her side and fast asleep. As soon as Mrs Badmus sighted the truck, she put away the eggs she had just collected from the cage, rinsed her hands under the tap beside her poultry cage and carried the sleeping child into the house, all at whirlwind speed. While Chinny waited for Mrs Badmus to come back out, she dusted off the sand and grass that had accumulated in her truck or 'cart' as she liked to call it. Eniola's mother thanked Chinny as she handed her the due fare. Chinny bade the woman goodbye and hurried home. Peppered fish soup for dinner hung in the balance.

On wheeling into the compound, Chinny spotted her father washing the Volkswagen car he called his 'jewel'. After his wife, his children and four-bedroom bungalow, in that order, it was the fourth-best thing to happen to him. While still in the middle of furnishing the bungalow to taste and negotiating to share a plot of land in the city with a friend, where he would build another bungalow, Dede suffered redundancy from work. He vacated the official apartment he previously occupied with his family in the city and returned to an unfinished bungalow in Abotiti village. Her husband's redundancy meant an automatic halt of Ama's contract of supplying lunch at the railway company. Dede's head of department never forgave her for beating his wife in the 'taste and bid' exercise, which delivered the contract into her hands in the first place. She admired her husband's strength through that period and supported him while they made the best of what life dumped on them – an unfinished bungalow could not be compared to Dede's father's dilapidated house.

Chinny greeted her father and parked her cart beside the house. She moved gingerly to avoid the water running down the concrete floor as her father scrubbed away at the wheels of his car. "How are the famous four?" Dede asked, wanting to know how his daughter's day went. He once referred to Chinny's current student-passengers as the 'famous four' and the alias had stuck since then. Chinny liked the sound of the name. She let out a soft chuckle and told him her passengers were doing great. In one quick move, Chinny removed the duvet from the cart to reveal the wooden structure. She got a big bowl from the back of the house and fetched some water with the hose her father was using.

The hose easily became his makeshift pressure washer by pressing his thumb over half of the pipe's opening. Adding some detergent from the pack lying beside the tap into the bowl of water, Chinny submerged the duvet, all the while humming a happy tune. After pulling the now heavy bowl to the side of the house, right beside the cart, she went into the kitchen through the back door to prepare dinner. She was done cutting the fish into thin slices when she remembered something. She washed her hands and cleaned them on the back of her denim trousers. From the chest freezer, Chinny took out six sachets of drinkable water, popularly called 'pure water'. For those who considered bottled drinkable water to be on the unreachable side of the living standards divide, 'pure water' presented a more affordable alternative.

She often questioned the purity of 'pure water' and wondered if they would become cheaper if the word 'pure' did not appear on the sachets and they were just called 'water'. They were all frozen rock-hard. She rinsed off a bowl and dropped all six sachets into it, hoping they thawed out before dinner.

They still did not own a refrigerator which, truth be told, currently sat pretty near the bottom of their priority list of things to buy. Eternally grateful for the chest freezer they got as their tenth-year wedding anniversary gift from Mr and Mrs Clarke, the Onas had come to accept freezing and thawing water in sachets as a fixture in preparation for meal times in their home. Chinny went back to cleaning the fish with some salt. She spiced it and put it on the stove to cook.

Not one to leave a meal lonely, she peeled the pineapple fruit sitting in the improvised pantry which Dubem and her father had carved out of the passageway leading from the kitchen to the backyard. Since it was a wide enough passage, they fixed some wooden shelves to the wall where fruits, onions, yams, potatoes and bottles of cooking oil were stored.

Right after Chinny set the plate of diced pineapple on the dining table, she went into her bedroom where her biology textbook caught her attention. Before long she became captivated by the illustration of the life cycle of the butterfly. It made sense to Chinny for the first time. After all these years, it occurred to her that the pupa, while appearing dormant, must have put a lot of effort into developing, and even more determination and hard work into cracking its hard shell before emerging as the most beautiful spectacle of creation. The sound of a door opening and closing startled Chinny out of her analytical journey.

She came out to the sitting room to see her mother walk in, with her father following closely. Ama looked beautiful and radiant in an orange-coloured print dress, fitted at the top but flared from her waist, all the way down to play around her ankles. False buttons ran from her neck to her mid-section, which held no tell-tale signs of childbirth, and her full hair stood tamed in one bunch by a matching hair tie. She looked gorgeous. Although it suited Ama to wear her hair in its natural form, Chinny could not boast of being endowed with her mother's hair genes. While Ama's hair came extra soft from infancy, her daughter was not quite as fortunate and therefore, had no real reason for her refusal to take the easy way out of simply stretching her hair. She was only being a mimic. But after one year of the sheer pain of combing through tough knots, thanks to her father's coarse creeper-plant-type hair, Chinny decided she had made her point of being proudly black and African. She would let her skin shade do the rest of the point-making.

"Welcome Nne'm," Chinny greeted her mother. Their cheeks touched briefly in that affectionate way. They were now about the same height. Ama handed her daughter the solid corn pudding wraps, popularly called *agidi,* which she had bought. Soon after, they settled down to dinner. This typified Chinny's typical day – nothing out of the ordinary. Just the plain old daily grind, save for the mounting excitement that welled up inside her. In a couple of months, she would sit for her general certificate examination. She registered to take the examination as a private student since she was self-schooled. All through the years, Chinny schooled herself with the aid of the books and past question papers that Ejiofor handed down to her and now considered herself ready to sit the examinations.

Easter was here again. Chinny opened the door to see Ejiofor standing on the porch with a huge grin. She squealed as they locked in a bear hug. It was twenty-five minutes after six in the evening and Dede sat relaxed on the porch, eating a plate of roasted breadfruit after he was done washing his Volkswagen Beetle. Ejiofor did not look bad for a twenty-year-old. He had become the bloke every girl wanted to associate with. It did not pose such a tough ride for him because he had evolved into a courteous and diplomatic young man. He related well with almost everyone, possessing the unique ability to compartmentalise each one. There were the social friends – the ones he exchanged birthday cards and graduation party invites with. The academic friends – he interacted with these ones on an intellectual level, but some of them managed to slide into the social friends' section. He had his close friends' compartment. This was for the friends who were even closer than his immediate family. With these friends, he shared his hopes, fears, dreams, joys and tears. This compartment had housed just one person for as long as he could remember. Ejiofor often referred to Chinny as his twin who lost her way at conception.

The friendship between Chinny and Ejiofor promoted a strong and cordial relationship between the two families, the benefits of which the Onas could not help but feel were tipped in their own favour, as they could afford to show the Clarkes no more than kindness when the occasion demanded. The only times the Onas felt any sense of accomplishment about their relationship with them were when they were able to gather fruits, plantains and fire-smoked fish for the Clarkes' journey back to Enugu after their Christmas or Easter break in the village.

Ejiofor and Chinny had been talking for a while when Chinny remembered the white yam she set on the stove to boil and ran off to the kitchen to check on it. Ejiofor followed her and watched as she pierced the yam with a fork to check that it was cooked. She strained the water from the pot before sprinkling a dash of salt on the boiled yam. "Is Dubem around?"

Chinny hesitated but answered, "No. He sent word that he had school work to catch up on. I think he flunked most of his papers last term. I guess it will have to be till Christmas." Her voice was rushed as she tried hard to hide her almost spilling emotions.

"What will the yam go with?" Ejiofor tried to cut through the mounting tension.

"Beef stew." Chinny took the clue, happy to evade the beckoning arms of gloom as she opened the smaller pot sitting on the second burner to reveal the stew.

In the mood for some friendly banter, Ejiofor asked, "Who made this stew? And no lies."

With her right hand on her hip, a slight tilt of the head and a smirk, Chinny retorted, "What exactly are you playing at?" She pulled him to her father for a testimony of her culinary mastery.

Dede, who since doing justice to his snacks now sat in the living room, listening to the evening news, could not help his amusement at their banter but was quick to inform Ejiofor that contrary to his assertion that Chinny could only boil eggs and yams, she knew her onions when it came to cooking skills. Pleased at the testament, even though Ejiofor said he still needed another witness before he could change his opinion, Chinny curtsied and took her leave with the gait of a peacock. The smile on Dede's face stayed on, long after the duo bantered back to the kitchen. He admired their long-standing friendship and wondered if it was the forever kind. His old head did not allow him the comfort of the delusion that their class gap would not ultimately widen beyond scope if he was not able to give his daughter the fighting chance she deserved. Amidst talk about Ejiofor's upcoming admission to the university, Chinny washed while Ejiofor rinsed the used pots and utensils.

Ama walked in and Ejiofor genuflected with a slight bend of his head and back. "Good evening ma."

"Eji, welcome. When did you return?" Ama's voice exuded fondness as she patted him gently on his lowered back.

Ejiofor beamed. "Late this afternoon ma." They barely sat down in the sitting room when the doorbell chimed. It was Ejiofor's younger sister, Zara, who had come with news of their Uncle Iyke's arrival.

As a project engineer, Iyke, Ejiofor's maternal uncle, worked with Drendon Petroleum. He specialised in building off-shore oil facilities for the world-class indigenous upstream and downstream company. With operations in various parts of Africa, North America and Europe, Iyke suffered countless transfers within and outside Africa.

Ejiofor promised to see Chinny the following day. He bade the Onas goodnight and skipped off to see his uncle. The last time they shook hands was two Easters ago.

A brand-new sports utility vehicle parked behind his father's car stood in impenitent splendour. Ejiofor wondered if his uncle had sold his old sports car before he acquired the impressive piece of work now on his father's patio. *There is no stopping Uncle Iyke and his machines*, he thought. In the house, the two men exchanged a firm handshake before locking in a hug. After dinner, everyone sat back to chat. Iyke talked about the new project keeping him busy at work. It was the construction of a compressed natural gas plant and a lot of work was involved. The project required his physical presence, especially at the preliminary stages where concrete thickness, pipe diameters and strict adherence to general structural designs needed tight supervision. Zara hung onto Iyke's every word while he talked about work. This did not come as a surprise to anyone since she intended to follow her uncle's professional path.

"Wow! It sounds like a lot of work, but fun all the same," she gushed, her eyes glassy with excitement.

"Yes," Iyke affirmed and continued. "It also means I must leave my base in Lagos for Bayelsa at least two times every month. I hope the project's life cycle is not stretched." But setbacks and undue hitches in Iyke's project were welcome to Chiaka Clarke, his sister. She hoped that they made her brother stay in Nigeria for as long as possible. She believed his closeness to home would end his 'single and actively searching' status. Iyke was thirty-two years old and Chiaka thought her younger brother was long overdue for marriage.

Later at night, after everyone else lay fast asleep in their beds, Iyke and Ejiofor settled down with a bowl of peanuts to watch *Indecent Proposal*. For no palpable reason other than perhaps in the spirit of 'movie-night' comradeship, Iyke confided in his nephew that he looked forward to shuttling between Lagos and Bayelsa. "I know that feeling! Exploring unfamiliar places, food, cultures… You know I should pay you a visit sometime and experience Bayelsa too. Never been there." Ejiofor's excitement shone through his rushed words and high-pitched whisper. Iyke nodded in agreement and added that shuttling between the two states also meant he could 'live free' in Bayelsa. The younger Mr Clarke shifted in his chair, gave his uncle a piece of advice and resumed giving the movie on the screen his full attention.

Iyke experienced a failed relationship four years ago, which slowly turned his once soft and naïve heart into an ugly chunk of ice. Even as Ejiofor told his uncle again that living free mapped out a dark slippery road to destruction, he saw the futility in his effort since his past pleas did nothing to stop countless innocent girls from paying for the hurt caused by another. Movie night ended at thirty minutes to midnight. Before Iyke went to his room, he told his nephew to strive to get it right the first time if he could. He believed that was Ejiofor's only ticket out of the looming 'mud-fight' for his heart. His tone dripped with solemnity.

Towards the end of breakfast time on Good Friday, Iyke was nowhere to be found around the house. Zara said she saw him go out on a stroll. Bemused at the prospect of strolling in the village so early in the morning before breakfast, Ejiofor walked out in search of him. *He could not have gone far. I'll just look around the compound*, he thought. His uncle was nowhere in sight, so he thought to peek outside the gate and was taken aback when he saw him talking with Chinny a few metres away. Waving cheerfully at Chinny, he made the eating gesture, mouthing food to his uncle who wrapped up his chat in a heartbeat to head back to the house.

In the evening of the same day, Chinny ran into Ejiofor at her father's gate. He had just left her house after being informed that she was not home. They began walking to Ejiofor's gate amid their usual chit chat. He asked if she was done reviewing the past question papers he gave to her. When she said she was, a rather pleased Ejiofor certified her examinations as good as successful. He then asked to know the date for her first paper. "I think sometime in October," came her uncertain answer. "You think?" Ejiofor scoffed. "Chinny, are you sure you want to make this happen?"

"I am, Ejiofor, but you know sometimes, the reality facing me is overwhelming."

Ejiofor appeared irritable. "What is this reality my dear Miss Ona?"

Chinny tried to put her thoughts into words. "Well... I ... You know, even if I sit for and pass my examinations, the money to do much with my certificate would not be available and that would just kill me." Ejiofor let out a snicker but looked contemplative.

"Secondly," Chinny continued, "People would find out I did not attend any secondary school... It would look like... like I got my certificate through the back door." Still no word from Ejiofor whose head now dipped further in thought. "Ehen," she went on,

24

"Somewhere in the corner of my mind, I also think that if I pass all my papers, it may put my parents under undue strain and guilt. Like the other day, I heard my father telling my mother of the bright idea he had, to make sure I went to a university. Guess what the idea was Eji? To sell his Volkswagen and timber shed! Thank God, my mother talked him out of it. She told him that whatever proceeds he got would not be nearly enough for my schooling and that his actions would effectively leave the whole family out in the cold – not enough to keep the family running and not enough to send Dubem and I to school."

Ejiofor had shutters over his eyes and seemed far away, but he returned with a bang. His words made Chinny bend over in loud and long laughter. "What was your discussion with Iyke about this morning?" he asked.

"E-ji-ofor! How did I not see that coming?" Chinny's voice rang out in humour. When her friend refused to share in her humour, she informed him that they had only been talking about her school plans. He wanted to know if she still intended to take the next GCE and had, on a lighter note, asked if the marriage proposals had started rolling in. "It was just a harmless friendly chat!" she chided in between bursts of laughter. By this time, Chinny and Ejiofor were back at the entrance to Chinny's compound. They stood in conversation for a while and started to walk back towards Ejiofor's home. They did this mostly when they had a lot to talk about.

"Chinny," began Ejiofor, "I think you have a lot of clutter around you."

"Like what?" she probed. Ejiofor hesitated before he continued, treading with caution. "Your transportation business." There was an undertone in Ejiofor's voice as he rushed on. "I wanted to pay for your GCE form, but you refused. Hey, my Uncle Iyke wanted to raise you some cash but you did not want to be indebted to anybody, let alone a man. Even when he asked you to consider it a loan, you adamantly refused. You seem to be having a ball at carrying children about in your glorified wheelbarrow rather than concentrating on garnering knowledge and exposure. Pushing that thing is not good for your arms. You are a girl for heaven's sa—"

"Now stop right there Ejiofor." Chinny's face became stern and her voice dropped to a whisper. Her eyes now sparkled, and Ejiofor knew this extra shine had nothing to do with excitement but everything to do with rage. "I have always looked up to you, not only as a friend but as a brother. Many times, even when in doubt of your judgement, I still went with it. Over the years, I learnt to let my guard down with you. The wall I built around myself to protect me from the intimidating odds stacked against me for being a female ceased to exist with you because I thought you saw me as a person, not as a female. I am awfully sorry you do not like my wheelbarrow business as you call it. But guess what? That wheelbarrow business is me embracing my current reality. I find fulfilment making sure little girls are given the chance to dare to dream. Little girls whose parents and guardians would have readily denied the most basic of educations with the excuse of lack of time and funds have been given the opportunity to find out what school tastes like. That way, they can make up their minds to fight for it or not." Pausing for a gulp of air, she went on, "Moreover, gathering as much funds as I can would not hurt a girl with my background. I try, God knows I try to immerse myself in as much knowledge and exposure as I can manage, given my prevailing circumstances and I will never stop. However, if I am too slow at it or if it seems chokingly embarrassing for you to hang out with the girl who pushes a glorified wheelbarrow for a living, you may very well look the other way. It would not be any different from being talked down to and being passed over for choosing the XX and not XY chromosomes."

Ejiofor's mouth hung open as his mind became a tangled mess. He could not tell how their chat degenerated into something that could now easily pass for a brawl. He curled his mouth with the intention of giving Chinny a piece of his mind, but because he stifled a bubble of laughter at the same time, a smile escaped and then the laughter bubbled through. He tried his best to stop but he found he could not and when Chinny could not take it any longer, she lashed out, "When you are done laughing, please tell me."

Ejiofor was able to rein in and with a face still contorted from laughing, he asked, "Choosing the XX chromosome? Chinny the babe!! Really?! Who told you anybody had a choice? Those chromosomes just happen in a zygote. You better go back to your biology or else you will flunk it butt-on-the-ground in your forthcoming examinations!"

"It was a slip of the tongue. I meant 'having' the chromosomes not 'choosing'." Chinny fought back for her ego.

Ejiofor laughed harder and chuckled, "A slip of the brain you mean." Chinny turned around and began walking towards her house. Not wanting to push his luck, Ejiofor backed off. What was it? Hell hath no fury like a woman scorned? "Hey!" Ejiofor called out. "Wait for me! I was just joking. Com'mon Chi!" Chinny did not react as though a fly buzzed. He tried harder for a reaction as he caught up with her. "How about those oranges you promised? Wait... truck pusher!" Ejiofor joked.

Not able to hold it in any longer, Chinny burst into laughter and said, "Coconut head, follow me if you are still interested." They could not stay mad at each other for too long. Moreover, Chinny's birthday was only one night away.

The conversation between Dede and an elderly man in his sixties suddenly stopped when Chinny and Ejiofor walked in. They said their greetings and headed for the kitchen to feast on oranges and the conversation between the two men resumed. Moments later, when they heard the visitor leave, Ejiofor took some oranges to Dede in the sitting room and thought he spotted a film of tears in Mr Ona's eyes. A while after, Chinny walked Ejiofor to the door, too engrossed in their chatter to notice her father's obvious gloom.

Dinnertime went by in silence. But that night, as Mr and Mrs Ona lay in bed, Ama knew all was not well with her husband. Not only was he turning in his sleep like a pregnant horse, she also noticed the absence of his snore. Ama tapped her husband on the shoulders and when Dede huffed, "Hmm? What?" in between sleep and wakefulness, she asked him if he was having a nightmare. He answered with a curt "No" and went back to sleep.

3

THE MORNING SUN TORE THROUGH THE SKIES, REVEALING THE beauty of dawn and Ama's eyes slid open a fraction to find her husband kneeling beside their bed in prayer. Her forehead creased as she watched his inaudible but fervent muttering. What bothered her husband and why he chose not to confide in her consumed Ama's subconscious for the better part of the day. When the moon came out again to play and Ama lay down to sleep, she caught her husband staring fixedly at nothing and realised that whatever ailed him still occupied a huge space in his mind.

Chinny had just submerged the duvet she pulled off from her truck and made to go into the house when she spotted the delivery man walking towards her. "I have a letter for Mr Dede Ona," he said. Chinny collected the brown package and signed on behalf of her father, who was home early. She could hear his heavy breathing from his bedroom and wondered if he felt unwell. After she knocked once and received no response, Chinny let herself in, to see her father on his back, his hands folded under his head while he glared into space. One look and Chinny knew something grievous worried her father.

"Nna'm, are you all right?" Dede sat up with a start, surprised at his child's *sudden* presence.

"Yes, my daughter. I am all right," he assured her as he collected the letter and left it on his bedside stool. His shaky hands and laboured breathing betrayed his fear at discovering the contents of the envelope he had just received. The Southern Rail crest on the top left side of the envelope made him certain of unwelcome news.

Once convinced that Chinny was nowhere near his bedroom, Dede tore open the brown envelope. It contained two smaller envelopes. The first held a letter from Gold Shore Bank, giving Southern Rail notice to pay the outstanding sum of 4,655,080 Naira before the end of the quarter or stand the risk of possible foreclosure of one of the twenty-five home units financed by the bank. If Dede claimed ignorance of the home unit being referenced, the second letter from Southern Rail spelt it out, informing Dede that his unit was the only outstanding debt they had with the bank. Southern Rail informed Dede of the option to pay up the loan on or before the stated date or apply for a personal loan from a bank to clear his debt.

Distressed at how much interest had accumulated over the years, he pored over some well-hidden documents to find that while the original mortgage cost 3,000,000 Naira, the additional 1,655,080 Naira was due to bank interests. A little slip showed another 800,000 Naira interest paid on his behalf to the bank by his former employers – this was also due for repayment. In closing, Southern Rail promised to make all supporting documents available to him if he requested them.

Beyond distraught at the thought of his house being repossessed, Dede's head churned out questions in their numbers. *Where would my family live? How can I secure a personal loan from a bank without a collateral? How will I come out of this mess?* Ama saved her husband from drowning in the pool of his own thoughts when she came in and spotting the envelope lying on the bedside stool, asked him where it came from. As Dede narrated the contents of the two letters to her in hushed tones to make sure Chinny did not overhear, his heart cringed in pain at the raw fear his wife's eyes reflected. Everything seemed to be going wrong in military sequence. He was having to deal with his inability to educate his very bright daughter while grappling with his son's school fees. How could he add homelessness to this mix? A mouthful of stones held no comparison to what he felt.

"Ama, I do not know what to do. Even if I find someone with such a huge amount of money, how do I pay back? Maybe withdrawing Dubem from school, selling my car and shed are the next things to do. I have run out of ideas," Dede sighed in exasperation. Ama did not see much use in selling the sawdust shed and car. She reminded Dede that the shed was their major source of income as a family since her small vegetable stall at the village market made only a slight difference. Dede agreed with his wife, telling her in the voice of a lost child that all his prayers came back

29

unanswered. When she asked her husband to explain what he meant, Dede admitted that he had prior information about the letter and hoped there would be some divine intervention or refraction of consequences.

"One Mr Peters visited a few days ago to give me inside information," Dede began. "He still works with Southern Rail. Remember I told you that they diversified into other realms of transportation and are presently working with the government to reinstate the system on a larger and more efficient scale. So, Mr Peters can be considered quite well off."

Ama listened to her husband with rapt attention as he narrated Mr Peters' visit, but she interrupted him after a while. "That man, what is his name again? Why did he come with such news before the office decided to formally inform you? Did he offer any solution?"

"I do not know my dear. And no, he did not suggest any way out." Dede's reply sounded like a distant echo. Their discussion went on until the wee hours but before their eyes gave in to fatigue, Ama and her husband decided that Easter Monday would be a good day to pay Mr Peters a visit and ask for help of any kind, as he may be their only opportunity to get out of the situation they found themselves in.

An hour and fifteen minutes after Dede sat down in Mr Peters' waiting room, he had still not been graced by the presence of the man who could be holding the keys to his shelter. The small room with two single cushion chairs had a lone painting on its white walls. It took Dede a while to figure out that it bore the image of a voluptuous African woman. The painting looked quite expensive and Dede would have taken a better look had the woman in the painting been given the smallest stitch of covering. He tore his eyes away, looking around to make certain no one had seen him staring and wondered if he should leave and return at a more convenient time. Before he could decide whether to stay on or leave, a young lady ushered him into the main living room where he was asked to wait a while longer. Though not particularly excited at the prospect of having to continue the waiting exercise, Dede sat to wait all the same, grateful for the more comfortable chair. He took note of the affluence that barked at him. The plush leather chairs and markedly high ceiling, made from plaster of Paris (commonly called 'POP'), spelt wealth. Not able to ignore how far away the ceiling appeared, Dede pondered on the deliberate waste of good space. All the side stools, the central and dining tables had pure marble tops. More puzzling was the source of the chill that threatened to send him outdoors. Dede now believed the cool air seeped through the walls since he had searched everywhere for the air conditioning unit and still could not find it. He was about to beckon on one of the many young girls bustling around with one task or the other to take a message to Mr Peters when he finally joined him, looking dishevelled but apologetic.

"I am so sorry Mr Ona. I was err… errr busy with err… something," he mumbled. Dede took his apology with grace but could not take his eyes off the young girl who followed Mr Peters out. He looked on as the girl disappeared from sight, her eyes tracing an imaginary line on the floor before her.

The two men talked at length. Dede took no time in laying his issue bare. He asked his host for a loan of 5,000,000 Naira. He planned to pay off the mortgage on the house and plunge what was left into buying a functional car to start a car hire business, the proceeds of which would fund his repayment plan. Moments after Dede recited his carefully scripted proposal, Mr. Peters spoke.

"I have no problem with giving you this loan, Mr Ona. I have the money but as a good businessman who does not pick his money from tree tops, I would like to go to bed knowing how and when my money is coming back to me and frankly speaking, your plan for the loan repayment seems like a castle of cotton wool. I mean we are looking at twenty years or more by which time I would most likely be dead. You can see I am not a young man, so why you make such a proposition baffles me." Dede winced and shifted in his seat. He was now in a position he hoped to never descend to, but grovel he would, since his family's basic comfort depended on it.

"Sir…" Dede began but Mr Peters stopped him with a wave of his right hand.

"No, no, no, Mr Ona. Coming to me for a loan should not make you call me 'Sir'. We are friends. Com'mon! Let us have something to eat and drink. I am sure we can work something out." Surprised, but grateful that their discussion which only moments ago had gone off on a less favourable tangent somehow found its way back to its intended course, Dede let out the breath he did not know he held in.

After a meal of boiled white rice and steamed vegetables, garnished with fire-grilled fresh fish and beef cuts that Dede partook of, even though he would rather have not, he politely declined the red and white alcoholic wines offered. He reasoned that he needed a clear head to assimilate what Mr Peters proposed to be the way around his seemingly hopeless situation. A very satisfied and hopeful Dede followed Mr Peters into his study – a smaller room adjoining the living area – and as soon as the door shut them in, Mr Peters told Dede his proposition.

"I can give you the money for the price of air but that is only if you act wisely. I want to marry your daughter Chinny. I have—" Dede's eyes shot up in surprise.

"Chinny? My daughter? She is only a child... I mean she is... I never... I—"

Mr Peters did not look in the least bothered by Dede's apparent distress. He interrupted him. "She is not a child at all. Any girl who is over fifteen years is no longer a child. Do you have any idea of how many of her mates get married every day? In fact, one of my friends from the North married one not long ago. I think his latest wife is twelve years or so. You see, I have been alone for too long. Since my wife's passing eight months ago, I have not had a real companion save for these young girls that are my beneficiaries. More than that, I want a son to take my place when I join my wife. Your daughter is young and vibrant. There is no doubt about her fertility and ability to produce male children. You are aware of how useless a man is without an heir."

Stunned beyond words, Dede looked on at the man who sat before him as one would a hydra-headed alien. He could now see how the young girls 'benefited' from the opportunist. He felt like regurgitating the food and water he had taken. He thought he would faint as he considered a barrage of reactions to the man grinning in front of him. When Dede finally found his voice, he drew himself to his full height, and looking Mr Peters in the eye, said, "I have a million thoughts to express to you, but I wonder if fighting an unarmed man is worth it because now I realise you do not have the capacity to think. But on the unlikely day when you

32

can think, I would like to hear about your experience so far with the human race, since visiting our planet. In the near future, I hope you find yourself and have the grace to be disappointed in what you find. There are many things I am ignorant of, but this I know Peters, that you are one of those people who would be enormously improved by death. You are living proof that gutter-mud can sprout legs. And if I have said anything to upset you, please be clear on one thing – it was purely intentional." Dede was shaking with rage as he turned his back on his once-upon-a-time host and slammed the door, an open-mouthed Mr Peters staying glued to his chair. He had the impudence to express surprise.

Dede decided not to flag down any tricycle. He intended to walk all the way home and after a few metres, he could stop the tears from flowing down no longer. Try as hard as he did, they were relentless in their rage as they pooled over his eye sockets and flowed down his face. Dede could only blame himself for not trying hard enough to give his family a decent life. He knew that most people may not consider a female child much of a force to reckon with, but he shook at the thought of anyone reducing a child, a human, to a mere commodity. If only he had not gone to this alien, his heart would have been spared the ache it now experienced. Why did life play games with people so? Why could things not just move on with natural gradient? Did life have to always present obstacles? Why did hard work not present the sure recipe for success? Engrossed in his turmoil, Dede went past his home. Wiping his face, he headed back and saw his seventeen-year-old daughter parking her truck and going through the routine of stripping it of the duvet, which she put in to soak. Chinny offered to take her student passengers to the school playground once a week as part of their holiday routine at no extra charge.

Pain lanced through his heart. "Why?" Dede questioned no one in particular as he resolved not to share his experience with Ama.

The months flew by and soon the long-awaited examinations timetable stared every candidate in the face. Chinny's papers spanned two weeks. Her first paper would be on a Wednesday – Alternative to Practical Chemistry. Confident in her many years of study, Chinny did not experience the usual examination fever typical of her counterparts who sacrificed study time on the altar of play and slothfulness. Ejiofor called to tell Chinny that he had been accepted to study medicine at the University of Ghana. He planned to travel in November for the registration process. Everyone in the Onas' home went insane with excitement for Ejiofor. Besides Chinny, being awfully disappointed that he shunned becoming an engineer like his Uncle Iyke; the promise of more distance between her and Ejiofor was not one she looked forward to being fulfilled. Nevertheless, nothing deterred the happiness she felt for her brother from another mother and her soon-to-be doctor friend.

As Adaiba saw her cousin off to the road, the two young ladies chatted animatedly about the forthcoming examinations. This would be Adaiba's second attempt at the private examinations. Chinny laughed at the naked terror in her cousin's eyes when they talked about mathematics, for hard as she tried to understand the dread attached to the subject, it remained a mystery to her. Grateful to be an art student, Adaiba said she did not mind a pass grade in the multi-tentacled monster of a subject. They said their goodbyes and went on their separate ways, Adaiba to the vegetable market and Chinny back to her house. A few metres from her house, Chinny spotted a car driving off in the opposite direction and thought she recognised the vehicle – and the driver for that matter. The car looked just like the one Iyke – Ejiofor's uncle – drove. She thought nothing of it since the Clarkes were not in the village. Ama was out visiting. She told Chinny it had to do with the grand sale she planned on hosting, so Chinny had some cooking to do and could not afford any waste of time, wondering who came or went.

Her examinations breezed by just like Ejiofor promised they would. All her subjects came and went in one piece, save for mathematics. Chinny could not wrap her head around what all the fuss was about. Almost everybody put on a pair of dark sunglasses inside the moderately lit examination hall on the day mathematics was to be written. The tension in the room was thicker than chunky beef cuts as people chatted with those they would typically not speak to. Fortunately, Chinny did not lose sleep over crunching numbers and she empathised with the unlucky lot battling with the 'monster' who they had allowed to thrive unnoticed.

34

Right before the examinations, much to the chagrin of the candidates, the invigilators shuffled their sitting positions. All plans for collaborative solutions during the examination fell through. What a disaster! At the end of the examinations, as the invigilators collected the answer scripts, three young men jumped into the hall and shoved aside the chief invigilator, causing the already collected answer scripts to fly in different directions. When the assistant invigilator confronted them, one of the hoodlums screamed, "E-ve-ry-body, leave this place!" With that said, all the candidates scrambled out with or without their personal effects. Chinny ran past the tricycle park and stopped only when she sighted some police officials jogging towards the examination centre.

With the frenzy of the general certificate examinations waning at the Onas' residence, their routine slowly returned. Chinny cleared the dinner dishes from the dining table and wondered what troubled her father. These past months, he laughed and talked a lot less. *Something is bothering him, but Mother does not care. She is so engrossed with sorting out her treasures*, she mused. In truth, Ama recently occupied herself with sorting wrappers and beads. Most of them belonged to her late mother. She planned on selling them off to make the money that would give Chinny a head start when she gained admission into a university. In Ama's opinion, no longer did Dede have the fighting spirit he once did. She found it impossible to understand why he appeared reluctant to go to Mr Peters for help. Deciding to take on the challenge herself, Ama thought through a few ideas, before concluding that her beads and wrappers sale took the first spot on the list. She had no clue that her husband's seeming nonchalance stemmed from an effort to shield his family from the real depth of the cruel reality they stood against. Thankfully, Southern Rail paid off the mortgage, so Dede's worry at an impending foreclosure shifted from the bank to the railway company. It appeared a change of course took place after all.

During the characteristically long church service, Chinny spent well over half the intercessory prayer time in deep slumber. As usual, once it was time to say the final 'Amen', she became wide awake. Sometimes she wondered if it was not too much of a coincidence that sleep often enveloped her during these prayer sessions and comically lifted once they ended. The sermon however piqued her interest since the topic

– Faith even when it makes no sense – resonated with a chord in her symphony. As they approached home, Dede spotted a figure sitting on the front porch. The Onas never looked forward to entertaining visitors on hot Sunday afternoons. They preferred to settle to a quiet lunch and enjoy their rest afterwards. The visitor was male, but nobody could make out the face. The tricycle got close enough, and the sitting figure looked up. "It's Dubem! It's Dubem!" squealed Chinny. Ama's face lit up but her forehead furrowed almost immediately, while Dede flashed an uneasy smile. Dubem got up and moved towards his family when they alighted from the tricycle. He had on a pair of dark sunglasses and greeted his folks with the customary side hug and shallow bowing of the head. An ecstatic Chinny threw both arms around her brother, oblivious to the portentous silence around her.

The resounding lullaby Dubem hummed while he slept made catching any more sleep a futile effort for Chinny. She cast a dejected glance at her little bedside clock as its arms crawled steadily towards 6:00 am. Looking at Dubem in the bed across from her, it seemed like ages since they slept in the same room. Since Ama's auntie had been childless for many years, she decided to take Dubem under her wings. So, he left home for Auntie Julie's house to conclude his primary education. Sadly, following her tragic death after a protracted illness, he returned home for his primary school leaving certificate at Future Bright Primary School. Life slowly became a tough patch for the Ona family. With time, Dubem not only became withdrawn and a shadow of his former boisterous self, but also stopped doing well in school.

Mr Oliseh had been Dede's friend for as long as they could both remember. Being an orphan, life threw daggers at him, but Dede was always there to support his friend. Oliseh abandoned school in the middle of his class three examinations to fend for himself. He started out being a farm hand and later began hunting for food and money at the age of fifteen. The returns were not remarkable, but he made just enough to live. He led a secluded life and did not relate with many people. He did not go out much, did not have many friends, never got married and never had any children. A little birdie said a ruthless swarm of bees attacked him on one of his hunting expeditions, making his reproductive organ area their sole target. For many, the story of the bees served as the connecting dots between Oliseh and the reason he preferred a secluded life.

Secluded life or not, Oliseh invested his time and effort to reconnect with his long-lost friend and had virtually given up when they ran into each other at DLSS (Demonstration of Light Secondary School). Chinny was in her third term in class one when Dubem eventually passed one of the toughest entrance examinations. To say that everyone was confused would be an understatement. In the end, a few called it a miracle while others inferred his younger sister's admission served as the much-needed push for him to get serious with his studies.

Dede had gone to Udu town to sign the acceptance form and pick up the billing information for Dubem's new school when he ran into his long-lost friend, who incidentally served as the chief security officer of the school. After exchanging pleasantries, Oliseh took his friend to the four-bedroom bungalow he called home. Thanks to DLSS, it was nicely furnished. Anyone who knew anything about setting up a house would conclude that DLSS did not take their staff welfare lightly.

"Oliseh, so you still cook?" Dede joked when his host served him a plate of steaming hot yam pottage garnished with fresh fish, mint and pumpkin leaves. With food and small talk off the plate, Dede confided in his friend. "I will not be able to bite this bullet." He handed the bill to Oliseh who after scrutinising the document, asked his friend why. Dede went on to narrate his entire financial situation and closed by saying that it may be best to let Dubem do something else which did not require cerebral competence, as the child took eight different entrance examinations before he could pass one.

"What is the guarantee that this is not going to be a dead end? What if Dubem's success in this entrance examination happened by chance? What if he begins to fail again? Anyway, what I am saying is that I cannot afford to pay boarding fees; this school is two towns away from home and the boy cannot walk to school. I will jus—" but Oliseh interrupted his friend's tale of woes.

"Dede, calm down. There is always a way. Look at my house. What am I doing with all this space? DLSS provided me with a fully furnished house. Why can't I help someone else? Let your son stay with me during school sessions and when the term ends, he can go home to you. Look, I will not stand by and do nothing while you throw away your son's future. I do not believe he is dull. There is something wrong somewhere and I personally think whatever it is has returned to where it belongs – in the past. Your son will have an education. He will not be a loafer. No! Not on my watch!"

Overcome with gratitude to Oliseh who had always been one with strong emotions, Dede recalled how his kind-hearted friend used to amuse him back in the day because his highly emotional personality could not be reconciled with his impressively intimidating bulk. When Dede expressed his fear about times when he may find it impossible to pay even the tuition, Oliseh told him that nobody ever achieved great feats without first launching out. "We will cross that stream when we get there. Relax my friend. Life is good, and God is great," he finished.

⟿

A happy Dede broke the news to his even happier family. Somewhere in the corners of their hearts, before now, they feared that on getting to the school, Dubem's admission would turn out to be an error. Oh, what a relief that it did not! But the most potent ingredient in their pot of excitement was the evasion of the heavy boarding fees. When they were alone, Ama asked her husband if they made a mistake investing in their son. Slapping a mosquito off the back of his ear, Dede said, "I do not know my dear. I wish I did. I guess time will tell."

Today, as Dede and Ama secretly regretted their decision to send Dubem rather than Chinny to school, Dubem turned in his sleep, adjusted his neck and continued his lullaby, only this time it went an octave higher. Emotions were ever at war each time Chinny thought about her brother. Most times, what she felt for him was pure sibling love but anytime she allowed herself the luxury of a journey down the dark, winding road of self-pity and frustration, she experienced fierce anger and struggled with resentment. This morning however, all Chinny had for her brother was pure sibling love – but it did not diminish her desire to reclaim her room. *Why did Mother decide to use Dubem's* room *as the sorting centre for her beads and wrappers, and why does Dubem snore like Father anyway?* she thought in exasperation. Since her brother did not show any sign of waking up any time soon, Chinny scurried out of bed. If she could not catch any more sleep, it made perfect sense to begin her morning chores.

"I did not lie to you. I just did not want to burden you with unnecessary information." On her way to the kitchen, Chinny froze and wondering what her father meant, leaned into their door. She stuck out her tongue at the voice of reasoning telling her that listening in on conversations one had not been invited to smacked of bad manners. Her parents seldom argued. Dede's voice sounded stern. She cringed as her mother retorted in a caustic voice Chinny did not recognise.

"Burden me? Dede, you did not want to burden me? You call selling our assets and considering such a revolting idea a burden on me? Why did you have that discussion in the first place? And if you were not considering it, why did you collect it?" Dede responded in a muffled tone. Ama's shrill voice made her words crystal clear, but it was difficult to understand the entire conversation. Suddenly Dede's voice boomed as he blamed Ama for her insensitivity to his frustrations, accusing her of resenting rather than supporting him.

Dubem placed his arm on his sister's shoulder, startling her. She turned towards her brother. The anguish in his eyes jolted her. "What is going on? Is it always this way?" he whispered.

"I do not know. This is new. They never fight aloud." Chinny's panic-stricken voice was barely audible.

By now, Ama was crying. Dubem feared the neighbours would hear. "This is a child that has been passed over in the most heart-wrenching ways all because she is female," she sobbed.

Chinny looked at her brother and whispered into his ear, "This is definitely about me."

Ama continued, "She is intelligent, purposeful and hard working. Against all odds, she learnt to carry herself with grace and has not once lost her love and respect for us. Now rather than come up with constructive ways to heal her crushed spirit or rekindle her hopes of the future we owe her, you come up with this unwholesome solution. Why have you refused to consider Mr Peters?"

Dede started to say that his proposed solution would not seem so bad if she paid attention to him, but Ama continued, "Are you not tired of always skilfully evading the core of the matter? Be the man I once knew and own this issue, Dede. Bring up a wholesome solution we can both work with." Neither Chinny nor her brother could understand the meaning of what they just heard.

"What did he collect?" Chinny whispered, not expecting Dubem to answer. Moments after their parents became quiet, Dubem and Chinny returned to their bedroom, each very troubled and actively imagining their individual theories. One thing was unanimously understood by the siblings; their father had plans for Chinny and from the way it sounded, they were not good ones.

With school break over, and Dubem due to return to his studies, Chinny braced for the usual lonesome air. Not much was given away by their parents as they tried hard to hide the tension between them. About to board the tricycle, Dubem hugged his sister ever so tightly as he promised to do everything he could to keep her safe and happy. To keep her brimming eyes from her brother, Chinny looked away as she waved him goodbye. She swallowed hard on the lump forming in her throat and wondered how Dubem proposed to fulfil his promise, considering the mud of uncertainty she currently waded in. Chinny did not see the thick mass of unbendable steel that lay beneath her brother's calm and unassuming mien.

Chinny carried on her usual activities although her typical sparkle appeared to be on recess. She started another fundraising venture where she distributed finely diced and fried beef, which she tied neatly in little transparent bags, popularly called santana. Besides her individual customers who loved her famous beef bites, the convenience stores were her major customers and bought most of the beef off her to sell at a profit. This business fetched her even better returns than her cart transport business and each day's sales pulled her closer to her dreams.

Delicious wafts of curry, thyme and bay leaf, coupled with the shrill protest of beef cuts as they lost their redness to super-hot groundnut oil roused Mrs Ona from her nap. Ama came into the kitchen and joked about people who preyed on other people's resources to run their business. When Chinny asked her exactly what resources she was referring to, her mother told her that she would soon begin serving her monthly tax invoices for using her site, cooking stove and pots. "You should be thankful that I buy my oil and spices," Chinny threw back giggling. Days after the quarrel between Dede and Ama, they observed a withdrawal in Chinny and tried all they could to lighten the mood around the house. Although they suspected she may have heard a bit, if not all, of their argument, they were not prepared to discuss anything with her. This frustrated Chinny even more. "Why is nobody talking to me?" she wailed at no one in particular, one of those nights when she cried herself to sleep. Chinny had perfected the art of crying herself to sleep and putting up a considerably bright and happy facade in the morning.

Lately, her father had been receiving too many letters that he read in privacy and was quick to either tuck away or tear into irredeemable shreds. Chinny's curiosity mounted with each passing day. So, on this day, not different from any other, while her parents were out visiting, Chinny spent time opening her father's bedside drawers to pore through files of letters but found nothing out of the ordinary. She gave up and started walking out the door when she experienced a brainwave. In a dash, Chinny reached for the mattress but found nothing underneath. As she set the mattress down, disappointment etched all over her, she heard what sounded like paper shuffle. She looked again but found nothing. She spotted the zip on the mattress and with fingers quivering like feathers, Chinny unzipped it and to her delight, found three envelopes. The contents of the first envelope informed her that they stood the risk of losing their home if certain payments were not made. The second letter did not make too much sense to Chinny. A certain Mr Peters informed her father that Southern Rail planned to repossess their home in a matter of months and that it would do his family much good if he reconsidered his stance regarding their last discussion. Chinny wondered what the discussion had been about.

The next envelope held a piece of paper that shocked Chinny to her toes. It was a cheque from someone called Iyke Uzor. Chinny hoped Iyke Uzor and Iyke – Ejiofor's uncle – were not the same person. Sweat trickled down the crease in her forehead and the back of her neck as she tried to understand why anyone would issue a cheque for 600,000

Naira to her father? The knock on the door brought Chinny's inquest to an end. Letters back in place, zipper redone, and bed laid back, she scurried out of the room to see who it was. Dede looked raddled and neither heard nor responded to Chinny's half-hearted "Good evening Father". He went straight to his bedroom.

As soon as Chinny got to her room, she dialled Ejiofor's number and went straight for the jugular. "What is your mother's maiden name?" Ejiofor, who was in the middle of lectures, gave her a curt reply and ended the call. Her heart sank. "Uzor." Humiliation washed over her. Had her father descended as low as begging Ejiofor's uncle for money?

4

THE DOORBELL CHIMED AS CHINNY LEFT FOR THE BANK TO make some deposits. She bade her father goodbye as she ushered her Uncle Kika in. Nobody heard Ama leave for her much-publicised beads and wrappers sale early in the morning and Dubem had gone back to school.

So, as soon as Dede made certain Chinny was gone, he blurted, "I cannot keep this in any longer. My family, my world is falling apart!"

"Dede, pull yourself together and tell me what the problem is. Where are Ama and Dubem?" Kika looked alarmed. Dede confessed his guilt to his brother. "The child whose future I vowed to protect graciously shook off the disappointment of having a father who cannot give her the one legitimate thing she craves."

Kika heaved with relief. "Oh! It is about Chinny. Dede, I have told you to stop bothering your good head. You have done the best you can. Do you want to kill yourself? You made the right choice so please concentrate on your son and you will be happy you did. Let her do something to help the family for now. You can marry her off you know."

Anguish tore through Dede's eyes. "So Kika, what you are saying is that despite Chinny being not only bright but resilient, I should leave her to drown in the misfortune which being a girl has thrown at her. What makes you different from the maggot called Mr Peters who would give me a loan of 5,000,000 Naira only if I let him marry my male-hatching daughter? Eh Kika? Are you any different?" Kika's tongue stayed glued to the roof of his mouth as Dede told him that he liquidated all his assets, his Beetle included and paid the insignificant sum of 850,000 Naira to Southern Rail. This would give him until next year, by which time the company threatened to sell off the house to recoup their funds.

43

Chinny forgot the spare house keys she always carried around just in case she came home before anyone else, which happened often. She came back to the house and nearly called out to her father to let her in but froze. Her heart picked up tempo in tune with the cultural dance troop, practicing a few blocks away as her uncle's words reverberated in her head. "It is a very hard pill to swallow especially considering the age of the man in question. That said, Chinny is a girl and will get married someday. Since this holds a promise of good returns for you, I suggest you take this chance my brother. Do you know what you stand to gain? The benefit of having this Mr Peters as a father-in-law will give your life the lift you have always wanted. The girl will grow to enjoy her new husband and if she does not like it, the old man would die soon anyway and set her free to marry any other man of her choice. Do not overthink it. I think it is a beautiful gift wrapped in rags. I wish an opportunity like this would come to me. Those who have buttocks do not know how to sit!" Kika finished with rue. The realisation that nobody outside his immediate nuclear unit really and selflessly had his interest at heart hit Dede and in that instant, the enormity of his error in confiding in his brother jeered at him.

After what appeared like decades, Dede broke his silence. "Thank you Kika. You are correct. I knew talking to you would bring my much-needed solution. As soon as we fix the dates for Chinny's marriage, I will let you know." Chinny missed the sarcasm in her father's voice as her legs, which now felt like the noodles she ate for lunch, moved as fast as they could to nowhere. She did not wait to hear the unprintable description of Kika as conceptualised and relayed by her father. Dede slammed the door behind his brother, shaking from the venom just spewed from his mouth. He regretted not confiding in his wife. He had lied so much to her both by omission and commission. Ama still believed that his Beetle, which now belonged to someone else, lay faulty at the mechanic's workshop and that their television, video cassette player and stereo set which Dede used as collateral for a loan from a mortgage bank would soon grace their sitting room once again. He did not tell her how close they were to being homeless. He regretted not telling her that his friend Oliseh has been the one paying the fees for Dubem's schooling. He regretted the different shades of lies he told Ama.

The chiffon blouse Chinny wore clung to her back, a testament of her over twenty-minute sprint. Exhausted and sticky, she boarded a tricycle and did not get down until the final stop. She continued walking for almost three hours before she realised she would faint from hunger and fatigue if she did not stop. She spotted a mini supermarket a few feet away and bought a bottle of soda and some crunchy pastry known as *chin-chin. Nothing beats the satisfaction of delicious coolness travelling down a parched throat after a long walk*, she thought, sitting on the shop's single step while giving her empty stomach its belated attention.

⤳

By seven o'clock in the evening, Ama was done with her sales and humming a happy tune, she walked through the door. With eyes as bright as the sun after the morning rains, she told Dede about the two wealthy strangers who bought her mother's coral beads at outrageous sums. "I think we have a headstart. Tomorrow, Chinny will take this money to the bank for me." Ama wanted to know if he was expecting any other person when she noticed Dede did not shut the door after her but kept peering into the night.

"Is Chinny not coming in yet?" he asked. Ama became alarmed as she had not seen Chinny the whole day but tried to speak with a calm tone.

"Maybe the Clarkes are around," she reasoned and went into her room to tuck her proceeds away in her wardrobe before rushing off to the Clarkes. She met a padlocked gate. Ama's breath could almost be heard a mile away. Her underarms clammed with sweat as she began to walk back home but met Dede outside.

"She may be with Adaiba," he said and suggested they go to Kika's house. The distance between their house and Kika's appeared to have halved by the time they arrived. Fear dripped through Dede's pores when his brother announced that Chinny had not come anywhere near their home the entire day. Hopeful she would have returned, Dede and Ama left for home.

An infinite number of thoughts sped through their minds as Dede and Ama gaped at their open door. Running into the house, the hair on the back of Dede's neck and arms spiked as he looked around for

Chinny or intruders. Ama dashed straight to her bedroom and let out a shrill cry. One look at his wife's ashen face, holding the open door of their wardrobe and Dede did not need words to confirm his worst fears. Her proceeds were gone! Somewhere between going to Kika's house and back, the ignoble guests of the night came visiting. Ama sat down on the floor sobbing and Dede stared on, the words to comfort his wife eluding him. The effort Ama invested in making the sales a reality could not be measured. Those coral and pearl beads she inherited from her late mother cost a fortune and he feared to ask her just how much she lost. The funds would have gone a long way in alleviating some of their present constraints. Somebody knocked and with a fast-beating heart, Dede went to see who it was but found a little boy not older than nine years.

"Good evening Sir. Chinny said I should give you this," he muttered, handing Dede a folded piece of paper and turned to leave. Dede held softly onto his shoulders.

"Wait. Where is... did you see her? When did she give you this? Where is she?" The boy said she came to their house sometime in the afternoon, asked for a paper and pen and scribbled a letter, which she asked him not to open but to give to her parents at 8:00 pm. The boy trotted off and with shaky hands and deafening heartbeats, Dede opened the letter and read:

I thought I could not have wished for a better home, but life and time have taught me differently. I put up a brave fight against all that fate threw in my path. I carried you along. Not once did I put the blame on you, accepting that life reflected whatever one purposed to make of it for oneself and not what it presented. In pain, my head bows and my bowels cringe to know that a pawn on the chess board of your life is a representation of all Chinetalum Ona is to you. I was only born to fulfil your selfish ends. My heart breaks into little fragments as I say this but dear Mother, go on and have a child for Mr Peters. That way, all your problems can come to an end. Take care of one another. God will take care of me.

Ama snatched the piece of paper from her husband's unsteady hands. She wanted to know what distressed him so much. The evening breeze shuffled the almond leaves that littered the grounds of the Onas' residence but the large beads of sweat rolling down Ama's forehead did not relent. She was broken and confused with no inkling of where her daughter fled to or why she had come to such harsh conclusions. Ama untied and retied her wrapper, peering into the darkness and willing Chinny out of hiding. She began to walk into the night but changed her mind and returned to sit on the front porch. Shoving away all thoughts of why Chinny may have left home, Ama tried to guess where her daughter could be, her stolen fortune forgotten.

Chinny woke up scared and unable to tell why the cold bit so hard. The insects fluttering around the light bulb in front of the shop chose to sing a symphony. Chinny reached for her phone only to find it had run out of battery power. When? She could not tell. The hour and minute arms on her wristwatch pointed to nine. Suddenly, the bulb went out and pitch darkness took over. Only then did Chinny assess her situation. Dread filled her, and in her panic, she began to walk. A flicker of light ahead infused her with the courage to keep walking and not give in to the alluring idea to stand still, hoping to melt into the night.

The light disappeared before she got to it. The roasted corn seller had just closed shop and busied herself with gathering her two little girls and what remained of her goods when Chinny approached her. Although sceptical at first, the middle-aged woman softened her stance once Chinny explained her plight and begged to be pointed in the direction of the closest lodging. But the woman, offering to lodge her in her home if she did not mind, told Chinny that the closest lodging was about twenty-five minutes away by foot and advised her against staying there, since the ladies of the night found it a comfortable environment for their nefarious activities. Chinny thought it through and took the woman's offer, hoping she had not made a decision she would soon regret.

Meanwhile, Ama and Dede suffered a dearth of tears and ideas. Ama asked her husband in a voice a little louder than a whisper, "What did she mean by telling me to have a child for Mr Peters?" Wide eyes stared at drooping eyes as Dede narrated his encounter with Mr Peters. He had not thought she deserved the agony that telling her about it would provoke.

Ama sighed, "I see! I thought she found out about Iyke's proposal." Iyke, Ejiofor's uncle wanted Chinny's hand in marriage, so he asked her father with an expensive bottle of champagne and a cheque of 600,000 Naira. The only snag rested in Chinny's ignorance of his proposal.

"So, who told her about the crazy old fool?" Ama's confusion mounted.

Dede narrated his meeting with his brother earlier in the day. "She must have stayed back to eavesdrop on your conversation. I told you to be careful with the things you tell your brother. He is not a bad person, but he just does not possess the ability to think through certain situations!" Ama's voice was the sound of broken chords. "But Dede, you should have told me about this. You should have told me. I am your wife. Here I was thinking that Iyke's suggestion was absurd. I did not know you had more to deal with. Chinny must have misunderstood your position on the matter. Oh God!!! My poor child, where are you? But why would she think I have a part to play in this awful plan?" Ama and Dede were confused, afraid and sad all at the same time.

Sparsely furnished but neat, the corn seller's house embraced Chinny as soon as she walked in. The woman greeted her husband and they both went out of the room to discuss the situation. Chinny noted the renewed kindness in the eyes of the man when they came back to the sitting room. After Chinny managed a few spoons of rice, she settled on the lone couch in the sitting room to sleep. Jolted out of the bliss that sleep promised, Chinny opened her eyes to see two other pairs staring at her. The corn seller and her husband grabbed two stools, sat in front of her and began hours of persuasion and reasoning. The odds, they told her, did not lean in favour of a homeless and defenceless young lady. Nothing could change her mind. She would never return to her family.

"They are a brood of vipers I had the misfortune of having as family. I'd rather live on the streets than live with them," she wailed. Husband and wife smiled, nodding in understanding. They let her cry for as long as she wanted. When they knew she was done crying, they spoke. Before now, Chinny only associated eloquence and depth with the rich and learned. But as the corn seller spoke to her, she realised that the concept of wisdom had no boundaries.

"Child, words are not always what they seem. Go back home and take as much time as you need to evaluate your options."

Cricket calls, bird chirps and sounds of shuffling leaves typical of the night went still as the corn seller's husband spoke.

"Mankind's life journey is pre-determined by the script writer who plots only happy endings. The only requirement is for mankind to prove they deserve to play out their script and it would all fall in place." Jolted into reality by the words of her hosts and certain her parents must be sick with worry, Chinny made up her mind to go back home. Nobody could force her into what she did not want.

"Tomorrow, at first light, I will return home," she promised, grateful for their uncommon kindness. As she went back to sleep, she thought there was something unusual about this couple. They were strangers to her, yet looked vaguely familiar.

In the morning, Chinny woke up to a note from her hosts to close the door on her way out as they were out for the day. "Remember, prove you deserve your script," the note ended. Disappointed at herself for being such a heavy sleeper, Chinny began her walk down the little path that led to a dirt road. For some reason, she could not recall how they got to the house the night before. The isolation of the house and the glances thrown her way by the passers-by who scurried off in what seemed like puzzlement or fear also did not go unnoticed.

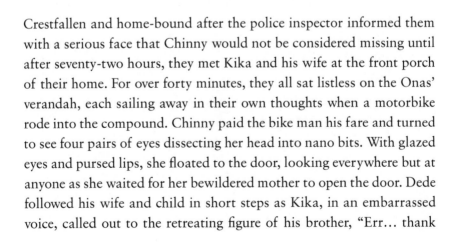

Crestfallen and home-bound after the police inspector informed them with a serious face that Chinny would not be considered missing until after seventy-two hours, they met Kika and his wife at the front porch of their home. For over forty minutes, they all sat listless on the Onas' verandah, each sailing away in their own thoughts when a motorbike rode into the compound. Chinny paid the bike man his fare and turned to see four pairs of eyes dissecting her head into nano bits. With glazed eyes and pursed lips, she floated to the door, looking everywhere but at anyone as she waited for her bewildered mother to open the door. Dede followed his wife and child in short steps as Kika, in an embarrassed voice, called out to the retreating figure of his brother, "Err... thank

God, she is safe and sound." The sound of the door as it closed in their faces told Kika and Violet that their own home beckoned.

Neither Dubem's return for the end of term holiday nor his parents' dry jokes eased the tense air in the house and nobody gave Dubem any details about his sister's odd disappearance and re-appearance. Gone was the flighty, boisterous and optimistic person he grew up with. In her place remained a dreadfully withdrawn being who believed that everyone she trusted had turned around and brutally stabbed her in the back. So Dubem, like his parents, perfected the art of walking on eggshells around her. Adaiba was away in Enugu through it all. It did not help either that Ejiofor did not make it home for Christmas. Chinny decided to leave him to his new life of higher learning. *We were never on the same playing field anyway*, she thought.

Weeks after her disappearance, the doorbell chimed and Chinny opened the door to find Ejiofor. On the night of her flight, her parents had called the Clarkes to find out if they knew anything. Although concerned, Ejiofor's parents could not be of much help. And though he learnt of the whole incident only after the fact, Ejiofor boarded the night bus back to Nigeria as soon as he could. School workload could wait. He needed to know in person what went wrong with his friend.

Ejiofor listened, spellbound at the surreal account Chinny gave him. "Do you know that till this moment, nobody has asked me anything about where I was or what happened to me the entire time I disappeared? These people care only about themselves. It is almost as though it is my responsibility to get them out of whatever it is they think they are in. Or… Eji, do you think I am being self-centred? Should I just go ahead with this plan? Sometimes, I think I may be thinking too highly of myself. I mean… many girls are doing it these days. Oh, I don't know. Oh God I am so confused," she cried in exasperation.

Cool as frozen waters, Ejiofor, regarding his weeping friend said, "When you are quite done crying, I would like to be informed, so we can both think about our next line of action." Chinny blinked back her freshly forming tears. What happened to her all-supportive and compassionate friend?

"I do not know, Ejiofor. I am so overwhelmed with pain, disappointment and hate and these emotions are alien to me. Sometimes, I feel like running endlessly. Other times, what I really want to do is knock some sense into everyone's thick skull."

Ejiofor let out a chuckle. "It is comforting to know that these are the only things you feel like doing. Believe me, there are more atrocious options, but we will not go that route. For starters, you must talk it through with your parents. They are probably terrified about bringing up any discussion with you for fear of scaring you into flight again. Secondly, Chinny, those people who took you in for that one night spoke the truth. Sometimes, life hands out sour pills, but I believe it is all in the grand plan to mould us into characters that can withstand the immense success intended for us. Now, if we cave under the mould, we do not get to that immense success but if we stand tall and weather the tide, then maybe we will prove that we truly deserve the success. Do not buckle. Give life your best shot. Nobody can force you into anything. Not in this era." Ejiofor advised Chinny to tell her folks – in clear words – exactly what she thought of their obscene plan and go ahead with her intention to study. "I am rock-stoic behind you," he finished.

The evening breeze brushed over Chinny's skin as she strolled back home from walking with her friend to his home, back to her house and once more to his home. Ejiofor was going back tomorrow. His father heard that he was in the country and his irritation at his son's mindless devotion to Chinny went sky-high. "You need to explain to me how rushing away from school at every flimsy opportunity adds up to you acquiring a sterling degree! First thing tomorrow morning, you will return to school. Have I made myself unequivocally clear?!!!" he boomed over the phone.

Ejiofor did not expect a less caustic reaction from his father anyway. He smiled as he said his "Yes sir, okay sir, I am sorry sir and good night sir," before hanging up the phone with a smirk. His mission was accomplished, and the old man could go suck on an unripe lemon if he so wished.

Something certainly smelled nice and it came from the kitchen. Ravenous, Chinny went into the kitchen to help herself to the beans pudding, popularly called *moimoi*, sitting in the pot. She settled on the little stool in the kitchen and unleashed the vengeance of the starvation she unwittingly inflicted on herself the entire day. Dubem stood in the kitchen doorway unnoticed, watching in delight as she gobbled her food and wondered if his sister had any idea just how much he loved her.

Sadly, nobody knew that beneath that aloof, self-absorbed and unintelligent exterior lay a perceptive, introspective and profound individual. Dubem had not always been mundane. The once happy-go-lucky Dubem began his journey of evolution the first time he realised that the odds may not be in favour of his little sister. "Speak gently, do you not know you are a girl?" "Take it easy! You are a girl. Things must not always go your way, you are a girl." "Shut up. Is that the way to talk to a boy?" These reprimands served as side dishes in his little sister's daily menu.

An event that marked the turning point in Dubem's perception of life, and which still stuck out like a sore thumb in his memory, occurred during one of their family reunions. Dede, his father, bought roasted breadfruit nuts. Aunty Violet shared the popular snack into portions on a big tray and asked the children to choose their preferred portion according to their ages from the oldest to the youngest. When Chinny stepped up to take her chosen portion, almost all the adults reprimanded her, saying that a boy, two years younger than she was, had to take his share first. She argued that, being two years older than the boy, it was her turn to choose her snack. That day, Chinny learnt from the adults that age was not material since the other child in question belonged to the masculine gender. The support she anticipated from her parents did not come. They kept their peace. Chinny cried so much and refused to take the snack altogether. The evening's chatter resumed as though nothing happened and she even thought she saw Dubem go for a second helping. Unknown to Chinny, her brother had returned his own snack to the tray. Eight-year-old Dubem refused to stand for a concept that robbed his sister of her right as an individual.

Thereafter, Dubem made it his responsibility to protect his sister and had since done everything to promote her cause. He lied, cheated and did many other things he dared not breathe to another soul. Everybody wrote Dubem off, after his failure in examinations seemed to have become second nature to him. Only after Chinny caught up with Dubem and gained admission into secondary school did he decide to pass his entrance examinations.

Shockwaves washed over Dubem when he learnt that Chinny, who was apparently more intellectually endowed than he appeared to be, would be withdrawn from school so that he could get ahead in life. That this decision was reached, merely because of their difference in gender, made it more painful for him. Dubem's resolve did not waver but only heightened as he continued to watch with keen interest the family a few blocks away – the Clarkes. They had not always been financially comfortable; Mr Clarke started as an administrative clerk in one of the private universities, took advantage of the learning environment and advanced his own education. He became a junior lecturer in a polytechnic, but his big break came when he landed a part-time job at a construction company. Ejiofor's mum, asides from being the head teacher in a primary school, ran a cleaning agency where she offered laundry, office cleaning and home cleaning services to her clients.

Dubem once asked his parents why they were not as comfortable as the Clarkes. They laughed at his sweet naïvety and introduced him to the two-group system of the world. One group received oranges, while tons of lemons were dumped on the other. The little boy bought their explanation, but not for too long. The passage of time was to present Dubem with two more groups. The first of which received oranges too, but never got around to the juicing process, becoming burdened with rotten oranges, which turned into their source of bitterness at life. And whilst the last group also got their fair share of lemons, they not only made lemonade which they drank for energy, they also stuck around those who got oranges, conscientiously picking up the fruit seeds that lay carelessly discarded, planting and nurturing them to fruitful trees, bearing juicy oranges. The Clarkes belonged to this last group, while the Onas' teeth had become brown with the corrosion of acidic lemonade. Dubem's time in Mr Oliseh's house presented him with the will to give up drinking unpalatable lemon juice and begin picking up his orange seeds.

Not until Chinny finished her sumptuous meal of moimoi did she bother to ask her brother, "Who made this?"

Dubem laughed heartily and answered with a question. "Who else makes moimoi this good?" Happy with his sister's renewed appetite, it no longer bothered Dubem that she now skipped using the dining table for her meals – a practice the younger lady of the house opposed vehemently in the past.

It was the usual wind-down mode at half-past nine that night at the Onas'. Chinny wrote down the new words she learnt for the day, 'obnoxious' and 'calaboose'. She tested them aloud, "What my parents propose to do is obnoxious and they deserve calaboose." She chuckled at the wobbly structure of her phrase and said it again before turning in for the night.

The harsh intrusion of the doorbell extracted a sigh from Dede who had begun to give in to the soothing comfort of sleep while listening to the news. Dubem rinsed off the last plate and hurried out of the kitchen to see who had come visiting so late in the night. "Iyke?" Dubem did not expect to see anyone in their house this late, let alone Ejiofor's uncle. He jumped when Iyke slapped his shoulder in what was supposed to be a friendly greeting. Once Dede saw who their visitor was, he lost his composure.

Something did not sit right. Did his father owe Iyke or did Iyke have something on his father? Were they in on something together? Dubem could not decide on what thought path to follow. He left the two men in the sitting room or so it would appear, and from behind the door, leaned into their discussion. Dubem's mouth fell open and his eyes became two big watermelons as the truth echoed in his ears. Iyke gave his father some financial aid and in return, Dede was to convince Chinny to marry him. Dubem could not believe his error in ever associating the word *decent* with Iyke. It all now made perfect sense. *Mother must have been outraged. This is why Chinny ran away!!* he thought.

He strained very hard to hear the rest of their conversation. "We need to tread softly, Iyke. My daughter is a very intelligent girl. If she suspects that you are being pushed her way, this will never work. The only reason I am even considering your proposition is because you profess to love and care about her. I suggest you try to win her by yourself."

Fair enough. He is a young, eligible bachelor but where does the money come in? Dubem thought.

Iyke remained silent for a while before resuming his near whisper.

"You know Chinny is very strong-willed. I have already sounded her out and she is focused on her own course. But why have you refused to cash the cheque I gave to you?" Dubem listened with growing pride as his father explained that in spite of the financial constraints that made it difficult to ignore his proposal at the time, he had taken a while to think it through and concluded that their arrangement reeked of nothing but manipulation, deception and slavery.

"If you can loan me the money, I would be eternally grateful, but it would be a favour from one human being to another. Not because you expect me to arm-twist or influence my daughter into getting married to you. I love her very much and will do everything in my power to be the father she once knew."

Iyke found it impossible to reconcile Dede's words. Not sure of what had happened since the last time he spoke to Mr Ona, it was clear to him that torrents of water had run under the bridge of their previous discussion. Dubem could not hold himself back any longer. He walked into the sitting room and began to draw the already drawn blinds and rearrange perfectly placed chairs. Iyke took the cue and asked for his cheque. Dede walked into his room and with drooping shoulders, returned with the cheque, handed it over and thanked Iyke who left as fast as his legs could carry him. With tired eyes and a bowed head, Dede made to retire to his room, but Dubem tapped him on the shoulders. When Mr Ona turned towards his son, who enveloped him in a hug, it dawned on him that his son must have heard everything. Dubem's arms around Dede felt like a balm over his aching heart.

In the bedroom, Ama asked her husband, "Is he gone?" He nodded with a thin film of tears in his eye. But that night, he went to bed an encouraged man.

The house needed urgent domestic intervention. For so long, it had gone without attention. But right after Iyke's clandestine visit and Dubem's narration to Chinny, her spirits competed with the eagles as she busied herself with cobwebbing, sweeping and mopping. As she worked through the chaos, she mused over how her boisterous imagination almost ran her into the wilds. She chuckled when she remembered

Ejiofor's loud and mile-long laughter after she narrated over the phone the misconceptions Dubem straightened out for her.

"Uncle Iyke has regressed into a child trapped in the body of a full-grown man," said Ejiofor, his voice a pitch lower than before. And to his suggestion that they feign ignorance of Iyke's failed attempt at cradle snatching, Chinny gave Ejiofor a loud virtual high five.

No longer did talking to her parents about the events that led to her dramatic flight pose such a grim task. Pride welled up in her at the clarity of what they thought about Mr Peters. Dede and Ama were vigorous with their apologies and regretted allowing the excruciating climb of their lives suggest options they chose not to rehash. The renewed confidence in the value her parents placed on her provided Chinny with the motivation to throw the past behind her.

The candle wax would not come off without leaving a scratch on the wooden table in the sitting room. So Chinny went to fetch a match box. The wax needed some heat to get it off. She had not quite made it out of the sitting room when her cousin Adaiba banged on the door. Puzzled by her cousin's obstinate ignorance of the ease a doorbell provided, Chinny opened the door and Adaiba charged in.

"Yes, just the person I wanted to see. Are you just waking up? Where is everyone?"

"Good morning to you too," Chinny laughed. Her cousin's boisterous and infectiously cheerful disposition never ceased to put a smile on her face. The twinkle in Adaiba's eyes could stop a moving train, or so one of her suitors had said. Adaiba swept past her cousin and heaved herself onto the most comfortable chair in the sitting room – Dede's comfort chair.

"Guess what?" she cried.

"What?!" Chinny's excitement mounted, but she reined in when she remembered Adaiba's proclivity for seeing invisible rainbows in pitch-dark clouds.

"Chi, GCE results are out!" Ama peered through the corridor doorway and grew anxious as soon as she learnt the reason behind their excitement. The weight of all the years of hard work Chinny slaved through suddenly grew bones and flesh before her eyes. Chinny asked Adaiba to give her a few minutes to take a bath. The day would not slide by without her knowing her fate and in minutes, they were off to the GCE secretariat. Almost right after the girls left, Ama followed. She glanced at her husband who sat, having his breakfast of bean cakes with corn pudding, and bade him goodbye. Life seemed to have settled back to normal since their talk with Chinny, even though the nagging issue of their meagre resources remained.

Ama still respected her husband, but as a result of the growing stickiness of their financial quicksand, resentment actively hovered and proved increasingly difficult to shoo away. But, rather than dwell on her emotions, she decided it was time to change her narrative. Her late father bequeathed five acres of land to her two brothers. His mind evolution regardless, he could not give his little girl any land. "The wolves of culture will eat her up", he had confided in his wife. However, when one of Ama's brothers disappeared into thin air just before their father's burial and the other died before he turned twenty years old, ownership naturally slid to her. But, the land remained in dispute between her and her uncle for several years and so lay unused. He did not see why a female should handle such a vast inheritance when there were still men in the family.

Ama began growing cassava, peppers, vegetables, corn and the likes for home consumption and sales at her vegetable stall without further confrontation from her uncle after he witnessed the birth and steady growth of her son Dubem. But the huge expanse of land had been grossly underutilised for so long and Ama set out to correct that. *Today will be a good day*, she thought as she flagged down a tricycle. With Chinny off to make the confirmation that would change the course of her life, Ama rode away to make changes that promised to positively redefine hers.

The heap of yams and cassava were impressive. One look at the unripe plantains and Ama let out a satisfied grunt. The labourers harvested four jute bags of pumpkin leaves and a bag of habaneros. She wondered why the peppers were mostly green. *I spotted a couple of red ones the last time I came here. One can never win with these labourers*, she thought as she paid all five of them and laid out her spare wrapper on the heap of yams where she settled to wait for the truck that would carry her harvested produce to safety. Ama planned to use the barn she constructed in her father's compound as a warehouse until she sold off all her produce. Finally, the truck arrived and when it was fully loaded, she began her journey to where she first called home.

As hard as the truck driver tried, he could not drive through the narrow gate of Ama's late father's compound. And to Ama's utter surprise, he ordered his assistant to give him a hand and together, they deposited all the produce right in front of the gate. Her pleas for them to take the produce into the barn she had painstakingly constructed amounted to nothing. She told them that the rains would destroy everything, but they jeered at her, asking her to brace up for the labour since she wanted to do a *man's job*. Ama experienced emotions that ranged from helplessness to panic and raving anger in quick succession. *If only Dubem was still on holidays*, she thought and dug deep for creativity as she watched the truck leave a cloud of road dust in its trail. At the back of the house, she rummaged for some wrappers and jute bags, which she tore open to create a bigger surface area. After she spread them over the heap of produce, Ama formed a ball with three wrappers and placed this on top of the jute-covered heap. She covered the entire pile with another wrapper. Next, she reached for a red scarf from her purse, folded it into a bow and masterfully placed it on top. After she placed a few odd-looking sticks around, Ama felt satisfied that most people would keep their curiosity in check, thinking that whatever lay under that heap was laced with 'juju'. She began a quick search for a tricycle as she walked as fast as her legs could carry her. As she walked, Ama thought about how best to go about her survival plan. She wondered what Chinny thought about breeding day-old turkeys or chicks for business. She would build cages and buy her first batch of hatchlings with proceeds from the farm produce she planned to sell.

Occasionally, Ama's head bumped into the tricycle's roof as the thoughtless driver tried to outrun the encroaching hands of darkness. But that did not stop the happy tune she hummed through the entire trip. Once at her stop, she got down, paid the driver and walked the short distance to the gate of her home. At the porch, Ama stopped midstride. She thought she heard someone sniffing at the side of the house. Taking cautious steps towards the source of the sound, Ama felt a chill when she saw who it was.

"Chinny, Nne, what is it? Why are you crying? What happened?" Ama rushed to her daughter's side as the questions came pouring in a panic-laden voice. She crouched beside Chinny, who sat dejected on the bare ground, and gazed into her daughter's eyes, bloodshot from crying. Ama's heart started to beat faster as she waited for an answer.

Chinny did not steer her wide-eyed stare away from space as she said in a hoarse voice, "Nne'm, I have no result. It was cancelled... all... my... hard work... it is all gone." The wind left Ama's lungs as she knelt beside her daughter. She gathered her in her arms and together they wept hard and long. When would fate stop playing games with them? Could life not see that they already had too much to contend with? Where and how could she get the courage to sit for GCE again? These questions plagued Chinny's mind as her tears gave in to the full force of the pain in her heart.

Dede came out for the fourth time to console them. "It is all right Chinny. Crying will solve nothing. Besides, I am optimistic that the results will still be released." When Chinny and her mother did not act as though they heard a word he said, feeling like a cuckoo in the nest, he went back into the house. But a while later, the night insects convinced Ama and Chinny to break up their pity party and go indoors.

After the intriguing events of the day Ama prepared the dinner, which went back to the pot untouched. Gloom's cold arms refused to let go even after Ama's warm bath. So, she lay awake, long after Dede began to snore, thinking about her next line of action. She believed life held a colourful promise on the horizon for her daughter and began to shuffle her previous plans around. Three of her many plots of land would go on a yearly lease to the telecommunications companies expanding their network to Abotiti town. What is left of one acre would be reserved for her own use while the remaining four acres would be used for industrial agricultural production. With such an air-tight prospective income plan, Ama could make sure Chinny would re-sit the GCE, take the entrance examination to the university of her choice and make a proper life for herself – or so she thought.

5

THE BURP FOLLOWING THE END OF MR OLISEH'S DINNER OF plantain pottage indicated deep satisfaction. "Thank you for this tasty meal, my son. With someone like you, who cares for a wife?"

Dubem gave his ever-scarce grin to his host. "We aim to please," he responded and took a dramatic bow. Seeing Dubem with Mr Oliseh would cause anyone to wonder why the words 'aloof and dull' were ever associated with him. In Mr Oliseh's company, Dubem bloomed like the sunflower at the first sign of the rains. It did not matter what anyone thought about Mr Oliseh, Dubem saw in him the definition of nobility and kindness, and remained indebted to the circumstances that brought them together.

Once done with the dishes, Dubem took a bath to rid himself of the sweat and grit which normally rode with the month of February. He made to have an early night when Mr Oliseh asked him to sit for a chat. Anyone would have thought a foul smell hung in the air with Dubem's grimace. He had an idea of the crux of the chat – the broken record of 'coming clean with his folks'. He dutifully sat down to listen to another one of Mr Oliseh's long lectures. He owed his benefactor that much.

So much had happened since Dubem's arrival. As the long-standing chief security officer of DLSS, the school allowed Oliseh to cultivate a huge expanse of land for an indefinite period. This, he used for minor domestic cropping in addition to the mini catfish farm he ran behind his house. On retirement, Oliseh planned on expanding the fish farm, which for now featured only two big drums made of reinforced plastic. He used these for fish farming at his leisure. His clientele included his ever-willing-to-buy neighbours. And those not sold, he used to prepare his favourite 'white soup'. This was why coming up with the funds for Dubem's school fees did not pose much of a burden.

Ready with rules, boundaries, consequences and a massive storeroom for disappointments and shortfalls, Oliseh equipped himself for the project before him upon Dubem's arrival. His understanding being that Dubem was one who, for reasons unknown, did not have any will to study. The shock Oliseh experienced when he learnt the truth can best be described as a high-powered jolt.

The first surprise came when Mrs Adun, Dubem's class teacher, who already knew about Dubem's 'peculiar case', informed Oliseh that there was either a mistake in Dubem's assessment or that the young man had experienced a monumental miracle. She came to this conclusion because besides being top in his class, Dubem exhibited profound knowledge of concepts in subjects taught two classes ahead of his. According to the class teacher, the young lad did not care much for needless chatter but gave lengthy and robust contributions whenever called forth to do so. When Mrs Adun mentioned that on rare occasions when Dubem decided to ask questions, her colleagues complained of being mentally stretched and strained, Oliseh let out a mischievous chuckle. He could almost bet his life's savings that Mrs Adun did not speak for just her colleagues. Following this revelation, Oliseh closed his book of rules and opened his eyes to observe the mystery called Dubem Ona.

Over the weeks following Mrs Adun's revelation, Oliseh found out that each time he pretended to have retired for the day, the daily papers which he often placed on the television stand took a walk a few minutes before the lights in Dubem's room came back on. They magically reappeared very early the following morning. Oliseh often smiled when he recalled with amusement the vigorous and hurried shake of Dubem's head each time he asked if he never received homework from school. The last straw for Oliseh was at the end of the school's first term, when he stared in complete bewilderment at Dubem's ridiculous attempt at altering his report card. The crooked number '3' that was squeezed in front of the number '1' stuck out like a sore thumb. More laughable were the alterations on his subject and class average scores.

Needless to say, Mr Oliseh paid Mrs Adun a visit the following day for a printout of Dubem's original result which, like he suspected, reflected an outstanding performance. He came out top in his class with an average score of 98.6 per cent.

After the second term, Dubem's teacher sent a proposal to the school's trust council for Dubem to be promoted to class three rather than class two after the third term. The council unanimously agreed with her that it would be a waste of time to promote him to class two, so they promised that her proposal would be given due consideration.

Only after Oliseh's coercion, cajoling, imploring and threats to send him back to his parents did Dubem confess to the age-long charade he thought would get his father to send his sister back to school. With liquid pain in his eyes, he took Mr Oliseh through the deep and lengthy journey of what birthed his web of lies. At almost the age of three, Dubem longed for a sister and sent forth his childlike prayers to whoever sent down children to please send them a girl. When Chinny came along the following year, Dubem almost popped with excitement. But as the months gave way to years, his sadness and confusion knew no end when he perceived that his little sister lived on the wrong side of 'favour-ville'. Almost everything the little girl did attracted a reprimand. Days gave way to weeks, months and years while Dubem looked on helplessly as his bright little treasure dimmed slowly but surely.

His answer, or the lack of it, when Oliseh asked Dubem what he would do if he was withdrawn from school did nothing to diminish his amazement at such dogged devotion. Being passed over in life due to factors entirely out of one's control was an experience Oliseh identified with. However, following his validation of Dubem's stance, he explained that men often had a knotty time articulating their frustrations – especially to the ones they loved the most. Oliseh asked him to rethink his state of mind and resulting actions.

After that expository chat with Dubem, Oliseh never bothered to go through the results Dubem handed him. He simply waited for the original copy, which Mrs Adun graciously made available to him without fail.

One day, Oliseh saw Dubem welding some metal behind the house and asked him what this was for. Dubem gave a nervous laugh and in an unsure, rushed voice explained, "It is a surprise sir, but please I will come to you next week for a loan of 6,000 Naira. I promise to pay you back to the last Naira as soon as I can. It is important and… it is for this construction. I know it may appear—" Oliseh cut in and calling Dubem a rascal, joked about him asking for the greater percentage of his monthly salary. Dubem's initial optimism nose-dived but that did not deter him.

The following week, he approached Mr Oliseh with his request for a loan and could not keep his heart from thumping with excitement when his host handed him the exact amount he asked for. In truth, Oliseh kept a rather stern exterior, but was pure jelly within and seldom refused anyone help. Dubem observed this part of him and jumped at it because a few weeks after receiving the loan, he asked Oliseh if he could use a part of his land that lay fallow for some cropping. Again, Oliseh said yes but was not prepared for what followed.

Dubem approached a settlement of fishers and arranged for them to become his farm hands. In payment for their labour, he would let them crop for their personal use, two out of the ten plots of land which Mr Oliseh gave him for his temporary use.

A rather confused Oliseh listened with rapt attention as the school's principal expressed his delight at his decision to take his love for agriculture a mark higher. He also told him to deal carefully with the settlers, as they have been known to exhibit violent tendencies when they feel short-changed. Oliseh masked his confusion with his vigorous nods and exaggerated smiles, having a hunch that the answer to the puzzle lay with the young lad who lived in his house. The principal went on his way but not before he made Oliseh vow that his new passion would not interfere with the school's top priority – to protect the students and staff of DLSS. Oliseh hurried home. He needed to have a word with Dubem concerning his far from conservative approach to actualising his dreams.

Unable to resist the delicious wafts floating from his Sunday dinner any longer, Oliseh tore his eyes away from the football match and went for his meal. He stared at what sat on his plate. "What is this?" he asked Dubem, whose eyes were glued to the television. "What did you do to the fresh fish?" Oliseh asked again.

"I dried it… with the kiln… the one I constructed. I used the loan you gave me to buy the… the remaining parts… sir," Dubem stuttered.

"The remaining parts?" Oliseh echoed under his breath as he took his first mouthful.

Later that night, Dubem took the liberty of explaining himself to his host, now turned friend. He had kept the individual parts of the kiln out of sight because he could not bet on the success of his contraption. He coupled the parts yesterday and to his delight, it worked. He decided to honour Oliseh with the first product of his construction. He hoped to expand the catfish production. He would buy six more drums, a hand-sealing machine, and print some labels. If the profits allowed it, he would construct more kilns and may even end up employing more hands. "I am sorry sir, if that was presumptuous of me," Dubem began to apologise, but Oliseh stopped him.

"No, no. Far from it, Dubem. You have been a box of pleasant surprises since you set foot in my house. I see in you the true meaning of determination, resourcefulness, resilience and dog-like loyalty. You… you illuminate unexplored possibilities. Please my son, know that whatever you do, I am one hundred and twenty per cent behind you. But you must promise me that nothing will affect your studies – remember, it is number one on your list." Dubem gave Oliseh his word.

Dubem planned to approach market channels for the sale of the plantains, cucumbers and watermelons he grew. Certain that adding his kiln-dried catfish innovation to the table held the promise of a bright future for his family, Dubem could never thank Mr Oliseh enough for the springboard he afforded him. With his eyes closing in to welcome slumber, Dubem's roadmap to success unrolled before him, brightly marked with rainbows and gayly coloured mountain peaks and hills. In the other room, Oliseh wept for joy at his second chance at life. "Blessings they say come in different packages," he mused. Since his life took the unpleasant tangent it did, Oliseh prayed and strove to get back on course. With each passing day, his chance meeting with his friend Dede seemed more orchestrated than coincidental but whatever the case, Oliseh decided he was going to enjoy every bit of the opportunity presented to him in Dubem. He turned off the light to make room for the future in the horizon of his mind's eye.

Ama opened the door to none other than Mr Peters and in a manner far from her character, gave a loud hiss and slammed the door in his face. She headed back to the kitchen to carry on with her cooking and collided head-long with Chinny.

"Who came Nne'm?"

"Nobody, my child. Nobody."

Chinny continued to the sitting room but Ama changed her mind and following her daughter said, "You know what? It is not nobody. It is that slimy excuse of a man who had the guts to show his decayed face here. A vulture with two legs and arms, looking for helpless and defenceless people to prey on." A scowl distorted Ama's tear-stained face as she shook with rage. Chinny shot a glance at the door, half expecting the object of her mother's expletives to walk back into the house. Only then did Chinny realise the agony and trauma her parents would have suffered, knowing that nothing but their shortcomings as parents could have given the likes of Mr Peters the impudence to approach them in the first place. Following this epiphany, every residual disappointment and disdain she held against her parents trickled away, never to return.

⸺⊃

The birds' tweets announced morning's arrival to Ama. She sat up in bed and became momentarily puzzled. For twenty-two years, she had woken up to her husband's snores. Ama tied her wrapper over her chest and walked half asleep to the sitting room in search of Dede. The sight of her husband on the dining table, writing vigorously on a sheet of paper came as a surprise to Ama. "Good morning Dee," she greeted him, looking at the litter of crumpled paper on the table and floor. Dede responded without as much as a glance her way as he continued scribbling. But he noticed the endearment in her voice. She called him 'Dee' only when hit by a surge of affection. The issues of life had made those moments far and few between. Yawning loudly, Ama drew a chair to sit beside her husband and asked, "What are you writing so early in the morning?" Dede drew a straight line across his words, took a fresh sheet and made to resume his writing when Ama placed her hand lightly on his.

"What is going on Dee? Talk to me," she insisted.

"Ama," he sighed and began, "I am done failing everyone under my watch. For reasons out of my control, I could not go on with school, but I used to be bright in my days. So, this is a list of our long-term goals, short-term goals and the resources I have to make them happen." He held up a sheet of paper which had a list of items like: Begin to pay off the house loan; pay Kika back his money; give my two children an education; pay John back his money; set Ama up in business; pay Madam Jacinta back her money; provide a weekly allowance for my home's upkeep; buy a car, a tricycle or a motorbike. On a second piece of paper were the items: God; my good head; my strong will and providence.

Ama stared at her husband as though seeing him for the first time and after a while said, "So you owe Madam Jacinta too? No wonder she always looks at me in that funny way." Dede hung his head as he drifted far away in thought, as was now his custom.

A bang on the kitchen door rattled through the silent house and Ama knew her daughter had returned from delivering her famous beef cubes to Thompson Supermarket. She often wondered if Chinny made any profit from her business since although they were fried crisp-dry to ensure a long shelf life, the beef cuts still came in impressive chunks. Never mind the plethora of spices she lavished on the meat while marinating. Humming a happy tune, Ama turned the lock on the door to let Chinny in and went about preparing breakfast – pap and moimoi from the night before.

Today promised to be a very good Wednesday indeed. Three rapidly expanding telecommunications outfits each wanted her property on a lease arrangement for their masts and were due to pick up the documents she had filled out. In the unlikely existence of some policy that red-flagged leasing from a prospect who already had a contract with competition, Ama arranged a meeting with the Breeze-links representative for 12:15

pm, while those for Starlite Mobile and Afrocomms would meet with her at 12:50 pm and 1:25 pm respectively that same afternoon. Exploring the possibility of becoming one of their major suppliers, Ama also fixed a meeting with the production manager at the yam flour processing factory in Koki town, situated two towns away, west of Abotiti. If she succeeded, it would be a profitable outlet for the yam plantation she had recently created on her huge expanse of land.

Ama had a plan. Once she secured a retainership with the yam flour processing factory, she would ask Dede to approach a bank for a loan using the plantation as collateral and, with any luck, they would be able to pay off the mortgage on the house. Hopefully, the proceeds from the plantation and other extra incomes like the land lease would fund the loan. Her brokenness over the loss of her family had finally mended. Everything would be okay.

Never one to pile up used dishes and pots, after breakfast, Ama washed up and got ready for the day. On her way out, Dede asked his wife, "Are you going to the farm?" Ama shook her head like one reprimanding an errant child.

"Ranch, Dede, ranch. They call it a ranch these days." Amused, Dede told his wife that ranches characteristically comprised plants, animals and a place to lodge. "Well, who is to say that one day, we would not have animals, processing sheds and a big lodge there? Exercise some faith oh good husband of mine," Ama said, brushing off Dede's call for her to wait so they could leave the house together. She told him she did not want to miss the early morning vegetable buyers. The back of Dede's ears hurt from grinning as he put on his shoes. Ama's decision to crop for commercial purposes on her land filled Dede with immense joy. For so long, the subject of the land had been a sore one as Ama could not get over the loss of her family. Other than that, he would have long made a defining move or at least offered a few life-changing suggestions. Walking out of the house, Dede pondered on his wife's high spirits.

"Could it be the list I shared with her? But it did not state any financial injection, so why would it cause so much hope?" Dede wondered aloud. But Ama's apparent belief in him sparked even more determination. His stance resembled a lion's as he strode along, resolving to reclaim and offer the life he once promised his family.

Ama stopped a few feet away to hand the documents to Mr Clarke. She begged him to be discreet about her dealings with all three companies as she was not clear on their organisational policies. With any luck, by the time they realised it, the contract would be long sealed. "But wait a minute. What is even wrong with me dealing with competitors of the same market? I do not work for them and there is no conflict of interest. Or is there?" she reasoned with Mr Clarke who in response, let out a dry laugh. "I will call the representatives and give them your number so that they do not go to my house at all," she said. When Ama also begged him to keep her husband out of her dealings with the companies, Mr Clarke's eyes twinkled, but dimmed almost as soon as she explained that she meant to throw it on him as a surprise once the deal matured.

Sitting in the bus to Koki town, a small smile stole across Ama's thoughtful countenance. They were going to be rich and Dede did not even know it. *I will shock him with my ability to make things happen,* Ama thought, as her chest expanded with the plans she held within.

6

CHINNY STEPPED OUT OF FORE-TRUST BANK WITH THE BOUNCE of a brand-new basketball, her trepidation long forgotten. Besides the steady climb in school fees, the number of primary six pupils unable to pass the secondary school entrance examinations also did not do much to help the crash in Chinny's school transport business. Grateful for the fall-back plan she had in her crisp beef cubes business, she reached into her bag for a pack of her scrumptious product. Chewing on her beef as she scanned for an available tricycle, Chinny grew nostalgic as she recalled giving out her cart to Abbas the goods transporter at the market. He moved goods in and out of the town market for traders. So, he promised to remit a fixed fee of 60 Naira daily for six days in a week to her, irrespective of how much he made. When Abbas realised that Chinny intended to strip the cart of its famous duvet, he begged her to forfeit the bell and ribbons since they would provide more visibility for his business.

The tricycle across the street filled up as soon as it slowed down and Chinny wondered where all the passengers had appeared from. More conscious of the dull ache in her stomach, which harped on the need to eat something besides her beef bites, she began walking towards a show glass filled with crust buns and bumped smack into a beggar girl standing by the sidewalk. Disarmed by the raw beauty of the little girl, not older than eleven years, Chinny wondered why someone with no obvious impairment would settle for street begging. Refusing to let her be, the beggar girl followed and called out to Chinny for alms. She went on about her two-day old starvation, and how Chinny's handout would be her life saver. Somewhat amused yet impressed by the beggar's creative persistence, Chinny shoved aside whatever concept she had about healthy beggars and gave her a ₦10 bill.

The beggar girl hesitated, then snatched and shoved the bill into the bag attached to her waist. Muttering, she turned to the next victim of her harassment. Wide-eyed with surprise, Chinny, who had begun to walk away, to place herself in an advantageous position for the next tricycle that would show up, walked back and in a voice a notch lower than her usual tone addressed the beggar, "Young lady, I have no clue about who you are, your story or what your expectations from life are, but I know two things. First, nobody owes you and is under any obligation to offer any assistance to you. Secondly, those who have risen above their circumstances are the ones known to have cultivated and maintained a grateful attitude for the little mercies that came their way – mercies as seemingly insignificant as breath." Saucer-eyed, the beggar stared as Chinny stalked off in time for another tricycle that had just pulled up, all the while wondering at the audacity of people with the incredible propensity to trample on the weightier things in life while bemoaning the lack of trivialities. She let out a long yawn and tried to remember if she needed to buy any cooking condiments before she got home. She had yam pottage to prepare for lunch and thinking about it made her mouth water in anticipation.

The three new carts that stood under the almond tree in front of the house drew a smile from Chinny as she walked towards the door. A lip-smacking happy Abbas, obviously pleased with the prospect of Chinny relinquishing ownership of the truck to him after twelve months, introduced his three friends to her. They also wanted to start the goods transport business in other market locations and found her arrangement enticing. Chinny took them up on their offer and contacted her truck constructor – her father – to build three more trucks. This, in addition to her flourishing beef business, made sure Chinny's bank account received impressive deposits in preparation for school. She now had a major customer who bought a hundred sachets of beef bites every week for the snack shop at the college of education in a neighbouring town.

Every so often, Chinny worked overnight on Saturdays to make packs ready for pick up on Sunday.

Dede did not see his daughter as she walked in and almost immediately out of the compound. She decided to go back a few blocks to ask Madam Cynthia, one of the caterers who outsourced the meat preparation bit of their food catering deals to her, for the number of chickens to expect from Mrs Badmus. Thankfully, Ama often threw her legs and arms into ensuring the timely delivery of her daughter's meat deals. These days, Chinny's bank account grew in giant leaps, and this thought filled her mind as she passed by, unaware of Mr Clarke sitting comfortably in his car, under the baking sun.

Mr Clarke sat parked a few metres away, poring over a newspaper and Dede looked out of his bedroom window for the fifth time, pondering on why his neighbour chose to sit in his car under the menacing heat, rather than the comfort of his plush sitting room to satisfy his thirst for information. At twenty minutes past twelve, a car pulled up beside Mr Clarke and a young man in blue denim and a smart shirt turned upwards at the cuffs came out and began talking with him. Dede could see that they were looking at some papers. Tired of straining his eyes and neck over people he could not hear, he went to the kitchen to help himself to a glass of water. He considered going out for a chat with Mr Clarke afterwards if he was still outside. Dede had put in a bid to supply brick casting machines at the construction company where Mr Clarke worked and wanted to find out if he should still set his hopes on winning the bid.

As he made to cover the bottle of water, the full glass of water now sitting on the counter slid off and landed on the ground with a crash. In a frenzy, Dede swept up the glass particles and with a napkin he snatched from the cabinet handle, mopped the floor dry. He shook the napkin vigorously to rid it of all the glass particles and started to wring it out but winced in pain. A glass splinter buried in the napkin had lodged in his palm where it joined to his wrist. Taking out the splinter with a safety pin proved to be trickier than Dede anticipated. For, as he attempted to make a horizontal bypass under the splinter in his palm, the pin made an unintended detour, tearing into his wrist. Judging by the volume of blood running off Dede's palm, he knew the cut was bad.

He put the napkin aside and, using another kitchen napkin, applied pressure to the cut. The once-blue cloth fast became damp and red with his blood and the entire arm now throbbed with excruciating pain.

Out of the corner of his eye as he walked back to his bedroom to lay his head, Dede saw that Mr Clarke still lingered outside, but with someone entirely different. With the pain in his arm as his current source of worry, Mr Clarke, his curious behaviour and strange visitors were the last things on Dede's mind. Giving in to the alluring comfort of sleep, he closed his eyes. *Chinny will bring me a glass of water when she returns*, was Dede's last conscious thought.

Chinny let herself in through the kitchen door. Deciding not to bother her father's nap, she went about preparing lunch like a mouse. As she cooked, she thought about the man snoring in the room and her heart warmed. She knew her father's back ached from bending over backwards to support the home but did not know that for each time a breakthrough prospect fell through his fingers, he died a little. Chinny did not know that after coming to the disappointing conclusion that his son did not have any interest in academic pursuits, he secretly regretted staking Dubem's education against hers. Dede did not want to imagine how bad Dubem's actual results were since even after severe mutilation, they still ended up so poor when he sent them home. Why Oliseh appeared happy to keep a total failure like Dubem in his house eluded Dede's logical mind.

Lunch preparation lasted till twenty minutes before 3 pm. Chinny knocked on Dede's bedroom door and when she did not get any response, let herself in to see her father shivering under the covers. She tapped him and when he did not move, tried to move him over onto his back to get a better look at him. Only then did she step on something sticky. Chinny went into panic mode when she realised the stickiness was blood from her father. She thought he had slashed his wrist but on closer observation, decided differently and began to shake him for response. Dede did not move, and the blood continued to trickle. The blood refused to clot, and this worried Chinny as she started to run out of the room. Almost immediately, she changed her mind and decided to place a call using her phone but one look at her father's immobile body made her change her mind again.

A few home remedies from a first-aid handbook which could speed up blood clotting flashed in Chinny's head and she dashed to the kitchen to return with a few items – tea bags, a block of alum salt and some black powdery substance. She sprinkled some water on the three tea bags she held and after undoing the now blood-soaked napkin from her father's hand, strained some of the liquid from the tea bags onto the wound. She waited for a heartbeat, wiped the wound surface with the napkin and saw the blood still flowed, but in less violent spurts. She dipped a small block of alum into water and placed it on the cut. While she waited, she touched her father's forehead and winced at his fever. Holding the alum in place with the bloodied napkin, she ran to the kitchen and came back with ice in a bowl of tap water. She grabbed her mother's wrapper from under the pillow, dipped it in the bowl of iced water and placed a cold compress on her father's head, neck and chest. Chinny gave a sigh of relief when she checked the cut again to see that the bleeding had almost ceased. She opened all three of the drawers beside the bed before spotting the object of her search. Taking a cup from the table, Chinny dissolved six tablets of the painkiller and without thinking, prised her father's mouth open by inserting an ink marker between his upper and lower incisors. She poured the dissolved medicine into his mouth, but he remained as still as ice. So, even though the blood no longer ran, Chinny braced herself and poured her last blood clotting aid – ground black pepper – on her father's wound. Dede winced and as he did, gulped for air. Chinny took out the marker and down went the medicine.

Chinny told her now-conscious but weak father that they had to go to the medical centre for proper care and went outside to flag a tricycle for the trip to the centre. Perplexed after three failed attempts at getting a tricycle driver to come into the house to move her father, Chinny went in to check on Dede to find that not only had the fever returned with a vengeance, he was also no longer responsive. She dabbed him with some iced water and ran out in confusion to seek for any kind of help. When Chinny found nobody in sight, she took out her phone and called Ama.

"Nne'm, father is injured. I have tried my best, but nobody is willing to help me. Nne, nobody wants to help me. I cannot lift him

alone. Father is not talking, his body... his body is limp. I do not..."
By this time, Chinny had her left hand on her head. Tears gushed
down her face as she wailed loudly, uncontrollably and without shame.
Unable to get in any more words through her daughter's outburst,
Ama turned hysterical at the other end of the line. In the midst of the
communication chaos, an oncoming car missed Chinny by whiskers.
The driver screeched to a halt and jumped out looking flustered. A
second man sat back in the passenger's seat.

"Do you have a death wish?" the driver bawled. Chinny cleaned her
face with the back of her hands.

She did not know the driver, but began in a rushed voice, "Please
sir, please sir... help me... my father... he is seriously injured. I cannot
carry him alone. Please sir can you help me to the hospi—" She took
two steps back when she recognised the still-seated passenger. It was
Mr Peters.

The driver, a younger man, asked pointing towards the house, "Is
that your house?" Chinny hesitated for a heartbeat. Two fresh beads
of tears slid down her face to her throat as she bobbed her head. He
followed her into the house and in no time, they were on their way to
the medical centre.

It did not take too long to locate a vein and set a drip line on Dede's
good arm. A total of five injections were pumped into the pack of
saline solution hanging on the stand beside his bed. The fluid dripped
soundlessly from the pack, through the transparent tube and into
his vein. Chinny wondered how long it would take the drip pack to
become empty. The tightness around her chest began to ease out since
her father lay stable and now snored lightly as he rested. The stranger
took complete control of the situation, insisting that Dede be kept
in a private room. He paid the registration fees and after making his
bank details available, asked the billing unit to charge whatever bill
was incurred to his account. Chinny was done filling in the required
documents at the registration desk and went to the reception area to
find the stranger and Mr Peters.

That Mr Peters neither empathised nor made any suggestions the
entire time did not elude Chinny's perceptive mind. She wondered how
Mr Stranger knew this vile man and looking pointedly at the younger

man, gushed her gratitude. Chinny's thankfulness radiated from her eyes as she told Mr Stranger that her father's temperature now read within the normal range and that he lay stable and sound asleep. But before he could respond, she continued, "Please sir, who are you? I mean what is your name and how much do I owe you?" Not one to be taken by surprise, Chinny had already begun thinking of possible ways to pay back if the bill became too much for her bank account to handle. She thought about services he may need; top of the list were house cleaning and laundry. She hoped he did not live too far away or already have someone who offered those services. Hopefully, whatever salary he paid for her services would be sufficient to offset her debt in no time.

Smiling genially, Mr Stranger responded. "Do not bother about the bill yet. I am Kenneth," and pointing to the man whose head now hung in an awkward angle, he finished, "and this is my father, Mr Nchedo Peters." The upward curve of the smile of gratitude that had begun to form again around Chinny's mouth dipped without warning. On cue, Chinny's phone began to ring. It was her mother.

"Nne, we are at the medical centre." There was a pause and she continued, "Yes, the one by the expressway, close to the water corporation. Yes, Mother. Okay. See you. Bye" She looked at Kenneth, the smile gone from her eyes and thanked him for his help but repeated, "How much do I owe you sir... for the registration and please do not worry, we will pay the bill. My mother will be here shortly." She made a mental note to transfer her father to the general ward the instant her mother arrived.

Kenneth noticed Chinny recoiled when he introduced himself and was surprised at her sudden mood swing. He glanced at his father and back at Chinny and in a measured voice said, "You have not told me your name... and wha—"

"My name is Chinetalum Ona," Chinny blurted. She was eternally grateful to Kenneth for coming to her rescue when he did but the thought of him being remotely connected to the man in the seat next to him proved to be a very rough morsel to swallow.

The air between them could almost be touched. "Ehm," Mr Peters stuttered, "I err... happen to be friends with err... Chinny's father."

"Who is Chinny?" Kenneth asked him, visibly piqued.

"That would be me. My friends and family call me Chinny for short and no, that man is no friend. He asked my father to trade me for a loan that would help offset the mortgage on our house. That is our relationship with him." Chinny's voice had risen an octave higher and sounded like it belonged to someone at least twenty years older. Kenneth rolled the information he had just heard around in his head and was mortified when the meaning of Chinny's words slapped him hard across the face. He turned towards Chinny.

"I did not know who you were when I almost ran into you and decided to help you. Please accept my offer to help and do not judge me by my father's gross conduct. I hope your father gets well soon." He did not wait for her response and walked out of the medical centre without as much as a glance backwards. Mr Peters started to say something to his son but neither halting nor looking in his direction, Kenneth stopped him with a raised hand. Chinny looked on as the two men walked out. She went back to peek at her father and by the time she came back to the reception area for some air and TV, she saw her mother talking to the nurse.

"Nne!!!" Chinny squealed, relieved.

Ama hugged her daughter. She was so worried and began in a rushed and nervous voice, "When I got home and did not see you there, I did not know what to think. I had called you up to four times before the call connected. These networks are so poor here. Where is he?" Walking towards the room, Chinny collected the carry-on bag from her mother as they made their way to Dede's room. She narrated the events of the day to her mother who was both grateful and angered that her daughter had to sit in the same space as the one person they all despised the most. Ama told Chinny that on her way into the medical centre, she ran into Mr Peters who, with the young man he seemed to be having an argument with, attempted to get her attention. Needless to say, the words she threw at them were ones she could not bring herself to repeat to her daughter.

Once in the room, Chinny examined the contents of the bag with visible appreciation. When Ama heard that they were now at the medical centre, her anxiety lifted somewhat, so she had packed up the yam pottage that should have been lunch and some essentials to take with her to the centre. Dede's eyes fluttered open. He still looked weak but managed a smile. He soon became agitated as his eyes darted around the room. Ama understood at once and offered, "Dee, you passed out. Your cut was deep, and you bled so much for too long. Maybe you tore a vein. It is a good thing you did not need a transfusion." Just then, a doctor came in. Chinny did not recognise this doctor. The first doctor who attended to them earlier was tall and light in complexion, but the doctor who now busied himself with examining her father's eyes and taking notes was dark-skinned and of an average height. She could not help but notice his striking good looks too. He had a set of perfectly white teeth. *Is that why he smiles often?* Chinny wondered.

The handsome doctor seemed pleased with his patient's progress. He smiled at the pairs of anxious eyes boring into him and said, "He is responding remarkably well. The cut will heal in no time. Unfortunately, his white blood cell count was over the roof. He was probably battling a prior infection. We would watch out for temperature spikes through the night and complete the full course of the antibiotics he has been started on." There was dramatic relief in the room at the doctor's words.

Chinny put the handsome doctor's smile down to professionalism because she caught a stern countenance replace the smiling face as he stepped out of the room. Ama asked her husband if he could manage some pottage and was happy to dish some up when he nodded. Chinny sat on the hospital bed, right beside her father, to eat her late lunch after she turned on the twenty-one-inch television sitting on the mini refrigerator, while her mother sat on the lone chair to have her meal. Dede ate every morsel on his plate while he listened enthralled as Chinny narrated the events leading to his admission. She reasoned that there would not be any need to move Dede to a cheaper bed since the doctor implied that he may be discharged the next day. They laughed at the tricks that life loved to play on mankind – fancy being saved by the son of the one man they wished lived on the dark side of the moon. Dede nodded off while they still chatted but this time as a result of exhaustion. Ama asked Chinny to return home while she stayed back at the hospital, but the young lady was having none of that. So, they both passed the night in the reception area, intermittently checking on Dede.

The next morning, the handsome doctor came to the room during his morning rounds. He did not seem as cheerful as he did yesterday. Groggy-eyed, he seemed in a hurry to go home. All the test results came back favourable. He flipped through reports, made notes, examined Dede's eyes and pronounced him fit to go home once the billing department gave the word. The doctor went on to reel out some dos and don'ts. "Stay off milk, nuts, tea, coffee, almonds and the like for at least a week. Eat more legumes, dark green vegetables and meat. Eat oranges every day right after taking your tablets." Dede, Ama and Chinny hung unto every word the doctor spoke. After the doctor left, Chinny said she was going to meet with the billing-desk staff but did not make it far out the door as she rammed head-long into Kenneth.

"Good morning," he laughed.

"Good morning," Chinny responded, out of breath. "My father has been discharged," she volunteered as she stepped back in and aside to let him into the room. Ama and Dede were relieved to see that he came alone. They began to offer their gratitude, but Kenneth brushed it off with a wave of his hand. When the pleasantries were over, Kenneth reiterated his decision to handle the bill. He said it was the least he could do for almost killing their daughter. He followed Chinny to the accounts department to make the payment and took them home afterwards.

7

THE DRIVE HOME STRETCHED FOR EONS. SOMEONE OF OBVIOUS influence and affluence was being buried and the ceremony spilled into the major road, causing a complete traffic gridlock. So, thanks to the sad loss of a human being, turned into a show of who is who, a trip that would ordinarily take less than fourteen minutes extended agonisingly into forty-eight minutes. The only occupant who appeared bothered by the delay was Kenneth, as Dede fed his eyes on the gaily dressed 'mourners', their beautiful cars and the condolence gifts they appeared happy to display to both interested and not in the least concerned audience. Ama and Chinny on the other hand took advantage of the air-conditioned, plush leather-seat-fitted car to make up for the discomfort they experienced overnight on the hard hospital chairs.

Kenneth's car pulled up outside the Onas' residence. Dede thought he recognised the man who stood in front of his house, his face to the locked front door. With hands akimbo, he exuded a somewhat confused mien. As the man turned towards the sound of the car, his face became distinct. "Oliseh!" Dede called out in a tired but excited voice. Oliseh's eyes lit up in surprise when he realised who rode in the lovely car.

"What are you doing here?" Dede beamed. The two men shook hands while Ama and Chinny took the bags into the house.

"Good evening sir," Chinny greeted the visitor.

"You are welcome," Ama said to him as she fished for the keys in her handbag. Dede blinked back his surprise when Kenneth bade them goodbye and politely refused Ama's invitation for a glass of water. Insisting they were exhausted from yesterday's drama, Kenneth said the Onas needed as much rest as possible.

"Moreover, Uncle here would like to catch up with his friend," he finished, referring to Dede. When all their persuasion fell on dead soil, they bade him goodbye, thanking him again for all his help. Mr and Mrs Ona ushered their guest into the house.

Chinny walked back to Kenneth. She took in his good-looking bulk, as her eyes swept over his pair of dark blue chinos and crisp, white long-sleeved shirt, turned up at the cuffs. His black authentic leather slippers accentuated his well-shaped feet. Dissociating Kenneth from the filth she had come to know to be his roots proved less gruelling, since the immense help he offered remained adamant in its tug at her reasoning. An overwhelming urge to give him a hug gripped Chinny but common sense got the best of her, so she took both of his hands in hers in a gesture of gratitude and began, "Mr Kenneth…"

"Ken is just fine," he chipped in, slightly amused by her boldness.

"I do not know how to make you understand what you did for me… I mean us… yesterday. I practically stood by hands-tied while my father slipped away. I could not do anything to save him and would probably have lost him if you had not come along at the time you did. Without an inkling about who I was, you gave your help and funds. Thank you so very much Mr Ken- I mean Ken. Thank you. I pray you find help and support in your time of need." A shy smile played around the lips of the twenty-six-year-old man as he regarded her.

She cannot be more than fifteen, he thought. "Chinny, I hope I can call you that?" When she nodded, he continued. "I did the least I could. And please, you are getting me embarrassed by your profuse thankfulness. It is what I am trained to do. Take good care of your father. I leave tomorrow for my base and if I am unable to pop by on my way, please wish him a speedy recovery," he finished, sliding one of his hands out to softly tap one of hers. Smiling, Chinny conceded and bade him goodbye. As Kenneth drove off, he tapped his temple in salute.

Chinny waved and called out, "Thank you again!" Smiling broadly, Kenneth shook his head in exaggerated resignation and waved.

Ama made some tomato sauce for the plain white rice she intended for lunch. No more beef cuts were left after Chinny gave out the rest of the meat to a long-standing customer as compensation for a previous late delivery. So, for the garnish, she settled for some sun-dried fish instead. Straining to make out what the two men chatted about, Ama tasted the sauce for salt while stirring vigorously. "You took a while Chi. Wash the rice for me," she told Chinny, who had just come in through the kitchen door. The young lady merely smiled and did her mother's bidding and in no time, Ama invited the men to the dining table.

With lunch over, Ama chatted with Dede and his friend Oliseh. For a while, they talked about Dubem and realised nothing had changed since the last time Dede visited Udu town. Dede found out from 'reliable sources' that his son's pact with hopelessness remained unwavering. His informants told him how Dubem spent the larger part of his time roaming the bushes bordering the school. That notwithstanding, he did not shy away from resuming sending the school fees, which Dubem at some point announced had been reviewed significantly downwards. As Oliseh shifted in his seat, stammering about Dubem's school work, his attempt at a cover-up for the monumental failure they called their son shone in all its brilliance for Dede and Ama to see. Rather than be relieved at the news of a downward review in school fees, Dede and Ama had shrunk further at their son's deception. In their opinion, since Dubem had failed out of school and lacked the gall to defraud them any longer, he developed a creative way to lighten the weight of his guilt for collecting fees for a school he no longer attended by inventing a slash in fees. But for as long as his son and his long-time friend did not bring the subject up with him, Dede decided to play the ostrich and see just how long it would take Dubem to earn a senior school certificate.

Besides dealing with questions about Dubem, Oliseh was having such a wonderful time with Dede's family and did not mind staying a while longer, but work commitments called. So, at 5:30 pm, he ruefully announced the end of his visit. Dede walked with his friend to the road to wait for a tricycle and as soon as Oliseh went on his way, he returned home at snail speed. Once indoors, he headed to his bedroom for some rest. Unaware of how precious her husband considered some tranquillity at that moment, Ama floated in, her voice ringing in melody. "Oliseh's visit seems so timely. It is as though he knew about the accident."

Dede managed a smile in agreement. "Yes. He said he had been planning on paying us a visit for too long and it was coincidental it happened today." But while they still basked in the lingering ambience of their friend's visit, a downcast Oliseh journeyed back to Udu town, uncertain of how

Dubem, who placed his faith in the success of this visit, would handle the disappointment. Oliseh concluded that the main purpose of his visit to the Onas had been difficult to achieve, given the circumstances. Remorseful and ashamed to face his family with the truth, Dubem had hoped his benefactor would help clean up the mess he had created.

"Some other time. I will go there and make this right for Dubem. Some other time," Oliseh decided aloud, swinging from side to side in rhythm with the bus swaying down to Udu town.

Immediately after dinner, Chinny handed her father his medication with a glass of water. A nurtured loathing for tablets, emphasised by Dede's grimace as he swallowed all six of them and stomped off to his bedroom turned Chinny's 'you better take your tablets or else…' scowl into a chuckle. Dede's face lit up with glee as Ama joined him, carrying a saucer of oranges. "Remember the doctor says they are good for your anemia." Two oranges lay sucked dry of all their juice and Dede settled into the bliss of tranquillity. It seemed like forever since he felt this relaxed. Today, a happy Dede lay in bed, and his spirit remained in that lifted state. His sleep-tugged mind's eye saw a brighter tomorrow in the distance as he floated off to dreamland.

Startled by the doorbell's chime, Chinny darted to answer it to find Kenneth looking every bit as handsome as the last time. But something about him appeared odd today and she could not quite put a finger on it. She let him in and offered him a seat. It finally clicked and referring to his white long robe, before Chinny could stop herself, she blurted, "Why are you dressed like a pastor?" ,

"Oh! It is called a cassock. I am training to be a priest," Kenneth offered with an ear-to-ear grin. Chinny's face fell.

"Oh! As in? You mean like… Are you? Wait! You want to be a priest?" Chinny gawked.

Considering the look on Chinny's face priceless and wishing he could cast her expression in stone, Kenneth's laughter rattled his torso. But Chinny's unyielding facial muscles made it clear she did not share in his midday amusement. He could never get over people's initial reaction when they learnt that besides his medical degree, he also pursued priesthood. Kenneth simply did not fit the mould of an aspiring priest. But Chinny's current state of shock dimmed in comparison to what she experienced when Kenneth informed her that his chosen priesthood path did not permit him to run his own family. Attempting to soothe her distress, he told her that it did not pose much of a challenge to him since his mother had passed on and there was no love lost between himself and his father. Chinny had a million conflicting emotions running through her mind and worse still, she did not know why. Her father broke up their quiet chatter when he entered the sitting room. Getting to his feet, Kenneth greeted, "Good morning sir."

"Good morning Kenneth. How are you? It is so nice for you to pay us a visit," Dede beamed.

"I am doing great sir," Kenneth replied and mentioned that Dede looked a lot stronger than he did yesterday.

"Thank you again. May God bless you," Dede said. Smirking at Chinny, Kenneth gave up on any hope of making the Onas stop thanking him.

"Are you a priest?" Dede asked.

"No, but he is training to become one." The disappointment in Chinny's voice was unequivocally eloquent.

"Really? The priesthood just gained a precious stone," Dede said. Walking out and into the early morning sunlight for a stroll, Dede excused himself. "Doctor's orders!" he called out over his shoulders as he shut the door behind him, wondering at Chinny's near-surly face and how much his little girl had grown.

Kenneth tried for some easy chatter and reeled in laughter when Chinny told him how she initially planned to pay the debt she assumed she would owe him from the hospital bills. It was her turn to laugh when he told her that an image of himself in handcuffs flashed before him when he thought he had crashed into and killed her. After a few more minutes of chatter, Kenneth decided to be on his way. They exchanged numbers. Chinny looked wide-eyed as Kenneth entered her number on his phone using something like a pen. He pretended not to notice as she stared open-mouthed at his phone and feigned not to understand why she preferred that he dialled her number rather than input it directly into her beat-up *unsmart* phone.

At the door, Chinny decided to take her head out of the sand and asked, "What did you mean when you said there was no love lost between you and your... err... father?" Kenneth's strides faltered momentarily, but he walked on to his car without a word. When he turned on the ignition, Chinny concluded he did not want to talk about it. Besides, his stance appeared a touch too coincidental, considering his father's illicit proposal. But to her delight, her stranger-turned-friend began to talk.

"My mother lost the one she called her heartbeat – my biological dad – shortly after my birth. She got married to Mr Peters – the man everyone knows as my father. The marriage did not last. They called it off after five years and she left with me. We have not had such a warm relationship, but he was the only physical father figure I knew so I kept in touch, mostly via telephone conversations. I only came around two days ago to formally inform him of my ordination which will be held in six weeks' time. As convenient as the story sounds, it is the truth, which I am not proud of. See you around Chinny."

Stunned and sorry, Chinny gaped as her new friend sped off. A hollow she could not understand formed somewhere in her stomach. Her initial bright idea of making vegetable-laced beans pottage for lunch suddenly did not seem as bright anymore. She went back into the house and got busy. She had to get to the meat market. Her biggest client would come knocking the day after tomorrow and was never in any mood for delays.

Two days after Dede's return home, his 'recuperation', as the doctor put it at his routine check-up, was commendable. Life slid back to normal and was generally easier since nobody needed to breathe down Dede's neck, with his medication or 'the right meals'.

After a breakfast of bread and bean cakes with tea, Chinny was in a hurry to clear the table. Saturdays were almost always very busy for her. In addition to the usual house chores, she had to fry and package her beef bites in readiness for her client who would come calling at noon tomorrow. This was the reason she always appeared to be in a rush to get back home after service on Sundays. Chinny did not like to keep her client waiting. Tray in hand, Chinny began to make her way to the kitchen when the bell chimed. She made to put the tray back down, wondering who could be visiting so early in the morning, but her father asked her to carry on while he got the door. "Ah! Oliseh? What a pleasant surprise!" But Oliseh looked nothing like his boisterous self as he sat in the living room. The two men exchanged some friendly chatter and began talking in hushed tones when without warning, Dede's voice boomed, startling Ama out of the kitchen and into the sitting room.

"What do you mean by you do not know?!!" Chinny stopped at the corridor that opened into the sitting room and peered through the curtain behind the adjoining door. Oliseh sat in a chair beside Dede, his head bowed while holding out a note in his hand.

"I did not meet him at home when I returned home that day. I found this on his bed. Read it please." He prodded his friend.

"No!!! I will not read anything. What do you mean Oliseh? What are you telling me?" Dede's voice shook in despair.

Ama looked from Dede to Oliseh in stark confusion. "What happened Dede? Oliseh, what is going on? Who is the note from? How... is Dubem?" Her voice quivered like a leaf in a storm. Chinny remained behind the door, the gentle movement of her chest as she took in mouthfuls of air the only indication she was no sculpture. She watched as all her mother's questions met with portentous silence. Taking the note from his friend, Dede read.

"I just saw it on his bed when I got home," Oliseh offered again. Ama moved like a flash.

"Whose bed?" she asked as she snatched the note from her husband. Dede looked up at his wife with pain in his eyes.

"Dubem is missing," he said in a cracked voice. The note slid from Ama's hand. Her legs refused to carry her any longer, so she heaved onto the next chair and began sobbing, all the while squeezing her knees.

Emerging from hiding, Chinny walked up to her father and in a voice that mirrored the hush of night asked, "Nna'm, what did you just say?" Looking at his daughter, Dede opened his mouth to respond but no words came forth.

Chinny looked hard at Mr Oliseh and demanded, "Where is my brother? How can you say you do not know where he is? You are the chief security officer of your school so how can you not know where he is?" Chinny was scared, confused and annoyed all at the same time but her tone could not be associated with rudeness, for accompanying those angry words were tears of uncertainty. A perplexed Oliseh blamed only himself. If he had let out all Dubem's dealings in the open for his family to see, he most likely would have received better guidance from them. And in one moment of revelation, Oliseh realised he had absolutely no knowledge of the revered field of parenthood. Chinny picked up the note and read aloud.

Thursday, March 2012

Dear Mr Oliseh,

If you are reading this note, it means I have been away for longer than I planned. Against my common sense and the warnings offered by my farm hands, I entered into a business arrangement with a man called Chief Utah. He is a very wealthy and well-known business man, but his business and wealth alone are not responsible for his fame. He is also known to be involved in unnamed shady dealings.

He approached me to supply watermelons and cucumbers for his fruit juice factory, telling me he had a passion to encourage young entrepreneurs. I was ecstatic and gave everything to match the demand his factory placed on me. After a lot of hard work, I supplied four tons of watermelon and eight tons of cucumbers over two planting cycles. As is characteristic of Chief Utah as I later learnt, he refused to pay the agreed sum of 1,100,000 Naira to me. My staff is still being owed three months' salary, but they stayed with me knowing the challenge I have been trying to deal with. All efforts to see Chief Utah met with futility. What broke my back was the news that my father had an emergency and the son of the world-renowned paedophile – a total stranger – paid his bills because they want to take advantage of my family (Yes, word travels fast. I heard even before Mr Oliseh left to visit you). I refused to sit back and watch my only sister being used as a bargaining chip because of penury. This same penury is responsible for eroding what is left of the man in my father, almost causing my mother to evolve into someone I barely recognise and slowly draining the life out of my little sister. I have gone to get my wage because I deserve my hard work's pay. Please tell my family that I love them and will get them out of this quagmire. I will pull us back on course and no matter how my meeting with Chief Utah goes, this is not the end. I will keep moving, breaking new grounds and forging bigger business relationships. Thank you, Mr Oliseh, for everything. I owe you everything. Thank you.

Your son and friend,
Dubem Ona.

In between sobs, Ama asked her husband and Mr Oliseh what Dubem meant by tons of cucumbers and watermelons. Oliseh explained that Dubem graduated from secondary school almost two years ago with straight 'As' but had all the while taken advantage of his free land to cultivate fruits and vegetables for commercial purposes. According to him, he intended to save towards a university education for himself and his sister. Dubem also confided in Oliseh that he planned on etching a significant dent on the house mortgage. Now sobbing louder, Ama asked how his explanation made any sense, putting Dubem's terrible results into perspective.

To this, Dede responded in an exhausted voice, "Our son deceived us. He believed that if we could afford to send only one child to school, it had to be his sister. He planned it all, Ama. Our son never had problems with his academics. Those results were forged. Dubem graduated best student in his school and Oliseh kept it all from us on his request. After Dubem stopped being angry at me, he did not want to strip me of what residual self-worth I had left by spraying my flaws on my face. On several occasions, Oliseh persuaded him to end the charade himself because he could not break the fragile trust he had built with our son. Dubem eventually broke his resolve and begged Oliseh to explain everything to us. The actual purpose for his visit the day I returned from the hospital was to put us all in the know. He came with all his original results." Dede paused. "Hmmm, it is my fault. I drove my son to this. Had I been half the man I meant to be, this would never have happened."

Silence reverberated through the room as Ama and Chinny absorbed Dede's words. A few clock ticks later, Chinny in a calmer voice asked Mr Oliseh, "This Chief Utah, do you know where he lives, sir?" Mr Oliseh knew that the chief lived in a villa in Item town, which was not very far from Udu, but did not know the exact location of the villa. He was also not confident about searching for Dubem by themselves, knowing how dangerous the chief was, and he told them so.

Ama was having none of that but before she could put her retort into a constructive phrase, Dede raised his arm in a calming gesture. "I think the first step is to find the exact address, make enquiries to be sure he is there and then report to the police."

Shaking her head, Ama reminded them of how process-driven the police always proved. "They will tell us to wait for seventy-two hours before we can consider him missing since he is over eighteen years old," she cried. Chinny moved towards her mother and placed an arm on her neck. Of everyone in the sitting room, Chinny seemed the calmest but her darting eyes betrayed her myriad of thoughts.

"Nne'm, it is seventy-two hours already. Dubem has been gone since Thursday." This piece of clarification ushered a fresh stream of tears down Ama's face.

The rattle at the door startled Ama, who hurriedly wiped her face with the back of her hands. Dede, his eyes closed in thought, asked in a tired voice, "Who is it?" The ever-lively voice of his favourite niece rang from the other side of the door as though she was their long-awaited parcel.

"It's me... Adaiba." Chinny made to open the door and nodded at her mother's eye signal to keep the news about Dubem to herself and with a smile pasted on her face, opened the door to her cousin. Adaiba breezed in, carrying a small nylon bag containing her famous home cooked *Okpa* – the moimoi variant made from Bambara nuts. Adaiba, knowing how much Chinny and her parents loved the meal had as usual saved two for each of them when she made it the night before. It was such a taxing meal to prepare, especially if prepared the traditional way – wrapped and steamed in plantain leaves. "Uncle, good morning, Auntie, good morning."

"Nne, good morning," they chorused in response. She paused, noticing the visitor for the first time.

"Good morning sir," she greeted. Mr Oliseh responded to her greeting and resumed brooding. She shoved the bag at Chinny, whose face lit up a fraction when she examined the contents of the bag. Chinny thanked her cousin with a hug.

"Two each ooo!" Adaiba warned with a knowing smile. The last time she gave them the meal, Chinny ended up eating four of the six wraps. She claimed she misunderstood her father's instruction to keep his share for him until the following day.

"Come, I have news," Adaiba said, pulling Chinny towards her bedroom. Once the door was shut, "We have letters!" Adaiba squealed, shoving a letter into Chinny's reluctant hand. She continued, "My brother received them in his mail box and brought them yesterday. I have been invited to GCE regional office for an oral interview to defend my results! Open your own!!!"

"Mmhh? Okay," came Chinny's unexcited response to the news as she placed the envelope on her bedside stool.

Stunned beyond words, Adaiba screeched, "Mmhh? Okay. That is all you can say?!" She playfully jabbed her on the shoulder. "What is wrong with this girl? Open your letter!" Adaiba chided. There was no escaping the boisterous claws of her cousin, so Chinny tore open the envelope and confirmed her interview invite. The outcome would determine if their results would be released to them or not, the letter ended. Chinny still looked aloof, much to Adaiba's perplexity. She sat down beside Chinny, turned her face to hers and placed her right arm around her shoulder so their noses almost touched. "Chi, have you decided to get married? You are throwing away your dream ehn? You want to leave me in the cold! All the inspiration to go forward is from you. How can—" Chinny was shaking her head as a tear brimmed over her left eye. Chinny regarded her sweet cousin for a bit and threw her mother's caution out of the window.

"Ada, Dubem is missing," she blurted.

8

ADAIBA PUT BOTH HANDS OVER HER MOUTH AS ALARM BELLS began to ring in her head. She cast her eyes around the room as if to draw strength from the walls. Turning to Chinny, she said, "When Chi? How? What happened? Who told you?" As the questions poured in, Chinny tried to keep pace with the answers but buckled halfway, the weight of the pain clutching her young heart too much to bear.

"It has been three days Ada! We pushed him to it. We pushed him to it, we pushed him, we pushed him," Chinny's voice dripped agony as her tears came gushing in uncontrollable torrents. Adaiba held her cousin in a hug as she, desperate to be the strong one for the first time, tried to gather her own chaotic thoughts. When Chinny's sobs abated, she walked Adaiba down Dubem's long and masterful charade. Several moments of complete silence threatened to stretch to infinity but Adaiba's eyes sparked with memory as she remembered a certain Chief Utah her brother mentioned a few months ago. She hoped he was the same person in question and promised to source the chief's address.

"Once I get the address, we will go and find the place. We will find Dubem. You hear?" Adaiba said, her chest heaving as she pulled back the sob threatening to break free. Chinny gazed at her cousin with a redefined perception. For someone who appeared overly flippant and flighty, Adaiba proved to be a sweet and compassionate soul. They were almost at the door when, telling her to keep a normal countenance, Adaiba stopped to wipe the tears off Chinny's face. In a sudden moment of appreciation and affection, Chinny hugged her cousin, before they joined the others in the living room. Soon after, Mr Oliseh left for home, with a promise to return soon while Ama and Dede left for the police station.

Once Dede paid the tricycle rider his fare, husband and wife went into the police station to fill a missing person's complaint form. After they answered a series of questions and narrated the whole account, the police officer's next words shook Ama and Dede to their toes. "Oga and madam," the officer began, "You both have to go to the town where your son was last seen and file your complaint there. What you are doing here is like going to Dubai to inform them that someone has gone missing in Kenya. Please go back to Udu town and lodge your complaint there." The police officer spat. They goggled in horror as the unkind police officer turned the form that Dede had conscientiously filled in into a paper ball and threw it into the waste bin, with the expertise of a seasoned basketball player. They left the station crestfallen and headed home where the news of Chinny's interview invite put a short-lived light in their pitch-dark sky.

⟶͡ͻ

Exhausted from long hours of prayers, Ama fell asleep on her knees in her bedroom. She woke up with a start to find she was still home alone with Chinny since Dede went to Item town for information regarding Chief Utah. The clock struck four with no sign of Dede and dread wrapped its fingers around Ama's chest. She peeped into Chinny's room to find her fast asleep and thinking the girl never slept enough these days, left her alone. Night drew closer; still no Dede. Ama shoved away the fast-forming ideas fighting for a space in her head. She dragged herself to the kitchen to start dinner preparation. A loud rattling of the door interrupted her. *Dede!* Ama thought as she half-ran to the door.

"Oh Violet. It's you." Ama's excitement went south. *Who else but Violet would rattle a door with a doorbell? She taught her daughter well,* she thought as she made to lead Adaiba's mother into the house. The two women existed in utterly different worlds. Besides Violet's lack of any formal education, she displayed a complete disinterest in anything that had the remote possibility of causing her any self-improvement. While Ama exhibited a positive and hopeful outlook towards life, her evening visitor often seemed to be in her dovecote only when she complained about how frustrating her marriage, children, neighbours, in-laws and finances were.

A defining moment in Ama's relationship with the wife of her husband's older brother happened just after Dubem's birth. Violet had come to the hospital to congratulate her with the traditional thin soup for new mothers. In between desperate gulps of water, Ama had asked her sister-in-law if the notion that the tear-inducing spicy soup washed out the remains of the placenta held any truth at all. "I do not know oo! But not long ago, I heard that if the soup has plenty pepper, it can help you have a girl next time," Violet answered. When an amused Ama asked her visitor why she assumed she wanted a girl the next time, Adaiba's mother with a truly bewildered look on her face asked, "So how will Dede get bride price money if he does not have a girl to marry off? If there is another way, please tell me so that I can stop trying to have a girl." Save for the relationship dumped on her by marriage, Ama would have been happy to put a sky-high mountain between herself and this woman's twisted concepts and negative energy. She usually wondered how Adaiba turned out to be such a joy and hoped life did not change the young lady for the worse.

Violet declined Ama's invitation into the house and informed her that she did not come on a casual visit. "Please come outside. Come quick." Alarmed at the note of urgency in Violet's voice, Ama dried her wet hands on the wrapper around her waist, closed the door behind her and did her visitor's bidding, all the while hoping she did not come with bad news about Dede. "Adaiba told me about the business you are doing with some telephone *compinis*."

Ama's answer was an "Mmhh". Though annoyed at how much more Chinny may have revealed to her cousin, Ama snickered at how the woman before her still pronounced the word 'companies', years after everyone, including Kika her husband, had tried to correct her.

"Which telephone *compinis* are they?" Violet probed. In utter shock that the woman did not know when to take her nose out of business that did not concern her, the furrow on Ama's forehead deepened as she killed an imaginary mosquito. But Violet was not letting her off.

"Breeze-links, Starlite Mobile and Afrocomms," came Ama's gruff reply, hoping the woman's porous brain maintained its inability to recollect information. When Adaiba's mother went on to ask if she shared her business intentions with any other person besides her family, Ama thought it was a case of a broken raw egg since her current audience and most

92

likely half the town already knew. But she answered her nonetheless. "No, I only gave the signed documents to my neighbour to submit on my behalf." Violet became alarmed and showed it by clasping both hands over her head.

"Chai, chai, chai!!!" her primitive lament rang through the calm evening. Completely ignoring Ama's puzzled expression, she continued, "I do not know many things oo, but I know what a telephone mast resembles and yesterday, they dug one into that land beside the expressway. The one that belongs to Mr Clarke, your neighbour. Today again, I saw him talking to one man wearing a green shirt with a telephone mast picture on it."

Ama began to hyperventilate as she cast glances between Violet and the Clarke's black gate a few feet away. The shirt Violet just described to her sounded like the Afrocomm's branded shirt. *It all now makes perfect sense. No wonder those companies have not contacted me till now*, Ama thought. The fear that her neighbour of over eighteen years and the father of her daughter's closest friend may have pulled a life-defining opportunity from right under her feet sent blood rushing to her ears. Shoulders drooped, Ama thanked Adaiba's mother for looking out for her and began walking back to the door. Violet felt nothing but untainted pity for Ama as she watched her *co-wife*, as she always called her, shut the door behind herself.

Back in the kitchen, Ama continued with dinner but with a lead-heavy heart and a sense of foreboding. Now awake, Chinny let her father in. There was welcome news. Dede succeeded in locating the chief's villa and they talked about the best way to find out if Dubem visited the villa or not. Bravely fighting through the rest of the evening, Ama decided to spare her family the pain of her recent discovery until the mystery of Dubem's whereabouts was resolved. Soon after dinner, all lights went off, but not all eyes were shut in sleep, each one buried in a pool of their own thoughts. Dede wondered at his son's whereabouts. He beat himself up so hard, fearing he may have driven his son into the waiting arms of predators. Ama wept for her son who was God-knows-where. She wept for her daughter whose life stood the risk of becoming a clone of hers. Her heart broke at the thought of their only hope for a better life, now in the far distance, nothing but a mirage. She wept for the husk of the man she adored once upon a time. Lastly, Ama wept for a budding rose, once full of life and promise, but which stood no chance against the raging storms, trampling feet and fiercely biting-cold hands of life. The rose flower lay forgotten, withered and torn to irredeemable shreds – for the first time, Ama wept for herself.

While her parents drowned in tears and despondency, Chinny's eyes were crisp-dry and lit with promise. She would leave early tomorrow morning for Adaiba's house, to tell her that they had the address. She believed that even the vilest of men possessed a modicum of kindness and would exhibit this if the right stimuli were applied. She intended to appeal to the chief to release her brother on the grounds of his ill health – schizophrenia. She would tell him that a few years ago, Dubem developed the disease responsible for his many troubles, ranging from being thoroughly beaten up to being locked up in school detention. Chinny planned to beg for the release of her brother to allow him to go for urgent medical attention. Certain of the believability of her well-crafted lie, Chinny anticipated a better life as she smiled at the big one – the land lease to the telecommunications outfits. "We will be fine," Chinny sighed as she drifted into the floating arms of the night.

Chinny woke up to the sound of wailing. She rushed to her parents' room where the cry was coming from and gaped at her father, holding her mother in an embrace. "Nna'm, what happened? What is wrong with her?" Chinny queried looking from Dede to Ama who appeared inconsolable. More agitated, she drew closer to her parents, asking again what the matter was.

"The Clarkes… the Clarkes, they are wicked people. All my plans. Hmm, wicked, heartless, back-stabbers. The Clarkes. Why did I not smell this a mile away?" Lost for words and unable to understand her mother's rant, Chinny sat on her parents' bed and listened to her father's attempt at explaining Ama's distress.

Struggling to put her thoughts into words, she forced her tongue off the roof of her mouth. "Why would Mr Clarke knowing how life-defining this opportunity was so callously rob us of it? Are our challenges not enough? Could it be that they delight in our lack? What would it profit them? A sense of importance and superiority over us?"

The gloom in the bedroom lay heavy over the Onas. It took a long while for Ama's tears to stop flowing but stop they did. Dede begged his wife to glean her lessons from the incident and move on with life. He appreciated her for the surprise she wanted to throw at him but reminded her that he remained as traditional as it got and had no intent on abdicating his God-bestowed responsibility to care for his family. His past shortcomings notwithstanding, Dede vowed to work his fingers to the bones doing just that. He took her two hands in his.

"I am onto something Ama. Please be patient with me. Let us find Dubem first. I will do right by you. I have a twig and with it, I intend to swim us all to shore. Do not let the tricks played on us by life rob you of the faith you once had in me." Ama and Chinny clutched to Dede's every word. Almost certain she had been living with an impostor, Ama stopped short of asking her husband at what point he left, for she felt as though her real husband just returned home after a long journey. She regretted ever thinking more highly of Mr Clarke than her Dede, who possessed a pure heart, compassion and honesty – qualities she believed were alien to many and most undeniably Mr Clarke.

Renewed hope filled the hearts of the Onas as they ate breakfast and got ready to go to church. It was a long sermon on 'Guarding against false doctrines'. A sudden scarcity in fuel sent all the tricycles into hiding and the Onas had no option but to endure the long trek home. "One never knows when petrol scarcity will strike in this country," Dede grumbled as he trod along. After a lunch eaten in silence, Chinny informed her mother that she was off to pay Adaiba a visit. Ama began to disapprove but stopped.

"Okay, take the key to the back door because I may go out," Ama called after her daughter.

Barely able to control the bubbles in her stomach, Chinny walked the few kilometres leading to her cousin's house. With Chief Utah's address no longer unknown, they could begin their search for Dubem as early as the next morning. She only hoped Adaiba had not developed cold feet, also known as common sense.

Monday had Dede up bright and energised. He donned a pair of black trousers and a short-sleeved plain brown shirt with a matching striped brown long tie. Looking every inch the executive he used to be many years ago, Ama could not hide her admiration. "Who are you going to impress at Udu town? Certainly not Oliseh," she joked. Dede was amused but grateful for his wife's humour, given how much she cried through the night.

Muttering something to her mother about seeing Adaiba and running some errands, Chinny rushed out of the house. Ama naturally thought Chinny's rush had to do with her inability to supply beef cuts the day before. Husband and wife left the house, Dede for Udu town, to confirm if Oliseh filed for a missing person at the Udu police station and Ama to the yam flour factory for a follow-up meeting. She returned home discouraged. The farm manager wanted an out-of-office arrangement that would create an enabling environment for the discussion of the *terms* of her yam supply contract. For Ama, a dense haze covered the true meaning of the *terms* he referred to, but she almost gagged when she thought about the possibilities.

On getting closer to the house, Ama cast an angry glance at the Clarkes' gate as she passed by, but constrained by her husband's prior appeal to glean her lessons and shun confrontation, she continued home. As she turned the key in the lock to let herself into the house, her hands began to shake with uncontrollable anger. Turning the key back in the opposite direction and re-locking the door, she stomped off to confront Mr Clarke. *God help him if he is home*, she thought.

Ama could taste the bile as she drew closer to her neighbour's gate. Revolted at the audacity of the so-called wealthy, she concluded that most of their success could only be attributed to the backstabbing and cheating they unleashed on their unsuspecting victims. She recoiled at Mr Clarke's sheer callousness. *The savage lived next door for eighteen years, watching us grind and struggle through life, extending a hand occasionally, but waiting with the patience of a predator for our chance at a headstart before viciously pouncing and tearing into thin shreds the very thread of hope I kept in his custody*, she screamed in her head. By the time Ama got to the gate, she rained loud bangs upon it and paused for the response, which was not forthcoming. Her repeated assault on the gate received no response other than the quizzical stares from passers-by. Blinded by rage, Ama had not noticed the huge padlock that kept the gate under lock from the outside. Realising her folly, she let out a dry laugh, wondering what to do with all her pent-up fury. She made to return home to wait for Dede when a shrill cry pierced through the stillness of the fast-disappearing morning.

Against her better judgment, Ama lingered to know what the cry was about but became alarmed when the shrill cry was followed by noise that sounded more like the hum of a thousand bees. With her eyes trained on the direction of the sound, she began to walk half-backwards to her house in quick clumsy steps. The sound drew closer and Ama realised that the hum was not from a thousand bees but from a stampede. She could hear indistinct chants, the sound of shattering glass and sticks snapping. No longer in need of further persuasion to run for her dear life, Ama turned to flee at the same time she spotted a boy, not more than ten years old, holding a red handkerchief to his forehead and running towards her. Dread filled Ama at the thought of a mob angry enough to cause such stark terror in the eyes of a little boy. She did a full 180-degree turn and fled to her house with the speed of an untamed squirrel.

Out of breath but safely tucked in her house, she peered through her window, over her dwarf fence at the mob in the distance and blinked back her surprise when she found that it comprised not only miscreants but young men and women whom anyone would think usually ate cake and drank tea for breakfast. Ama could see the little boy, out of breath as he ran, casting a helpless look at her house. The mob had almost closed in on him and within that window where motherly compassion takes over self-preservation, Ama turned the lock, slid the door open a fraction and beckoned to the boy. Blind fear gave the little boy extra speed and as Ama helped him up her porch, someone called out her name. She looked up to see none other than Mr Clarke and almost succumbed to the tempting urge to slam the door in his face. *He deserves whatever they do to him and even more*, Ama thought, but the thread of conscience that strongly held her subconscious in place tugged hard at her, so she let him in. Once in the house, Ama took a better look at the boy and froze. The red handkerchief used to be white but was turned into a piece of blood-drenched cloth by the big gash on the child's forehead. She asked him if he knew what sparked the stampede and the boy, obviously still terrified, narrated what he knew. A sports-utility vehicle knocked down and killed a woman and her two toddler children. Vandalising all nice-looking cars and houses, the mob began a march against the mindless speed with which 'the rich' drove their big cars around. As the protesters smashed the window of a vehicle, a stray glass fragment gashed the young lad's forehead. Worried about her husband and children, Ama's depression almost grew arms and legs.

Mr Clarke stood by the door since Ama refused to offer him a chair and began to condemn the recklessness of drivers but Ama halted him in a voice she hardly recognised as her own. "You will please keep your opinions to yourself, Mr Clarke. You are in no position to point accusing fingers. I let you into my house not because of our enviable neighbourly relationship but because it is required of me by conscience to always do what is right." To Ama's increased anger, Mr Clarke feigned surprise at her less than courteous response to him. Now in front of Ama's house, the mob appeared to be having a tough time deciding on whether to unleash havoc on her house or not. All three froze in fear but relaxed moments later when the mob, still chanting, moved on to more beautiful houses. It took a long time before gun shots rang through the neighbourhood, for as had become expected of the police, they only showed up after considerable damage had been wreaked. The tranquillity, though welcome, was laced with bales of suspicion. They were still contemplating whether to remain behind doors or not when Mr Clarke's mobile phone rang out. He cast an embarrassed glance at his unwilling host and hastily picked up the call.

"Hello Lance... Yes, I am home... I parked my car at the police station. Well not really... No but I am pretty close. We had an incident in the neighbourhood, so you must be cautious... Oh, thank goodness... It depends on where you are coming from... Only three houses away... All right. I will stand outside. You will see me just before you get to my house. Bye bye."

After his call, Mr Clarke informed Ama that according to his friend, the demonstrators had been dispersed. He hurriedly apologised for the way things went with her business proposal, explaining that all three organisations thought her lease charges were too high and would have cancelled the contract altogether if he had not stepped in with an offer almost half her cost. He thanked her for allowing him into her home, shielding him from the rioters. "I hope to make it up to you one day soon," he finished. Disgusted at his lame explanation, Ama chose not to dignify his short speech with a response and stared the other way as he left her house. Although a lot calmer, the little boy still held the bloodied cloth to his forehead.

"Do you know where your parents are?" Ama asked. He told her that they were together minutes before the demonstration began but did not know which way they went when the chaos started. Ama hurried off to fetch some gauze, cotton wool, methylated spirit and iodine tincture to clean the cut. She tried to distract him with questions while she dabbed the wound.

"What is your name?"

"Arghhhhhhh... Chimdi!!!" yelped the boy, his eyes shut in pain.

"Chimdi, how old are you?"

"Ooowwww, eleveenn yeaarsss!!" Done cleaning, Ama was delighted to see that the gash did not go beyond the dermis. In Ama's typical nature, she would have offered him something to eat but certain that the faster he got home, the earlier his parents' worry abated, she ushered the boy to the door. On opening the door, Ama found her husband about to hit the doorbell. Relieved to have him back in one piece, she held him in a warm embrace as she bade the little boy goodbye. Thanking Ama and offering a greeting to Dede in quick succession, Chimdi skipped off to his home.

Once she shut the door, Ama rained questions on her husband. "So, what happened? Any news? Did Oliseh file at Udu police station? Did you see the demonstration?"

Dede waited for Ama's stream of questions to stop before he responded. "Nothing happened. There is still no news and yes, Oliseh reported the case immediately. Dubem is still nowhere to be found." Dede did not meet the demonstration. Disappointed that her husband brought back no news but thankful that he returned to her unharmed, Ama went on with her chores wondering why Chinny's phone kept saying it was 'switched off' and hoped she also did not meet the demonstration. The spark in Dede's eyes, even though he returned with no news about their son, got Ama thinking into the wee hours of the morning.

⟿

The praying mantis would have a hard time matching the speed with which Chinny's eyes darted around with unbridled excitement. Item town looked nothing like Chinny's hometown. Adaiba did not appear in the least affected by the bustle around her. Chinny asked if she did not find the town captivating and stared open-mouthed when her cousin informed her that she was not the only one saving up for school. Adaiba's father did not have any plan to train her beyond secondary school, so she became creative. While her parents thought she trained to become a seamstress in a tailoring shop in Item town, Adaiba took up house-cleaning jobs on different days of the week with four clients. Over-the-rooftop happy for her cousin, Chinny resumed observing the wild hustle and bustle around her. "Abotiti town is nothing like this place. Item does not have the easy air we have," Chinny mused. She had heard so much about the private university here and hoped for an admission to study the course of her choice one day. She wanted to become a genetic engineer but would need to study biochemistry as a first degree. The school's high tuition being the only snag in her lofty dream, Chinny did not quit pushing but kept her dream and hope alive regardless – yes, that was Chinny Ona.

The bus stopped at the final park. They got down and boarded a tricycle, which took them to Itolo district. At Itolo district, getting another tricycle to the outskirts of the district where the villa was situated proved to be knotty as only very few people lived in the outskirts. So, Chinny and Adaiba sat in a tricycle to wait for two more passengers to board. The tricycle driver seemed well accustomed to the wait as he munched on his egg roll snack. Advising them to drink in a good dose of patience, he explained that the part of town they were headed to belonged to the *rich few* and that only some of their domestic staff who operated from home or who needed to run errands took the public transport.

The tricycle driver went to buy himself a sachet of cold potable water and the two young ladies settled in comfortable silence. After a while, Adaiba yawned, "So Chi, what exactly is the plan? From what I hear, I do not think that villa is a place we can just stroll into. I heard the gate is manned by heavily armed and uniformed security guards." Chinny told her cousin about how she planned to persuade the chief to release her brother, much to Adaiba's amusement.

"I really pray the man buys our story. But wait oo! Chi, are we even sure that Dubem is there? We just assumed by reading his note that he is still there. What if he left the place?"

Chinny became flustered. "Okay if he is not there, where else could he be?" she asked, expecting an answer. Wishing away the unpleasant thoughts crowding her head, she told Adaiba that their first step would be to locate the villa. "Chance or good luck should take care of the rest," a yawning Chinny finished. Chinny accused her cousin of infecting her with her yawns. Adaiba let out a hearty laugh and forced her cousin to admit that hunger pangs also knocked on her stomach walls.

Chinny conceded. "Okay, let me find a quick snack to buy. I have some dried beef but that won't do," she chuckled and ran along, escaping the greedy hands of her cousin as she tried unsuccessfully to grab the bag with the beef cuts.

The lady with a tray of bread loaves caught Chinny's eye. She watched in amusement as the bread seller expertly cut the bread in half, leaving a thin layer of crust to hold both halves, after which she lavishly splattered some baking fat in between before she sold each loaf. *Bread should do, but without the butter*, Chinny thought as she waded towards the bread seller. The last time Chinny ate bakery fat in the name of margarine, it felt like chewing on stale, solid oil. A man in the opposite direction clanged two metals. He stood in front of a book stand, calling on passers-by to buy books. Chinny looked back at her cousin in the almost-empty tricycle, cast a quick glance at the bread seller and decided she could make a dash for the book stand, get back to buy the bread and return to the tricycle in reasonable time.

The book stand stood a few feet away from where the tricycle was parked and Adaiba had been intermittently stretching her neck in the vain hope of seeing Chinny return with something to eat. She would never have known that her cousin dearest now stood engrossed in a book titled *Improving Your Public Speaking Skills*. As Chinny battled with the temptation of parting with 180 Naira for the book, she heard a sharp reprimand, "Stay off the road Eniola and stop looking around!" Chinny smiled to herself as she paid the book vendor, thinking that whoever Eniola was, found the town as mesmerising as she did. Beside herself with excitement, Chinny found the recipient of the reprimand to be none other than her very own Nini Okoye, whom she ferried to school in her cart for close to three years. "Nini!!!" Chinny squealed. Eniola and her mother turned to see Chinny waving vigorously in excitement. The bustling noise of the park must have made it difficult for Chinny to recognise Mrs Okoye's voice right away. They quickly crossed to the other side of the narrow road to say hello. Eniola was both happy and proud to inform Chinny that she passed the entrance examination into Royale Academy and was going to the school to sign the acceptance form in preparation for the coming academic session. Eniola had always shown promise and Chinny knew she would go above even her own expectations.

Eniola's mother watched her daughter in amusement as she showed off to her mentor, but caught herself. "Ehen," she began, "it is good I have seen you. Please keep an eye on Eniola for me while I find somewhere to ease myself." Eager to know all about Nini's school, Chinny agreed with enthusiasm. Giving her handbag to her daughter, Mrs Okoye hissed, "All the toilets in this motor park are disease camps," before meandering through the crowd to find a decent place to empty her bladder.

Was Royale Academy the only entrance examination she passed? How much were the fees? Would she be a day student, or would she board? Chinny's excitement knew no limits. Not all the children she ferried to school made it through to year six and only a trickle acquired their first school leaving certificate. The duo chatted animatedly. A fly perched on Eniola's cornrowed head and Chinny made to shoo it with the book in her hand. Only then did she remember the bread seller and Adaiba. "Chimoooooo!!!" She exclaimed, turning towards the general direction of the tricycle. She saw Adaiba stomping towards her with an exasperated look on her face. Chinny clasped her hands in a conciliatory manner when Adaiba got to them.

"I am so sorry. Please forgive me, my sweet cousin. I forgot and got carried away when I saw Nini." Hands akimbo, Adaiba tried to sustain her angry stance but failed woefully. She could not decide which made her angrier. That Chinny wandered off and left her waiting and costing them their spot on the tricycle, that hunger pangs now sang in addition to banging on her stomach doors, or that it was practically impossible for her to stay mad at her cousin for long enough. The small smile that formed around Adaiba's mouth indicated that Chinny had already been forgiven. Not many people who Chinny knew could offer themselves so freely. They did not have many childhood memories together as Ada was shipped from one aunt's house to the other from as early as aged four. Her parents' excuse for such a thoughtless act stemmed from their belief that rather than spend her holidays with her brothers, she stood to gain more in the homes of relatives who had female children. This, by their own postulation, would help her grow into a more rounded female. By the time Adaiba could clearly express herself, they realised that they unwittingly sold their daughter off to relatives who used her for varying forms of child labour, ranging from bar-soap selling to ice-water hawking. More heart-wrenching were the unclear memories of molestations which Adaiba tried to piece together. Her mother had wept bitterly and begged her to never mention it to any other person. Her bond with Chinny began to grow when she confided in her the childhood memories she had kept buried in parts even she sometimes found hard to reach.

"Good afternoon," greeted Nini.

Adaiba responded good naturedly, "Good afternoon my dear. How are you?" Once the pleasantries were over, Adaiba informed Chinny that the tricycle driver abruptly changed his mind about making the trip. He ordered her to get down from his vehicle and get another transport option. While they discussed other alternative means to get to their destination, Nini became bored and busied herself with enjoying the view around her.

Chinny suggested they hike to Chief Utah's villa and Adaiba erupted in uncontrollable laughter much to Chinny's consternation. "What is funny?" she asked. "So what if it is a long distance, could you not have said so rather than laugh like you just saw the king's fool?" Out of options, Chinny found herself in a strange terrain and felt like a child trying to get bubble gum out of her hair. Adaiba stopped laughing and was about to say something in retort when Nini, tense with fear and without looking away from whatever had caught her eye, pulled at Chinny's arm.

The air tasted like ash in Nini's mouth as she said in a high-pitched whisper, "I just saw something... I just saw something happen!"

"What is it?" chorused Adaiba and Chinny as they tried to follow Nini's eye line. All three were now aware of an agitated crowd slowly gathering in the distance. They could see Nini's mother returning from the direction of the agitation. She reached them, looking quite relieved but soon sensed their unease.

"Why do you all look like the dreaded *mporokiki* masquerade just appeared?" she asked, taking her handbag from her daughter. When she realised they were worried about the gathering crowd, she told them that the agitation was just about a certain Don Kay who stopped to fix his flat tyre but decided to dole out Naira notes to his fans amid their chants of "Don Kay... Don Kay... Don Kay."

"It appears," she continued, "that while he busied himself with spraying Naira notes and his driver concentrated on changing the flat tyre, somebody in the crowd stole his briefcase containing an undisclosed sum of dollar bills and now, the town's champion is awfully distraught," she ended, without as much as a shred of sympathy. Nini's mother thought the man called Don Kay deserved the theft for so blatantly brandishing the wealth he got from heaven knows where.

"Oh, my goodness!" Wide-eyed, Nini whispered in a terrified voice as she cupped her mouth with a palm. She resembled a scared cat. Adaiba and Chinny were still taking in Nini's mother's narration when the little girl said something that had three pairs of eyes boring into her forehead.

Her mother asked slowly in a stern voice, "Eniola Arabella Okoye, what did you just say?"

9

ENIOLA DREW IN AS MUCH AIR AS HER LUNGS COULD MANAGE and looking her mother square in the face repeated, "I can tell who took the case and where he kept it." Pointing at Adaiba, she went on to explain. "Ten steps backwards from her, turn left, continue with your eyes till you spot a lame beggar sitting on the ground."

"Is he the one with the case?" Chinny whispered.

"Not a 'he' but a 'she' and yes, she is sitting on the case," said Eniola, her heart doing a rumba. Six eyes followed her instruction and as sure as the morning trailed the night, they spotted the beggar. Chinny started to ask how the lame beggar got hold of the case but froze as her heartbeat began a dance without rhythm.

"I recognise that girl!!! I know her. I met her once outside the bank. She was not lame then. How come she is not able to walk now? Did something happen or is she pretending?"

Eniola's mother would have preferred to go on her way. The complications of being a key witness in any criminal case made the idea of being an ostrich attractive to Mrs Okoye as she tried to modulate her daughter's testament. "Did you see her take the case? Remember she is lame or is at least pretending to be?" But her daughter explained that the girl did not take the case. A man passed the box to the girl who appeared reluctant.

"Where is the man?" Adaiba asked, looking around.

Ruffled and scared, Nini jerked her head in the general direction behind Chinny, who now stood beside her cousin, and said, "I am not sure! Maybe he went that way." Mrs. Okoye's eyes darted around and over her shoulders.

"This is what I do not want. Nini, if you say anything, the police will use you as a witness, fast turn you into a suspect, then the thief.

I say we go on our way. The man is rich and will find a way to handle himself. We have an appointment to meet, Nini, let us go." Taking her daughter by the wrist, she made to leave.

Chinny stood in front of Eniola's mother. "Sorry ma, but you cannot just leave. I once had a friend who told me that if I see evil and make no effort to correct it, I am the same as the evil-doer. We must do something. We owe it to our existence to stand for what is right – even if it makes us uncomfortable." Adaiba and Eniola nodded their assent. Feeling somewhat small, Eniola's mother knew the young lady was right and slowly released her daughter's wrist. Asking them to keep their eyes on the beggar and raise bedlam if she made any sudden movements, Chinny almost looked taller than her five-feet-six inches stature. She began to walk in the opposite direction and when Adaiba asked where she was going, "To tell Don Kay where his case is," Chinny responded, marching off with determined strides.

Nini's mother did not exaggerate regarding Don Kay's state of mind. It was an agitated man who responded when Chinny spoke in a loud voice, "Please, I want to speak to Don Kay." She did not explain for too long before he swung into hyper-activity. He asked his driver to position himself at a safe distance to the beggar. He dialled a number on his phone and the speed with which two plain-clothed police officers arrived on power bikes deserved a standing ovation. *It is in one's interests to be rich and influential. Things get done pretty fast*, Chinny thought.

Adaiba, Eniola and her mother observed with growing trepidation from afar as Chinny talked with the policemen. Much to Adaiba's shock, her cousin began to meander through the crowd until she stood before the beggar who, rattling the coins in her plate, called out in a small voice, "Please help me."

Chinny took out some money from her pocket and began counting at snail speed. She stared the beggar straight in the face and barely moving her lips, said, "This place is surrounded by the police. Someone forced a briefcase on you. Hand it over now and tell the police everything." To Chinny's disappointment, the girl started a fierce denial. Chinny could not imagine why this child had become so immersed in the world of crime. But the stream of tears accompanying the beggar girl's denial indicated otherwise and Chinny's thoughts took a different leaning.

She must be terrified of whoever gave her the case, she thought, but pretended the girl's tears did not tug at her heartstrings. In an even sterner voice, Chinny asked, "Who gave you the box you are sitting on?"

The fast throb between her collarbones at the base of her neck bore testament to the beggar girl's unease as she let out a torrent of words. "Auntie, please you have to help me. My name is Nasa. My... err, the man. He gave me the box. He is my guardian – Uncle Godwin. I do not know where I come from because he refuses to tell me, and we move from one place to the other. I do not have parents... Uncle has been the only one taking care of me." Looking over her shoulders, she continued. "He says I have no one else, that I must do what he says... always if I want him to continue to care for me." She shuddered but did not stop talking, an increased urgency in her tone. "He is a devil. He makes me pretend to be blind, lame or mad in different places so that people will give me money. Then he collects everything in the evening. Any day I do not bring back enough money, he will not give me any food and I will sleep in the toilet. Any time he steals money, phones or earrings and watches, he will make me hold them until it is safe for him to collect them. He calls me an ingrate who does not want to face the reality of her destiny anytime I ask about my parents. And... and he carries a gun about. He told me that any day I tell anybody what he does, he will kill me. Please Auntie, you must help me... Please, help me. I beg you pleeeease!" the beggar girl implored.

Chinny's eyes grew large and darted around, her initial courage now safe home and under the covers. A gun?! She thought this was a case of petty theft, but the beggar's uncle was a full-fledged armed robber. "Can you tell me exactly where your uncle is hiding?" Chinny asked the teary-faced girl who now looked younger. Nasa jerked her head to her left and told Chinny her uncle hid somewhere behind a rusty zinc shed a few yards away. The policemen watched Chinny and the beggar with the stealth of vipers and picking up on their body language, began a furtive close-in on them from two opposite angles. A tad handicapped since they did not have any visual description of the man in question, the police called for back-up.

Nothing in all eighteen years of her existence prepared Chinny for the trepidation and uncertainty that tore through her. Certain they had an audience in the armed robber who would soon be forced out of hiding, she inhaled gulps of the fear-flavoured air, pulled the girl into a standing position and took the case. This got the attention of the few bystanders who began pointing and talking animatedly. The ensuing minutes went past in a flash.

Not about to allow an amateur girl-thief to rob him of his just-earned cash, Uncle Godwin scurried towards Chinny and Nasa and began crossing over to the other side of the road to intercept his money. At that moment, a toddler ran for his ball, which had rolled onto the road as he played with it. The toddler's mother screamed, waving her hands at an oncoming truck with a full load of builder's sand. The driver saw the toddler in time, took a left swerve and bumped into a cart parked against a tree, missing the child by a fraction. The cart's wheel came off and began to roll, hitting the bread seller who Chinny never got around to patronising. The bread seller's tray went up in the air, sending her loaves in different directions as she tripped, running straight into Godwin. He fell flat on his back and tried to get up at once but not before the two plain-clothed policemen reached and pinned him to the ground.

"Gun! He has a gun! He has a gun!!" cried a petrified Chinny. When one of the two policemen searched the thief and brought out the gun tucked in his pocket, the two officers burst into wild laughter.

"So, this is your gun?" they jeered at him, one officer knocking his head with the gun. They informed a relieved Chinny that she had been terrified of a dry toy water-gun. They roared in laughter as they placed handcuffs on the bewildered thief.

Don Kay and his driver met up with Chinny and the policemen who had now been joined by Eniola, her mother and Adaiba. Everywhere was a flurry of activities. People talking, picking up their scattered wares and others still running for safety, but the little toddler who caused it all seemed content at his mother's feet, playing with his retrieved ball while his mother hurriedly packed up her vegetables. Home called. For the poor woman, it was enough trouble for one day. Moments after, a van came on the scene to take the thief, the beggar girl and the briefcase to the station for further investigation. The chatter petered out. The policemen respectfully asked Don Kay, Chinny and her friends for a brief stop at the police station. Everyone got into the passenger section while the beggar girl and her uncle were hurled into the barbed trunk of the van.

As would be expected the usual bureaucracy in public offices went on recess once the Divisional Police Officer identified Don Kay. Since Nasa did not have anywhere to go, they were told an orphanage would accommodate her temporarily, pending the conclusion of her background investigations. With all the statements signed, Eniola and her mother started towards the door. Chinny and Adaiba tried to figure out how to continue their journey. Not wanting to disclose their mission to anyone, they kept their ignorance to themselves. Outside the station, Eniola and her mother bade Chinny and Adaiba goodbye and had started on their way to a nearby motorbike park when Don Kay rushed out of the station panting, "Wait, wait one minute please," nearly choking on his breath. They all shook their heads, declining his invitation for a brief chat and some drinks in his luxury car. Not able to contain his excitement, Don Kay implored, "Please, can I at least know who you are, where you are from and what I can do to show my appreciation?" Chinny was quick to tell Don Kay that helping him retrieve his briefcase of dollar notes served as their own little way of correcting the plethora of wrongs in their immediate environment. She told him that, but for the strength of character of the people she had learnt to surround herself with, she never would have been able to be of any help to him.

"We do not ask anything of you sir. That we rescued that little girl and retrieved your briefcase is enough incentive for us to continue to do the right thing," she finished, looking pointedly at Mrs Okoye. Chinny's impeccable diction was undisputable.

"Fair enough. At least, tell me where you all are from," he conceded and Chinny made the introductions. Don Kay tried another shot at convincing his new acquaintances. Pointing to the taxi park right beside the cluster of motorbikes, he asked them to allow him to hire a cab that would take them to wherever they were headed. It appeared the man found it impossible to understand the word 'no'.

Eniola's mother spoke for the first time. "We are going to Royale Academy." Lightly touching Eniola's shoulder, she continued, "My daughter here passed the entrance examinations, so we are going to register for the interview."

"So, what was your examination score?" Don Kay asked, his eyes on Eniola as he gave her a congratulatory handshake. The twinkle in his eyes as he looked at the little girl did not escape Chinny. *Was this world filled with paedophiles? Why is this old man looking at Nini like that?* The disgust Chinny tasted in her mouth escaped, spreading across her face. Nobody but Adaiba took note of her changed countenance as Eniola proudly rattled off her scores.

"A hundred and eighty-seven out of two hundred! Forty-five out of fifty in English, forty-seven out of fifty in science, forty-seven out of fifty in general studies and forty-eight out of fifty in mathematics." Don Kay's mouth formed an 'o' in amazement. He asked for her name again and told her he was sure her parents were proud of her. Eniola said her mother was, but could not tell her father's disposition towards her academic success since he died when she was only eight months old. Don Kay nodded and whispered to his driver who went off in the direction of the taxi park.

Chinny noticed that rather than feel sorry for the little girl who just mentioned she lost her father as an infant, Don Kay's eyes rested on Chinny with an obscure look on his face. He took Eniola's hand as he congratulated her yet again. Flummoxed by everybody's ignorance of the lewdness that shone through this man's eyes, Chinny became incapable of further self-restraint and yanked Nini's hand away from Don Kay's. She shoved her towards Mrs Okoye who took the cue and after thanking Don Kay and bidding everyone goodbye, got into the now waiting cab with her daughter.

"Thank you, sir, for appreciating us. We will be on our way now." With the look on Chinny's face as she spoke those words to Don Kay, one would think the air reeked of something offensive. He looked somewhat confused at her clear displeasure at something but did not dwell on it. *Of course he is comfortable with the disgust people show him when they realise the kind of degenerate he is*, she thought with indignation. Don Kay said something about selfless acts like those of today being refreshing. Chinny figured why Don Kay needed refreshing. *He must be choking from his own stench*, she thought, carelessly tucking the business card he held out to her into the back pocket of her denim trousers. She had a mission and was in a hurry to leave. She would ask the motorbike riders a few metres away for directions to Chief Utah's villa. As Chinny scurried off with her cousin, she regretted wasting precious time in assisting Don Kay to find and retrieve his briefcase while her brother's whereabouts remained unknown. The motorbike rider charged Chinny and Adaiba 70 Naira to Chief Utah's villa. When they bargained, he argued that carrying two grown ladies would cause a lot of strain on his bike's engine and that it made sense to make the trip on one bike rather than go on separate motorbikes at 50 Naira each.

When the bike rider stopped and pointed to a black gate some distance away, Chinny asked why he stopped them so far from their destination. An air of importance surrounded him as he listed a set of rules governing the vicinity, one of which prohibited tricycles and motorbikes from going any further. Chinny took out some notes from her pocket to pay for the fare, the diameter of the gulf between the rich and the poor heavy on her mind. "*Auntie, your paper fall for ground,*" the bike rider said in Nigerian pidgin, referring to Don Kay's business card which fell out of Chinny's pocket as she took out his fare. He continued as he zoomed off, "*I beg pick am. If environmental force people see paper for here, they go ban us oo,*" vehement about not making the environmental tax force agents place a ban on bike riding in the area because of littering. Chinny smiled at the retreating bike rider and picked up the business card. She chuckled at the real reason behind the bike man's aversion to littering – not his immense love for his environment, but the potential consequences that non-adherence posed to his means of livelihood. *Heavens forbid I cause anyone's job loss*, she thought, tongue in cheek. She was dusting off the dirt from the card as Adaiba informed her that if they did not get to a place where she could ease herself, she would have a huge embarrassment to deal with. Chinny did not respond. Her breathing had become laboured as she stared at her cousin with eyes nearly twice their original circumference. Alarmed, Adaiba shook her cousin's shoulders.

"Chi, what is it? What is wrong?"

Still in shock, Chinny did not blink as she said, "Ada, Chief Utah… Chief Utah is D… Don Kay."

"How?" an incredulous Adaiba asked, snatching the card from Chinny. One look at the card and she exclaimed "Chimooooo!"

But for Adaiba's vocal intervention, the two ladies would have stood staring at Chief Utah's gate till nightfall. "So, what do we do now? He believes he owes you for helping with his briefcase, but you were rude to him before we left the police station. You behaved rather poorly Chi," said Adaiba. Disappointed that neither Adaiba nor Eniola's mother picked up the leer in Don Kay's eyes as he looked at Eniola, Chinny gave her cousin the eye and told her what she thought of Don Kay. Adaiba gawked open-nosed and open-mouthed at her cousin. She thought Chinny had allowed her unfortunate life experiences to feed her paranoia and told her so. A heated argument ensued.

"What gives you the impertinence to judge me? The fact that I confided in you?" Chinny barked.

Steam escaped through Adaiba's ears as she fired back, "The world spills with people who have been hurt at one point or the other dear Chinetalum Ona. I also shared my confidence with you remember? But I refuse to allow them to shape or flaw my perception of any or everyone. Get your foot off the pedal because at this rate, the same qualities which draw people to you will also send them far in the opposite direction." Stung by the words she just heard, Chinny's smart retort stuck in her throat as she began walking towards the gate. Adaiba felt sorry at once. Her words must have hurt since her cousin was seldom speechless. She volunteered of her own free will to come on this mission and fight or not, she would see it to the end. Adaiba shrugged and followed a now sullen Chinny.

Rows of beautifully kept short trees flanked both sides of the paved walkway leading from the road all the way to the gate. As soon as Chinny stepped on the walkway, Adaiba increased her pace to meet her. Patting her softly on the shoulder, she implored, "Chi, let's not fight. You may be right about the man being a pervert. Maybe I missed it. But at the same time, you may be terribly wrong. What if Eniola looks like his own daughter?" Chinny's sullen face eased up a tad. She reasoned that her cousin could have a point and shrugged off her initial anger as she admitted to being more horrified knowing Don Kay was the infamous Chief Utah.

"Do you know the nasty stories going on about him?" she asked Adaiba.

"Hmmm!! Remember the speed with which the police arrived at the park? Only the rich, powerful and influential can command that kind of attention," Adaiba added. They were puzzled that such a callous being could exude the disposition of a kind gentleman, even though the look he gave her precious little Nini still stuck out in Chinny's mind's eye.

They were now at the gate but hesitated to knock, wondering if he was already back or still on the way. Two unsure and terrified young ladies stood with their backs to the gate. They deliberated on whether they should both go in or if Chinny should go in first while Adaiba stayed behind as 'insurance'. They were so deep in conversation that the soundless opening of the pedestrian gate went unnoticed. A uniformed guard with a baton in hand peered into the walkway and seeing the two ladies asked in an attempt at proper English, "*Yes? What you want?*" He looked like he would rather be doing whatever he was doing with the paper in his other hand than talking to two lost ladies. Chinny and Adaiba jumped at the sound of the guard's voice. They turned to face a disgruntled middle-aged man whose countenance changed the minute he saw their faces. Elated, the guard shouted, "My friend!!"

Matching the guard's excitement, Chinny shrieked, "Oga Rufus!!" Adaiba took one step back. She yawned and rolled her eyes skyward. Something told her she was in for another getting-to-know-you session. She decided her cousin knew at least one person in all six towns around Abotiti. With his financial obligations now sky-high – thanks to the adorable set of twins his wife birthed a year and a half ago, Rufus left Future Bright Primary School to become one of the many guards in the Utah villa. The school did not give any indication of leaning towards plans for better pay for him. The salary at the villa was good, and the work conditions were not bad either.

Thankfully, this reunion session did not stretch beyond reason as Chinny soon explained the situation to Rufus, who became instantly agitated. Although not certain if Dubem was in the villa, he told them of the various 'happenings' there, many of which were not pleasant. "*Chief don't know anything. He be very very good man, but you see*

113

this people," surreptitiously pointing at the two uniformed guards manning the inner gate, each holding a two-way radio and a couple of less-obvious guards that could be spotted through the second gate, "*dem wicked well well,*" he continued. He told them that Chief Utah rarely stayed in town, but left the villa in the hands of the villains he called his staff. He advised the ladies to walk further down the road and flag down the chief when he passed by. A two-way-radio-holding guard walking towards them presented the stimulus they needed to draw the curtains on their quest. Thanking Rufus in a rush and thoroughly amused at his still-terrible English, Chinny pulled Adaiba along, evading the scowl of the radio-holding guard. They settled down under a big tree a good distance away to wait as Chinny thought about ways to recreate the parting impression she left with Chief Utah.

10

A T 6:25 PM, NOT ONE VEHICLE HAD YET GRACED THE ROAD leading to Chief Utah's villa. Adaiba sacrificed all reason and properness, as right on the dirt road, she relieved her bladder of the pressure that threatened to tear it apart. And when the mosquitoes turned up for their blood cocktail party, they decided it was time to answer Abotiti's call.

Chinny cast a sad look at the gate, which she was certain held her brother captive as they began the long walk in search of a motorbike out of Itolo district. Drenched in depression, no words passed between the two ladies throughout the journey back home, save for when they got to Abotiti and Adaiba asked when best to repeat the journey. Now aware of her cousin's finance-building commitments, Chinny told Adaiba that she was forever in her debt and could not ask for more. Grateful arms squeezed a reluctant frame, and each headed to their individual homes.

At exactly 8:45 pm, a distraught Dede opened the door and would have been shoved into Chinny by a more distraught Ama. Uncertain of what to presume in view of the last time Chinny left home without warning, her parents had been beside themselves with worry. When it became obvious that Ama and Dede were not about to let her brood in peace, Chinny confessed to her whereabouts. It took six clock ticks for her gaping parents to find their voices. "Chinetalum, you should have told us. It was mindless and dangerous for you to go off on your own." Ama's voice sounded like Dede's former Volkswagen Beetle after taking a dip in a flooded road during the rains.

Dede added, his tone more controlled, "You know our hearts would not take it if anything happened to you. We will find Dubem but before then, please be safe, not just for you but for us. Everything will be fine." Deep in Dede's heart, he could not blame his daughter for trying to solve issues on her own. He thought he had failed her enough.

Narrating her previous encounter with the chief, Chinny tried to assuage her parents' fears, adding that she did not go to the villa alone. Ama and Dede could not decide on how to receive that extra bit of information. They were only certain that if Adaiba suffered the misfortune of being salted by some of her mother's character traits, the entire town would have all the juicy details by the morning of the next day. After their child became dry-mouthed from persuading them of the rationality of her plan, Mr and Mrs Ona decided that she may have a better approach to solving the mystery of Dubem's disappearance. "Since that security guard knows you—"

"Rufus, Father. The guard's name is Rufus," Chinny corrected her father who modified his phrase at once.

"Yes, Rufus. Since Rufus knows you, if anything funny happens, we have someone to hold onto." Not half as optimistic as her husband, Ama pointed out that even if they had "someone to hold onto" as he put it, it would be after "the something funny" had already happened.

"God forbid!!" Ama's self-reprimand was as sharp as the tip of a needle. Chinny seemed bored with her parents' brainstorming exercise and this further reflected in the way she jumped in excitement at the sight of the new phone on the dining table. Ama joked about her father finally deciding to buy a mobile phone in his old age. As she took her mother up on her invitation to help her with dinner, Chinny laughed when she heard the details surrounding her father's recent purchase.

"He rushed out earlier this evening like a goat in labour pains, came back with a new phone and has been reading the manual like an interesting book all evening," Ama narrated in between chuckles. They ate their food in silence, each relieved at the baby-step progress towards finding Dubem. It had been an exhausting day and as Chinny closed her eyes in sleep, thoughts of her brother's whereabouts plagued her tired mind. Tomorrow held new promise. Chinny decided she had taken a sufficient helping of the day's worries.

It did not rain, it poured on the Onas. In addition to Dede's creditors breathing down his neck and Ama's failed arrangement at leasing her property to the telecommunications companies, her farm with all her growing yam seedlings was set ablaze by the vandals who demonstrated a few days ago. Hands tied and with no fall-back plans, they stood by as all their projections fell through. One would wonder at Chinny's apparent oblivion to her family's distress, for in her bedroom she lay poring over the eight subjects she sat for during her general certificate examinations. Unclear about the implications of or requirements for attending an oral interview, she assumed everyone invited would be tested for their competence in the subjects they sat for and thought it best to be overprepared rather than underprepared.

The days sped by and Udu town police station still offered nothing tangible regarding Dubem's whereabouts. With Chinny's interview with the General Certificate Examination Board due in a couple of days, she lay sprawled on her bedroom floor, her eyes narrowing at the gradient of her just-completed graph. She was certain she had not got the scale right. The door creaked open and slammed shut, indicating somebody had either come in or gone out. Chinny went to the sitting room to see who and found her mother in a chair, humming a sad tune. "Has Father gone out?" she asked.

"Yes. He went to follow up on a job he is trying to secure." Ama feared that even if he did get the job, with the debts, children's education and home upkeep, his 'twig' may give way to the sheer strain. The doorbell rang and Chinny hurried to the door, thinking Adaiba had come for some revision but was pleasantly surprised to see Kenneth. As she let him in, she could not help but notice his immaculate white cassock. Kenneth had barely sat down when he began a flurry of explanations.

"I am so sorry. I should have come earlier than now. I did not see your message about your brother when you sent it because I was in seclusion – it's something I do occasionally in preparation for priesthood. During these times, I typically cut myself off from all outside communications.

But as soon as I saw your message, I tried to call your line, but it kept disconnecting." Chinny was somewhat amused at the panic in the voice of her stranger-turned-friend.

In one moment of distress, Chinny sent a text message to Kenneth about her brother. As far as the Onas were concerned, the entire Clarke family could not be trusted. So, talking to Ejiofor did not present itself as an option. Not that Chinny had too much confidence in Kenneth. He had an indelible history with Mr Peters that still brought bile to her mouth each time she thought of him. But there was something about Kenneth that made it utterly impossible to hate him – try as one might. It probably helped that Mr Peters' father-figure status to Kenneth stood far away from being biological. Kenneth continued, "So, what's up? Has he been found?" He rubbed his knees as he asked the questions. The crease on his forehead and the squint in his eyes indicated genuine concern.

"No, not yet and it has been over eight good days since anybody heard from or saw him. Chief Utah has been out of town since Tuesday and has still not returned. I am sure Rufus has grown tired of my incessant calls." As she spoke, Chinny's eyes brimmed with tears. Kenneth felt sorry for her. He tried to console her but within, knew that the only way to make her happy would be to find her brother. He asked her to tell him everything she knew about Dubem's disappearance. By the time Chinny paused from talking about her childhood, education, the huge mortgage loan, family petty debts, efforts to ride the tide, theft of her mother's fortune, their long-time neighbour's betrayal, the fire in her mother's yam plantation, Dubem's charade and business venture, her trip to Item town, her encounter with Chief Utah and her plan to get the chief to release her brother, Kenneth stared, speechless. He could not fathom how she could keep a calm exterior, especially after throwing his father's unwholesome proposal into the mix.

Appreciating her grace even more, he mused, *How can such a beautifully sculpted being have these dark clouds looming over her?*

After moments of staring at her in complete silence, Kenneth told Chinny that he believed everything would ultimately turn out fine for them and to lighten the dense gloom in the room, he told her a little more about himself. "My mother never recovered from the loss of my biological father. She later confessed to me that she married Mr Peters in reaction to the sudden void she felt after my father died. She left the marriage as soon as she realised she had barked up the wrong tree. Six years ago, after years of battling a stroke attack, she died." Kenneth measured Chinny's reception of his line of conversation and decided to go on. "When my mother passed, I was just in my third year at medical school. Thanks to her savings, my inclination towards paintings, which I sold for extra income, and Mr Peters' almost regular and well-appreciated financial support, I finished medical school. Thankfully, there were no setbacks, so here I am, a fatherless, motherless medical doctor, torn between specialising in gynaecology or paediatrics and yes... headed towards priesthood."

Chinny laughed and masterfully ignoring his reference to working towards priesthood, quipped that whether the babies liked it or not, he planned to handle them one way or another. "Bullseye!" Kenneth called and gestured animatedly, pointing two fingers at Chinny in excitement. He liked her wit. But when, without warning, Chinny asked why he decided to be a priest, the shutters slid over Kenneth's eyes and he told her in a dismissive voice that he wanted to be of service to God and man. Chinny would have probed some more but sensed they had come to the end of their friendly chatter.

"Have you tried to call the security guard again today? You know, to find out if the chief is back in town?" Almost dizzy from the speed with which their conversation switched lanes, Chinny made an attempt at recovery, saying that as of the morning of the previous day, Rufus confirmed the chief's lingering absence. Ama, who had been discreet in being a part of their conversation, came in carrying a tray to the dining area. Kenneth stood up at once to take his leave, but she stopped him.

"Please do not go. Stay and have lunch with us. Even if you are not hungry, just push the food around on your plate. It is good yam and I tell you, the sauce is tasty! Please stay." Chinny found her mother's attempt to recreate her first meeting with Kenneth amusing. Although Ama blamed her initial disposition towards Kenneth on Mr Peters' offensive personality, Dede and Chinny secretly thought she had herself alone to blame for how she chose to come across, Mr Peters or not. After some subtle coercion, Kenneth sat down to a hearty meal of boiled yams and vegetable sauce and his taste buds attested to everything Ama promised it would be. No amount of dissuading stopped Kenneth from taking his plates to the kitchen for washing. He argued that not clearing up after a meal typified poor behaviour and did nothing to show good upbringing and gratitude for such a sumptuous meal. Ama decided she liked him nearly as much as she used to like Ejiofor. *What a shame he is training to become a priest*, she sighed to herself.

By ten minutes to four in the evening, Kenneth announced his departure and asked Chinny to call Rufus one more time, but neither Rufus' line nor Chief Utah's line connected. He offered to take Chinny to Item town early the next morning, to see if by any stroke of luck the chief had returned. To avoid sending a wrong message of confrontation, Kenneth planned to park at a safe distance and if twenty minutes after she went into the villa he called her line and did not receive any response from her, he would assume the worst and alert his military friend to move his 'boys' in.

"If in truth, Chief Utah is holding Dubem within his property, I hope he is half the man you are compelling everyone to believe he is and that your story about schizophrenia would get him to release your brother, because only the stars know in what condition he is being kept," said Kenneth, his voice grave as he repelled the unwelcome thought that Dubem may no longer be alive.

When Chinny learnt that Kenneth had no intention of spending the night in Abotiti, she asked why he chose a lodge on the outskirts of town over the comfort of his father's house, but Kenneth only smiled as he walked to his car. No way would he tell her about the volcano that erupted when he found out the details of how low his father had gone with the Onas. Neither would he mention that they had not spoken since the fight and that he intended to keep it that way. Kenneth zoomed off waving at Chinny, who had a chin-straining grin on her face. As she walked back to the front door, she spotted some cobwebs at the top right corner of the wall just above the door. She went to the side of the house and returned with a long broom. Satisfied that she just rendered a poor spider homeless, Chinny turned to return the broom but bumped right into Ejiofor. Almost throwing her arms around him in her usual welcoming hug, Chinny caught herself and instead, stepped back to serve him a cold stare before offering a clipped "Hi", and Ejiofor's face fell.

"Hi Chi. I... I am... err... having an early Easter. My folks are coming back in a couple of days," he replied in an uncharacteristically small voice. After a few awkward moments, Chinny let him into the house. She tried for a simple chatter but Ejiofor, not being one to hop from one foot to the other, went straight to the point. "My mother told me Chinny and I am so sorry." She was not sure of what he referred to. Could he be talking about Dubem or about his father's betrayal? Ejiofor continued. "My father... Chinny, he is just who he is. He is a crude businessman with an unexplainable phobia of poverty, to the extent that the line between loyalty and self-preservation has become blurred if not non-existent. He has lost so many good friends in the process and acquired new ones who share his *drive*. I will never be able to fully express how sorry I am. If... if only I had known about your mother's plans. I would have warned her." Ejiofor seemed frustrated as he clawed for the words he needed. "Chinny... please apologise to your family on behalf of mine. What he did was callous. It was cruel. And yes, it is difficult no doubt, but please I beg you, try to find it in your hearts to forgive him... I mean... us."

Ejiofor's words put a crack in Chinny's wall, for somewhere within, she knew Mr Clarke ran a one-man squad and that his family existed between a rock and a hard place. Assuring her friend that time healed most wounds, she told him about Dubem and Ejiofor went into overdrive. He wanted to head for the villa at once but felt kicked as soon as Chinny told him that she had other plans, which she thought best to keep him out of.

Chinny explained, her tone softer. "Please Ejiofor, we are still experiencing life in a tough place. With time, we will learn to live with how we presently perceive your family. But you must understand that 'heartless' does not come close to the description of what your father did. You know our story. I hid nothing from you. You know how much and how hard we scraped, and are still scraping through life. You know the odd jobs I engaged in just for us to get by, singing from one market stall to the other for cash appreciation from my audience, transporting children to school in trucks, frying and selling beef cuts, the list is endless. Have you forgotten the day you visited and saw me preparing what was to pass for dinner? You met me pounding dry maize in a mortar because we neither had beans to prepare moimoi nor the required 30 Naira to send the maize to the mill for proper grinding. You Eji… you gave me 50 Naira that day. Have you forgotten coming home during the Christmas period to find that along this whole stretch, our house was the only one not brightly lit with Christmas lights, thanks to a four-month old disconnection from the power grid, as a result of our pile of unpaid bills? A certain secret Santa known to you and I paid the bills. Your father cut in pieces the lifeline my mother handed to him in confidence. We are only human and must be allowed the luxury of licking our wounds, if only for a while. Maybe afterwards, we can pick up from where we left off as friends but for now Eji, I think we would rather be left alone." For the first time since either of them could remember, Ejiofor had nothing intellectually stimulating or witty to say.

⌐⌐⌐

Ama lay in bed, brooding over Dubem's disappearance when Chinny came in to ask her what she should prepare for dinner. "Let us have some fried plantains. Is Ejiofor gone? I heard his voice," Mrs Ona said, her tone distant.

Chinny said "Yes," and made to leave but her mother called out to her, "Nne, never mind. The poor boy should not pay for his father's sins. I forgive all of them. Moreover, not forgiving is not charging people for staying in your heart."

Chinny smiled and rephrased the quote. "Unforgiveness is people living in our hearts – rent free."

"Same difference!" chuckled Ama. Chinny continued to the kitchen to get on with dinner. She had not quite finished with slicing the plantains into flat, wide fingers and setting the pan on the stove when the bell chimed. She wiped her hands and rushed off to the door.

"Father! Welcome," Chinny greeted in delight. Dede looked happy as he patted her lightly on the shoulder, asking how her day had been. He went into his bedroom. He had a spring in his steps.

The frying pan on the stove became hot at the same time as Chinny's phone started to ring. What displayed on the screen as the caller identification drew goosebumps from her skin. Her breathing reverberated in her head. Ama came into the kitchen to check on dinner but became alarmed at her daughter's ashen face.

"What is it? Who is calling you?"

Chinny's voice was barely audible when she answered her mother. "It is... Chief Utah... Don Kay. I... do not err... How did he get my num... number? Nne'm, what do I tell him?"

"Pick it up! Pick up the call!" Ama cried, oblivious of the increasing warmth in the kitchen, thanks to the frying pan left forgotten on the stove.

11

"GOOD... EVENING MR... SIR... I MEAN CHIEF UTAH SIR."
She shuddered when the voice on the other end of the line
boomed, "Am I speaking to Chinny?"

"Yes, yes sir," she stuttered.

"Okay, my security guard – Rufus – gave me your number. He
told me about your visit and your effort to contact me over the past
week, yes?" Ama was stock-still in uncertain anticipation as she tried
to make sense of the one-sided dialogue. "I only just got back late this
afternoon from a short trip outside the country. Can you come over
at your earliest convenience? I am indoors throughout the weekend."
Still awestruck but grateful for his call, Chinny asked if it was okay
to visit him the next day by noon and the chief confirmed he would
be available.

The call had ended but as Chinny relayed the details of the call to
her mother and her father who came rushing in as soon as he heard
the high-pitched voices in the kitchen, she realised her trepidation
was far from over. In truth, it had only just begun. The enormity of
Dubem's danger grew flesh and poked her in the face. What if this man
was a heartless brute? What if he was above the law and Rufus totally
misjudged his character? Was Dubem still alive? The questions would
not stop popping and she broke out in large beads of sweat.

Turning off the stove, Ama spoke. "Breathe Chi. Try and breathe.
Let us not be too agitated. You said you met this man at the park...
You did something good for him... Surely, he must remember. It is also
impossible that Rufus completely misread his boss' personality. Deep
in my heart, I believe there is more to Dubem's disappearance. I am
confident my son will come back to us unharmed. No, Dubem is fine."

Ama's words did not help much, since discerning who they sought to comfort between herself, Dede and Chinny proved difficult. Chinny's breathing refused to return to normal. She told her parents about her plan to visit the villa the following day and they both hoped the chief's call had just cast a silver lining.

Sleep eluded Chinny. She tossed and turned in bed throughout the night, her mind a battlefield of troubled thoughts. Picking up her mobile phone, she checked the time. It was 1:30 am in the morning and two unread messages blinked. The first message came from her diced beef client, a response to the text message Chinny had sent to her the day before informing her she may not be able to deliver again this week due to some serious family emergencies. The lady was sympathetic, wished her luck in resolving the family issues and asked her to inform her once she was able to make ready the order. The second message was from Ejiofor. It read:

> *Chinny, I apologise again for what my father did. I understand and accept that it will take a long time, if ever, for you and your entire family to accept us as family like you once did. But please, if your friend for any reason decides not to go with you, let me go with you tomorrow. I am not sure why, but I am uneasy about your trip to Item town. Please think about it. Be safe and good night.*

Convinced of the bleeding pain her friend suffered as a fallout of the choices his father made, Chinny made up her mind to be deliberate about putting Mr Clarke's betrayal behind her and vowed to convince her folks to do the same.

The early morning rains sent out a waft of freshness and riding on its wings was a mild chill. Chinny woke up with a start and at once became pensive. *Today is the day*, she thought and scrambled out of bed to get prepared. She did not want Kenneth waiting for her when he arrived. By the time Chinny was ready, in a cream knee-length flared skirt and a black sleeveless fitted top with cream polka dots, the clock had almost struck eight in the morning. She hurried into the sitting room and stopped midstride at the sight of her parents, fully dressed and waiting.

"Father? Mother? What... Why are you dres... Where are you going so early?" she asked, looking from one to the other. They informed her calmly of their intense deliberations through the night, which led them to decide that there was no way they would let her go to Item town by herself. Chinny stared speechless. How would she go about convincing her parents of how terrible their idea was? And in one moment of bare-faced desperation, she fell on her knees and begged them to let her go alone. If Dubem still lived, their decision to go with her would cause the chief to panic and that could be the final nail in her brother's coffin.

Ill-prepared for the depth of emotions their daughter displayed, Dede and Ama were helpless as they tried to make her understand the risk embedded in letting her go off all on her own. They reminded her that she was all they had for now and of how totally broken they would be if any harm came her way. They went back and forth for the next few minutes until the duo caved. "If you insist Chi, we cannot throw away your reasoning, but we want you to understand this. Not minding how it might appear, we not only love you and your brother from this lifetime into the next but will gladly give our lives for you. We will wait... Hmm... We will wait for your return," Dede said.

"And Chinny, you better return. You have beef to fry for your clients. Did you hear me? Chinny. Your clients are waiting for your fried beef cuts," Ama finished, almost in tears.

With eyes smarting from threatening tears, it dawned on Dede that had he two daughters rather than a son and a daughter, it scarcely would have mattered. His well of emotions almost choked him as he came to the realisation that he had custody of two children he did not deserve. Chinny, who had been squatting the entire time, got up and hugged her folks. Grateful for their change of heart, she bade them farewell as she made her way to the door to wait for Kenneth outside. On getting to the door, she cast a backward glance and saw her parents looking bereft, her mother's eyes two pools of misery. Taking brisk steps, she walked back to hug them again but as she straightened up, the words escaped her lips before she could stop them, "Please, let us pray."

Nobody expected this, not from Chinny at least, but they were more than happy to pray. As nominal Christians, the Onas prayed individually, especially with their mounting issues, but it had not always been so. Morning devotions used to be a primary feature of their daily routine, but this revered family tradition, finding it impossible to keep pace with the tempo of the family's 'dance of survival', sought a dwelling elsewhere. As they made to kneel, the sound of a car pulling up outside announced Kenneth's arrival. Rattled by his punctuality, Chinny started to say a brief and rushed prayer to avoid not only keeping Kenneth waiting but also their awkward moment from being shared with an outsider. But Ama stopped her daughter's prayers in a stern voice.

"Let him in Chinny. Let him come in. We are not ashamed of who we are. Is he not training to become a priest?" Her tone could not be argued with. So, as soon as Kenneth reached the door, Chinny got up and let him in.

Kenneth wore a black cassock today, looking every inch as dashing as ever. He said his greetings to Chinny's kneeling parents and without another word joined them on the floor and Dede prayed.

Our dear merciful God, thank you for today. Thank you for your protection over us and our loved ones through the night and all through these years. We thank You for where we are coming from, where we are and where we are headed. Thank You for the help You sent to us in the form of friends like Kenneth. We are grateful for life and good health. Although we believe our circumstances could do with some improvement, we know of countless people who are dealing with a lot worse. We are sorry for taking for granted, the life and the mercies you daily adorn us with. We are sorry for hating our offenders. Please give us the heart to truly forgive our offenders and to cultivate the culture of gratitude to You oh God, so that when we come before You in supplication, we would be before a God who is pleased with us. Today, my family, our friend and I are asking You to please keep Dubem safe. Keep Chinny and Kenneth safe as they go to Item town. Please bring Dubem back to us unharmed. You own the entire world and all that is in it, including man. So please, when Chief Utah sees Chinny today, let him see in her, his own daughter, grant her audience and respond to her favourably. We will never forget to say thank you in the end. And Lord, please bless Kenneth more than he ever thought was possible. In Jesus' name, Amen.

Ejiofor lingered outside his gate but soon began a slow walk towards the Onas' residence. Although not sure of what to expect, he wanted to be of any kind of help. Besides, he missed his friend. The Onas and Kenneth had just come out of the house when Ejiofor reached their patio and was lost on what to make of the almost-warm smile and hug Chinny gave him. Dede greeted him and Ama gave him a measured pat and rub on the back by way of customary greeting. Kenneth gave Ejiofor a courteous nod. This outranked what he expected. After Chinny briefed Ejiofor on the chief's call and her decision to go to Item alone, he sounded diffident when he asked if he could stay with the Onas while they waited for their daughter's return, and sighed in relief when they assented.

The drive was done in comfortable silence and as soon as the villa gate loomed in front of them, Kenneth stopped at a safe distance and said, "Chinny, remember, twenty minutes. I have informed my friend of this visit. If in twenty minutes I call your number three times and get no response, I will ask him to move his boys in." She nodded and stepped out of the car, flashing a small smile as she waved to Kenneth. But he neither smiled nor waved. Chinny turned to begin her walk towards the gate and Kenneth called out after her, "Twenty minutes." He did not stop looking at her as she walked away, interpreting the strange feeling he had in the pit of his stomach as a sense of foreboding.

Unsteady fingers dialled the chief's mobile number when Chinny reached the gate. She thought to inform him of her presence before subjecting herself to the scrutiny of his fierce-looking guards. She knew Rufus was off duty since he mentioned that except on rare occasions, he always got time off work on Saturdays. In the voice of someone under water, she informed the chief of her presence, apologising for coming a few minutes earlier than was arranged. Chief Utah assured her it did not matter. "I'll just ask security to let you in. You will wait for me at the guest chalet and within a couple of minutes, I will join you."

"Thank you, sir," Chinny exhaled as she hung up. *Why does his breathing sound so laboured?* But Chinny did not have the luxury of pondering on the many possibilities of what the chief could be up to because, before she could think any further or gather her terribly racked nerves, a guard she did not recognise opened the gate and let her in.

Once within the four walls of the villa, the folly of her decision to face the chief alone became clear to her. For starters, the villa sat on an endless expanse of land and ominous silence enveloped the entire grounds. She figured that screaming at the top of her lungs for hours with all her might would only attract the attention of more tranquillity. Three uniformed guards walking around noiselessly, did not go unnoticed. There were four buildings within the compound as far as Chinny could see. The entire ground was paved with beautiful stones designed to interlock. The best of houses she had ever seen had gravel-covered grounds. There were trees with large leaves in the compound and this created a coolness that masked the morning sun's intensity. The main house was a large building that appeared to have two floors. It sat far into the grounds and away from three smaller bungalows. All four buildings were painted in rich cream. Capped with mud-grey roofs, they all had white-trimmed and vertical rectangular windows. Besides the deafening quietness, Chinny thought the villa looked breathtakingly beautiful.

A middle-aged lady in uniform took her to one of the smaller buildings. She had large, kind eyes. Nothing Chinny had ever seen or read about prepared her for the chill and stark splendour that greeted her on stepping into the guest chalet. It was picture perfect. The expensive marble floor reflected light and images. A black glass table sat in the middle of the room, which was well lit with a single white-lighted chandelier hanging in the middle of the ceiling. Chinny thought the plaster of Paris ceiling seemed higher than usual. The uniformed lady pointed her in the direction of one of the four single leather chairs and, to Chinny's relief, left, closing the brown steel security door behind her without as much as a word.

No matter how long she scanned the room, Chinny could not find the source of the cool air. "Where is the air conditioner?" she wondered aloud. There was indeed an interminable gulf between the rich and the poor. Chinny knew on which side of the divide her family fell but could not quite place the Clarkes or Kenneth for that matter. She checked her wristwatch. She had been inside the villa for only ten minutes and toyed with the idea of dialling Ken's mobile phone to say she was fine but decided against it as her attention shifted to two other doors besides the main security door. Certain that one led to the kitchen, she wondered what it looked like. Distracted by the cold-induced goosebumps fast forming on her arms, Chinny chuckled at the fact that she still could not find the air conditioning unit responsible for giving her the chills and rubbing her palms over her arms, she sank deeper into the leather chair.

Chinny's heart almost jumped out of her chest when the security door creaked, and Chief Utah walked in, wearing a pair of joggers, a white T-shirt and trainers. Though covered in a thin film of sweat and still breathing heavily; like someone who had just done a sprint, Chief Utah appeared a tad younger than she recalled. Chinny stood, taking the chief's outstretched hand in a handshake, her knees a mass of rubbery tangles. He had a genuine smile as he greeted in return, "I am so sorry I kept you waiting. I was having my morning run. How are you? Really good to see you again and under better circumstances. Now what brings you to my home?" Chinny began to respond in a very nervous voice but he interrupted her, asking her to sit back down and make herself at home as he sat in the chair almost opposite her. He hit a switch on the wall right beside him once and a male voice filled the room.

"Sir?" It was an internal communication system. Chinny sank deeper in her chair.

"Who?" Chief Utah asked.

"It is me, Simon, sir," came the response.

"All right Simon, please fetch some fruit juice, almond nuts and coconut cookies. Thank you."

"Right away sir," Simon responded. Chief Utah hit the switch again and the room fell silent.

Giving Chinny his full attention, he continued. "Yes, Miss Chinny, where were we? What is this critical issue you want to discuss with me? I remember you could not wait to get away from me at the police station. Anyone would think I belonged to the group of unscrupulous men looking to take advantage of females one third their age," he finished with humour. At once, Chinny felt small and gave a rushed explanation that she hoped sounded plausible.

"Please sir, I am so sorry for my conduct. There were things on my mind, better kept to myself. On a typical day, I am not that person... Chief Utah... sir. Please sir, prior to me helping with your briefcase, I did not realise who you were. It was only after you gave me your card—"

He interrupted her in excitement. "Yes! Thank you again. You have no idea what you did, do you? Apart from the large sum of money you saved me, do you know the little beggar girl only served as an instrument in the hands of that crook? He was no blood relative of hers. He confessed to abducting her after an accident left her parents dead. Her only living close relative, an auntie who had been frantically searching for her, had almost given up on ever finding her niece before that day at the square. The police briefed me that proper investigations carried out on her auntie found her to be genuine. The lady is married and successful but has no children of her own. She is the younger sister of Natalie's mother." Chinny, whose eyes were bright with unshed tears of joy was listening with rapt attention, but it was her turn to interrupt.

"Natalie? I thought her name was Nasa."

The Chief sighed. "That crook will spend a long time in jail. The girl was born Natalie Bello. She is from the North. You know she was quite young when the accident happened. My theory is this; the thief could not make out the name when the little girl said it to him, so he christened her with his own version of whatever he heard. She is still being prepared and sensitised for adoption. Her auntie is in town with her husband and I hear they visit her every day at the orphanage where she is being cared for. You know, building bridges in preparation for her new family. God knows that if she did not have a living relative, I would have adopted her myself. Please go on. What can I do for you?" he finished.

Kenneth began calling Chinny's mobile phone and she excused herself to take the call without getting up from her chair. In a clipped voice, she told Kenneth that she was fine and would talk to him soon. Chief Utah regarded her silently. It was difficult to guess what was on his mind. She apologised after she ended the call.

A refraction had occurred in the lens through which Chinny viewed Chief Utah. This man had an easy air! She almost asked him if he did not have children of his own but checked herself. She did not want to push her limits. She began with a pea-pod version of her childhood. From her early life as she remembered it, family struggles, her hope for an education, her vicarious academics, her parents' frustrated efforts at a headstart and finally, her brother's attempt to salvage the situation. Chief Utah did not understand where her narrative was headed but he listened, waiting for her to get to the point. Chinny eventually got around Dubem's involvement with him, which not only confused Chief Utah but made him ask for clarification.

"How do you mean? Am I supposed to have met your brother?" Chinny shifted in her seat and continued, exasperation lurking in the corner of her head.

"Nobody at home knew about Dubem's charade until recently. From what we have been able to gather sir, Dubem claims he entered into a business arrangement with you. He said he supplied a large quantity of produce to your fruit-juice-making factory and that you owe him a huge sum of money. But of course, we do not believe him. He has his bouts of schiz…" Chief Utah looked anything but easy and genial at this point. He had an incredulous look on his face.

"Hold on for a minute young lady. Your brother, Dubem, where is he? He sent you to me I suppose? Did your family put you up to this? You told them about the incident and now, they want you to extract a piece of the pie huh?" Alarmed at the sudden turn of events, Chinny could swear she saw steam coming out of the man's ears.

"No sir, no sir," Chinny whimpered but a knock interrupted her outburst as a steward walked in with a tray of refreshments. He set it on the central table with nothing but a bow to his employer and his guest.

As soon as they were alone, the chief continued, "You should not have done this. I would have been happy to show my gratitude in cash, but now, I see your previous rebuff was all an act. Go on, call back the person or people who called your phone moments ago. Tell them your plan worked. Your claws are digging in… How much do you want? One hundred thousand? Five hundred thousand? One million? Com'mon…"

Now sobbing, Chinny cut in, "It is nothing like that sir. My brother has been missing for over a week now. We believe he is here." The terror etched on Chinny's face looked genuine. She reasoned that if Chief Utah spoke the truth and her brother was not being held on his premises, then the situation was far more hopeless than they thought. As soon as he heard her brother was missing, Chief Utah's eyes shot up in alarm. He held out his hand, motioning for her to stop talking.

"What do you mean your brother has gone missing?" he asked cautiously.

Now dead quiet, he listened as Chinny read Dubem's letter to him. After what seemed like a lifetime, Chief Utah spoke, his voice sounded softer, even conciliatory. He admitted to having a fruit-juice-producing factory but told her he did not concern himself in its operation and had never met Dubem. He wanted to know why she was certain enough that Dubem really had any business with his juice company and that he was indeed being held on his premises to put herself in supposed harm's way. As soon as Chinny began to respond with her invented schizophrenic theory, he stopped her, telling her to tell the absolute truth if she expected any cooperation from him. At that, she paused and dredging all the courage within her recesses, told him of Rufus' admission to her about his misgivings regarding the running of the villa.

Chinny told him of Rufus' claims that some of the guards carried out suspicious activities when the chief was out of town – and this happened often. On one occasion when he thought they brought in some bulky things tied up in jute sacks, he ventured towards the back house where they have their quarters and was harshly reminded of where his duty post began and ended. Chinny did not forget to add that Rufus swore on his life that the chief knew nothing of these activities. Chief Utah suddenly got up and began to pace the length and breadth of the sitting room. The large room now felt too small. "Sir, please do not punish Rufus for this. He is a good man. I promised never to mention his involvement. Please sir."

"I see. I see. Hmm. I see," Chief Utah muttered, all the while pacing with both hands folded to his back. Chinny did not know what to make of his countenance as she twiddled with her hands in her lap. He stopped pacing for a moment, scratched his head, glanced at Chinny and resumed pacing. He began heading for the door but stopped midstride and reached into his joggers' pocket for his phone. He dialled a number. Chinny watched in palpable fear as he spoke to someone on the other end of the line. "Godwin, yes. There is an emergency. Deploy OPS VOID. Yes. Right away. Thank you." *What is OPS VOID? What have I got myself into? Was this all a mistake? I should have just placed my faith in the police.* Chinny's phone ringing again cut through her stream of questions. It was Kenneth.

"Who is trying to reach you?" Chief Utah blurted. He appeared angry, alarmed and confused all at the same time.

"It is my friend," said Chinny. The chief wanted to know if he was anywhere around, and Chinny hurriedly answered. "Yes. He is outside, but he just offered me a lift. He does not even know the details of my visit. Please... sir..." she lied. Chief Utah could practically slice through the tension around Chinny, so he offered some respite.

"Relax. You can breathe. I believe you. It is possible I have misjudged and placed too much faith in my staff. You see, I am hardly in town and try not to bother myself with affairs which I believe are under control. You heard me on the phone. I have ordered an override of my entire staff and security. Call your friend and ask him to join us at once. It may be unsafe for him out there in a moment."

Chinny was too flustered to fully understand the chief's last words but she called Kenneth and asked him to drive into the villa while Chief Utah informed the security guard on duty to let him in. As soon as Kenneth took the seat beside Chinny, he turned towards her with large, questioning eyes and in as few words as she could manage, she filled him in. Chief Utah observed them as they discussed in hushed tones. Just then, there was a loud, unusual chime. A few seconds later, the chime came again, and Chief Utah tapped that switch on the wall twice to ask the security guard to let the guests through the gates. A black van drove into the premises. The word 'FUMIGATOR' screamed in bold white letters across the van. Four men and the van driver, all suited up in thick, black overalls, came out of the van. Each had a tubular backpack. Their hands were covered in strange black gloves, and they had on heavy boots and head masks. Chief Utah immediately went to meet with them but not before instructing Kenneth and Chinny that on no account should they leave the chalet. Kenneth and Chinny peered through the window as Kenneth asked himself if he did not plunge too soon and too deep into the lives of these people he knew too little about.

12

C HIEF UTAH SPOKE AT THE TOP OF HIS VOICE TO TWO OF HIS staff outside. "This is an absolute negligence of duties. I saw a huge python this morning and judging from the six or more eggs under that shrub over there, we may be dealing with more of them in the not-too distant future," he said, pointing to a clump of St John's wort in the corner. Continuing, he said, "The fumigators are here, so I need everybody outside. They have to get to work at once." In that moment, Kenneth and Chinny realised that Chief Utah's higher-than-usual pitch was for their benefit.

One of his security staff spoke up in a rather pensive voice. "We are sorry sir... err... Yes sir... bu... but sir... err... sir, they would need some... someone to go around with them... You know err... to point out corners to them... sir." Chief Utah agreed, saying he would be happy to take the fumigators around himself. But when the staff insisted on a member of staff following the fumigators, suggesting that the chief may not be conversant with all the nooks and crannies, disappointment spread through Chief Utah. Contrary to what he hoped, deploying OPS VOID was not a wolf cry. His staff had something to hide.

"You are correct. I cannot possibly move furniture around. Maybe two of you can help them out," Chief Utah said, deciding to carry out a staff overhaul at the end of the operation, 'snakes' found or not. With arms folded to his back and a drawn face, Chief Utah began to walk towards the second chalet in a slow and non-obvious manner.

Soon, all fifteen staff stood outside the villa grounds. Cooks, gardeners, drivers, laundry personnel, stewards and security guards. And besides the occasional eyes darting around in anticipation of their slithering intrusive guest, most of them appeared to be relaxed and in a chatty mood.

Chinny and Kenneth peered as two masked fumigators took positions, one of whom manned the second gate, which now stood ajar, giving a clear view of the buffer zone, while the second masked fumigator stood at the back end of the perimeter fence. Yet another opened the back door of the black mini-van and began to let the staff in, one after the other. Soon all thirteen staff were tucked away in the van, slowly bringing the chatter to a halt. One fumigator marked Chief Utah at close range, his eyes darting around, while the last of them hovered within considerable distance to their two would-be fumigation escorts. Judging by their furtive disposition, the two guards fretted about something graver than a python and its six eggs. But, nobody besides Chief Utah and the fumigators knew there was indeed no python to catch. The so-called fumigation team were members of a private security agency. OPS VOID was set up as a fall-back plan in the event that Chief Utah's highly intelligent and empowered security detail went rogue. He had hoped there would never be a reason to deploy the team, but the allegation put forward by Chinny and Rufus could not be dismissed with the flick of a finger.

In truth, OPS VOID comprised six and not five fumigators in total. The last of them lurked in the chloroform-saturated mini-van and as the staff came in one after another, he doused them further with a regulated dose of the gas. This would allow a fifteen-minute time lapse for a thorough search. With any luck, anyone found to be a part of the mess going on in the villa would not be in any position to fight back or resist arrest. The private security agents figured that the two villa guard escorts were no threat in comparison to their own physical strength and professional expertise. The masked fumigator who had been letting the staff into the van reached into his backpack and produced three face masks. He gave one to each of Chief Utah's guards, explaining the need for protection from the fumigant and handed the third and biggest mask to Chief Utah.

At the back, the fumigator began spraying some mist as his designated villa guard showed him various hidden corners, while the other fumigator began to spray the buffer zone and the gate areas, at the direction of the second villa guard. Lost in the haze of activities, Kenneth and Chinny could not understand what Chief Utah's plan entailed or what its purpose was, seeing that he appeared content prowling the entire stretch of his property, looking anything but perturbed.

Chinny noticed that Kenneth no longer observed the fumigation process as he fiddled with his phone, but something else distracted her from speculating on what he was doing. The fumigator at the back turned a corner with the villa guard, leaving a trail of mist in their wake. Kenneth resumed watching and without losing view of the fumigation activity, began telling Chinny something about his military friend when they both froze. The fumigator spraying the front grounds of the villa was walking towards the chalet, and without warning, the villa security guard escort in front of him faltered in his steps and, before they got to the chalet's porch, doubled over and crumbled to the ground in one big mass. The fumigator beside the van, who before now had been actively scanning the villa grounds, took out a gun from his backpack, walked briskly towards the chalet, and with the help of the other man fumigating the front grounds, heaved the now-unconscious guard into the mini-van. Chief Utah stood aloof with both hands folded behind him, and other than the occasional exchange of whispers between him and the fumigator who closely marked him, they were as silent as the night. Terrified to the point of insanity, Chinny's teeth rattled while Kenneth's forehead shone with large beads of sweat.

The sound of trickling water gave Kenneth some respite from his thought process as his eyes flicked around, looking for the source. They rested in shock on a mortified Chinny whose detrusor muscle having contracted in her fear, caused her to stand in a puddle of her own urine. Tears of humiliation brimmed over Chinny's eyes as she gratefully accepted the black cassock Kenneth pulled off and handed her. He had on a pair of black chinos and a round-necked white T-shirt underneath. Ducking behind one of the other doors, Chinny tried to retrieve some of her lost dignity and came back wearing the cassock. It did not matter that the hem of her new adornment swept the floor of the chalet. She was grateful that her badge of shame with which she discreetly mopped the floor now sat in her bag.

A loud bang rang out. It sounded like a gunshot and Chinny ran back to where she had just emerged from while Kenneth crouched, his head below the window. A few moments passed, and the bang came again. They could hear humping and thumping. It seemed there was an altercation. Once again numb with fear, Kenneth wondered if his text message, asking Sam to call off the deployment of his military boys was sent out too soon. Nothing made sense to him anymore. The thought of how thorough *or not* Chinny and her folks may have been in assessing Chief Utah's character filled Kenneth's head as he decided it may be time to put an escape plan on the table.

More grunts, a shriek, and thuds came from the far back of the main building. A loud bang crashed on the gate. The bang came again accompanied by metal rattling and shouts of "Open this gate!!! Open this gate now!" Chinny crawled out of hiding. The humour was not lost on her companion as he watched her scurry towards his crouched-on-all-fours self. BANG! BANG!! BANG!!! rang through the now quiet villa. Words were not needed to express the terror in their eyes as their sweaty foreheads and palms did the honours. Summoning all the courage he could manage, Kenneth dared to peer above the windowsill to see Chief Utah and one of the OPS VOID officials, his gun held in position, walking cautiously towards the first gate. He observed that the second villa guard lay immobile on the villa grounds. Chinny who still crouched under the window with her eyes shut tight in fear, summoned courage to open them and had just asked Kenneth what he could see when the villa gates swung open and four military boys swept in.

More gunshots rang out and Kenneth whispered in alarm, "Oh no, no, oh no! It is Sam's boys. Sam didn't get the message in time!"

Stretching out flat on the floor, Chinny asked in quick, short gasps, "Who is Sam?"

"My friend in the army," said Kenneth, not taking his eyes off the chaos outside. Chinny was going to ask if they were the ones shooting when she heard Kenneth curse with a word she believed just terminated his pursuit for priesthood. The next words from Kenneth jolted Chinny into a kneeling position. "Whaaaatttt!!!?" she cried as she confirmed the arrival of her parents and Ejiofor to the villa. One of the military boys moved the villa guard on the floor with his boot to check his consciousness. They appeared agitated and somewhat confused.

"I want my children! Where are my children? Chinny! Dubem!" Dede bellowed like a mental-asylum escapee. Her heart thumping in her throat, Ama marched in right behind her husband, intent on tearing down every wall till she found her children. But something stopped her in her tracks. She stood transfixed, staring at Chief Utah for several moments; he looked familiar. And then, it all happened so fast. The atmosphere outside became hostile once again. A face-off erupted between the OPS VOID agents and the military boys but just before it went out of hand, one of the OPS VOID agents called out, "Kamal!... Kamal! Wait. It's me... I am the one... Sydney." As he made to remove his head mask, he motioned to his colleagues to stand down while the military officer who he addressed raised his hand to stop his already advancing team. As soon as Sydney revealed himself, Kamal's eyes lit up with recognition. They bumped shoulders and soon, the two groups flashed their different identification cards as Sydney explained the operation to the military. They were OPS VOID and came on Chief Utah's request to uncover a suspected misconduct in his villa's operations.

One of the villa guards who took them around for the supposed fumigation lay unconscious inside the van from the chloroform-laced mask he wore, but the other guard's bulk required a higher dose of chloroform in his mask, so he did not go under. Realising the situation, he tried to put up a fight and took a blow on a particular spot on his spine. This explained why he lay motionless. Unconscious, the remaining staff were in the van, affording time for a proper search. Kamal explained their presence as an intervention assignment, directed by their boss but while he spoke, his phone rang and after the call, he halted their mission and began to retreat with his boys.

Ejiofor started to walk towards the chalet and at the same time, the OPS VOID agent who knocked out the villa guard began to tell Chief Utah about something that needed his urgent attention when the doors of the mini-van were flung open. The military boys on their way out turned back to the villa grounds in one flash, taking formation with the OPS VOID agents.

Fifteen minutes went by fast and all the staff being held in the van regained consciousness. Amidst all the chaos, a few of the staff had rained a myriad of punches on the OPS VOID agent whose watch they were under and made sure he lay injured, before they retrieved their confiscated guns to attack the agents and military boys. The innocent villa staff huddled together in the far corner of the van while a fierce but short-lived gun battle ensued. An agent provided cover for Chief Utah as he ran into the third chalet. A cluster of flowers beside the chalet that Chinny and Kenneth peered from gave refuge to Dede and Ejiofor. But as Ama ran towards the safety of the buffer zone, she fell backwards. "My mother has been shot!!" Chinny screamed and without thinking, flung the chalet doors open and, running to her mother, pushed Kenneth aside as he tried to stop her.

The OPS VOID agents and the military working in unison, brought sanity back to the villa. A situation assessment showed that the two villa-guard 'fumigation escorts' had got caught in the crossfire and lay dead, while the other five suffered injuries of varying severity. One of the staff inside the mini-van had an arm injury while an OPS VOID agent suffered a flesh wound on his thigh. All other agents and military boys were fine.

As Chief Utah emerged from the safety of the chalet, Dede and Ejiofor who did not have the time to nurse their scratches – a testament of the bravery they expressed in crawling on paved floors and around rough flower shrubs, ran towards the buffer zone with Kenneth in hot pursuit. Dede looked frantically over his wife and child and let out a relieved sigh when he did not find any gunshot wounds. Ejiofor gently helped Ama to her feet. She had only slipped and so had Chinny. Kenneth stretched out his hands to Chinny to do the same but became alarmed when she neither opened her eyes nor moved. Dede scampered to his daughter's side and tried to rouse her. The alarm in Kenneth's eyes as he felt for Chinny's pulse and prised her eyes open to examine them betrayed his calm exterior. Something appeared terribly wrong with Chinny and Ama let out a shrill, anguished scream. For some inexplicable reason, Chinny lay on the villa grounds, unconscious.

The military and OPS VOID operatives immediately swung into overdrive. While some talked animatedly on their phones, others scanned the villa perimeter for possible intrusion or ambush. Abuzz with everyone talking simultaneously, it was impossible to understand what any of the operatives said over the phone or to know what to expect. Chinny was carried into the chalet. Her parents and Ejiofor were asked to stay with her while they waited for the ambulance, which was already on its way. On confirmation of Kenneth's medical background, he was asked to further evaluate the state of the injured staff on the villa grounds and those in the mini-van.

Led by the private security agents, Chief Utah walked to his basement which could also be accessed from the back of the building. The military boys stayed vigilant, their eyes darting around the villa grounds and perimeter fence. Chief Utah could not contain his anxiety as he dragged his unwilling legs to the one place he tried his utmost to avoid like a plague. They got to the huge metal door that guarded the basement. The door had a security feature and needed a combination of numbers to be accessed. A security agent explained to the chief that on getting to this part of the villa, his security guard, who now lay dead, told him that there was no need to fumigate that area as it had neither been used nor opened in many years. When the agent insisted, the villa guard informed him that only the chief had the combination. "This made me even more suspicious, so I insisted on asking you for the combination. I think your guard became certain then that something more than a fumigation was going on. On our way to you, he tried to *jump me*," the guard finished.

This further confirmed Chief Utah's suspicion since his security detail and all his domestic staff – including his two cooks, knew the combination. Once he entered the set of numbers, the door to the basement that his late wife once used as her budding perfumery swung open. After his wife's tragic death, he stayed away from the basement and plunged himself into making as much money as he could, giving some back to various charity organisations, one of which was Royale Academy.

At the point of admission, parents would sign a non-disclosure agreement, prohibiting them from divulging to anyone – even the children involved, that no admission, accommodation, boarding and sundry fees were required. Chief Utah's decision on this process stemmed from his observation of man's bent to soon despise whatever cost little or nothing. Royale Academy comprised one hundred per cent of students who possessed outstanding intellectual capacity, eighty per cent of whom came from indigent homes. The status of this clear majority was often confirmed after a series of remote investigations had been carried out on the individual families. And so, thanks to Chief Utah, over-the-moon-at-her-admission Eniola Okoye would never suspect that the so-called funds provided by her late father for her education would never have gone the distance.

13

THE THICK STENCH THAT ENVELOPED THEM AS SOON AS THE basement doors flew open would cause even pigs to run for cover. Revulsion-laced nostalgia swept over Chief Utah. Fond memories of bright white lights, floating in the intense blend of sweet wood, nut and fruit clashed with the present murk and stench. Not able to handle the unpleasant smell any longer, Chief Utah stepped aside to allow the agents to move further in. While he relaxed in the welcome ambience of fresh air, he wondered if Dubem would not have passed out inside such stench. His thoughts dwelt on Chinny and what may have caused her unconsciousness. Three of the security agents came out of the basement with a trail of sixteen teenagers, all walking in a daze. As the other two security agents came out after them, Chief Utah snapped out of his initial shock and told them that the boy who was the reason for the operation – Dubem – was not part of the sixteen. They were all girls.

One of the agents walked back into the basement mumbling, "That means we need to search some more. These girls are not in any position to answer any questions right now." Another agent followed. The girls sat on the floor in the front yard, while Chief Utah waited, hoping Dubem would emerge with the agents the next time they came out. Not able to wish the sinking feeling in the pit of his stomach away, Chief Utah sensed rocky days lay ahead. The crime had happened on his property, with the perpetrators either dead or in a critical condition.

The ambulance arrived, whisking Chinny and her protesting folks to the hospital. They wanted Dubem to be found and brought to join them. The military called for more ambulances to take the girls to the hospital, and the police to take the remaining staff to the station for questioning.

Chief Utah's hopes crashed when the agents came back without Dubem. Concluding they may have to wait for the injured staff to recuperate before opening any investigations regarding Dubem's visit to the villa, the agents began walking to the mini-van. But when Chief Utah remembered the secret safe, he knew his days of evasion were over and led them into the basement. He tore off a life-sized wall painting to reveal a steel panel with number-engraved buttons, which he punched. A hidden door slid out and downward to let them into a hole in the wall. There lay Dubem, battered beyond recognition, hidden in a corner of the life-size safe in one unconscious heap. Within minutes, Dubem lay outside waiting for the next ambulance. His wounds looked septic.

Thankfully, Halfeet Security Agency – the group responsible for deploying OPS VOID – were on hand to give a full professional statement at the police station. This validated most other statements. One of the villa guards, after receiving the well known 'detention induction', sang like a canary and confessed to the entire crime.

"After Chief Utah lost his wife, we took advantage of his pain and growing aloofness. His incessant trips and continued withdrawal from most of the businesses he ran with his wife before her death gave us the opportunity to run the villa and his other interests. We also ran other 'deals', using him as a front. The basement is our collection point for the err... girls we trade." Most of the girls who came from polygamous or underprivileged homes were either abducted or received from their willing parents after a promise of a better life through their children, who would be taken to work abroad.

When asked if there were any actual plans to take the girls abroad and if so, how they intended to fund their travel, the staff said, "We tell the families that the chief is running a charity program and would send their daughters to either America or London where they would work. We promised that their children would send monthly returns from their salaries. When the girls are in the basement, we brainwash them by telling them every day, that they are the luckiest girls in the world and that nobody is looking for them. To keep them calm, we infuse cannabis into all their meals and add the juice from the leaves of St John's wort plant into their water. After four weeks, we transfer the girls to the Dominican Republic." The near four-week wait afforded them the time to tie up all the logistics before they sent the girls off to Greater Santo Domingo by sea.

Over time, a few families grew wiser and began to question the authenticity of the chief's so-called charity program but were cruelly informed that Chief Utah had the police and the military on his pay roll and would pulverise their entire lineage if they pushed for any more information. As would be expected, these families often slid back into their shells and suffered their grief in silence, hoping their children would find their way back to them someday. The villa staff outside the crime web lived in constant dread, never discussing the happenings in the villa – even amongst themselves. Chief Utah's reputation had been thoroughly maligned by his trusted security detail.

On the day Dubem delivered his letter, Chain – the lead villa security guard – was out on other 'business.' Rake, his second-in-command, reckoned that letting Dubem run free after his visit may be a bad idea as he did not appear to him as one who would back down and forget about his money after a few shoves. So, he decided to detain and ship Dubem off with the girls. He planned to ask their partners to drown him in the North Atlantic. Thanks to the villa staff's working relationship with a handful of the officials at Sabana de la Mar wharf, so far they had successfully transferred four 'consignments'. This foiled attempt would have been their fifth, after which they had planned to go on a long recess – foreheads and eyebrows had started to furrow.

Torturous days followed the crime bust, ruffling Chief Utah's dovecote of a simple existence. The investigations grew convoluted and showed no signs of going away any time soon since international human trafficking could not be ignored. A report made to Abuja Police Headquarters caused an immediate invitation of the Enugu State Police Commissioner and Chief Utah for further investigative chats. A formal appearance at the Dominican Consulate in Abuja also seemed apposite.

Once at the hospital, Chinny regained consciousness but would not stop screaming in pain. X-ray scans showed a swelling in her brain from the impact of her fall and this made a drug-induced coma necessary. Once Chinny and Dubem were settled in the hospital room, Kenneth left for his base, with a promise to call frequently and check in on them as soon as he could. Ejiofor went home a few hours after and said he would come with some breakfast the next morning.

Dede and Ama spent agonising hours praying fervently for their two children. Hospital policy neither permitted relatives to spend the night in the reception area nor allowed two patients to sleep in one room, but the hospital management stepped down the rules for the Onas who could neither afford separate rooms for their children nor an extra room for themselves. The hospital waived the usual standard deposit and allowed husband and wife to pass the first few nights on the hard reception chair and lone chair in their children's hospital room interchangeably. They also gained access to the hospital facilities like the bathroom and kitchen area. The style and maintenance of Safe Trust Hospital – the biggest and most equipped hospital Item town could boast of – could not be compared to anything Mr and Mrs Ona were used to.

At almost ten-thirty the next morning, Dede, much to his disappointment, realised that Ejiofor may have decided on better things to spend his time on other than bringing breakfast for the parents of his sick friend. Marvelling at how unreliable man could be, even with his best intentions, he went to the hospital kiosk to buy some bread and two sachets of powdered milk. The hospital kitchen in their magnanimity lent him cups and spoons. Ejiofor showed up late in the evening with an unconvincing story and under-dressed apology. He seemed distant and in a hurry to get away at the first opportunity. Ama and Dede did not dwell on Ejiofor's behaviour longer than necessary. They decided he owed them nothing. Besides, they were thankful their children were still alive.

This whole time, the Onas could not communicate with anyone that would have cared. Nobody could find Chinny's phone. Ama's was destroyed during the chaos at the villa, Rake seized Dubem's while Dede, a man still in the process of getting used to carrying a mobile phone, had left his at home. Dede bought a few essentials at the hospital's utility store with the hope that they would be on their way home soon. Grateful for the unusual generosity received from the hospital, Dede and Ama moved around the building like mice, not wanting to tip their receptacle of benevolence. Future insight would later prove that the overly accommodating disposition of the hospital towards Mr and Mrs Ona was due to the welcome influx of sixteen female patients, traced to the involvement of the Ona children in uncovering a crime web. More welcoming was the pledge by the state government, to be financially responsible for the hospital bills of all sixteen girls.

On the second night of their stay at the hospital, Dede confided in his wife. He had been employed to work in a vegetable oil processing company.

"When?" exhaled Ama, almost falling off her chair. It took the patience of a saint for her to sit still and listen to her husband's explanation.

"Dear, please do not take it the wrong way. I would have told you earlier but on one of those nights when I tried to tell you, you thought I was fishing for some mutual benevolence and shut me up. The following days came with one trying wave or the other. When the terms of the employment were made clearer to me, it sounded like a 'fever dream', so I decided to keep it to my chest until I knew for sure that I was not leading you blindly to sea… again."

Sensing Ama's growing impatience, expressed by her heavy breathing, Dede's words became rushed as he explained that after upper school, he lost contact with an old friend called Lancelot but fell into luck's path when they met again after almost twenty-five years. While on admission at the hospital following his domestic accident, Dede took a stroll to the accounts department of the hospital after his discharge, to re-confirm that his bills had indeed been settled when he saw his friend. He had come to visit a member of his staff, also admitted in the hospital. Lancelot had done so well for himself and owned many business ventures around the country. Before he left, he gave Dede his number but since Dede still had not got around to buying a mobile phone at the time, he kept the piece of paper with the phone number in his pocket. Of course, he lost the paper.

They re-established contact on the day of the demonstration, when he met Mr Clarke and Lancelot close to his house. "To cut the long story short, I got the position of Logistics Manager in his vegetable oil processing company. With a rather short interview and no employment letter, I did not have a clear understanding of the terms of employment. A day after, Lancelot told me I would undergo some training and would be paid an advance of 75,000 Naira. He said that after the training, my position would be confirmed and would attract a monthly income which would be disclosed in my employment letter. He also said that once I start work, I would need to go through a series of courses on the job."

Ama could not believe her ears. "Oh! Is that the reason you rushed off to buy a phone that day? You needed to save Mr Lancelot's number?" she exclaimed. "But you should have told me nonetheless," she continued. Dede apologised again. Ama knew her husband only meant well and was doing all he could to reclaim his image as a husband and father.

A streak of silver lining shone in the dim clouds of the Onas on the fourth day when the doctors certified Dubem fit for discharge from the hospital. The intravenous antibiotics pumped into his body kicked in fast, giving the bacteria responsible for his infection the boot. Dede took his son home after his discharge but stopped at the bank to withdraw the required 30,000 Naira part-payment for the hospital. The tricycle stopped a few metres from the house. Concluding the trip was not profitable to him as Dede and Dubem were his only passengers, the driver asked them to disembark, informing them of his decision to take a detour. Miffed at his audacity, Dubem blamed the driver's effrontery on his father's inclination towards paying his transport fares upfront. Dede did not mind much as the house no longer sat too far away, and he liked to walk. Moreover, he needed time to think. As they made the few metres' trek home, Dede pondered on how to raise the balance for his children's hospital bill. For reasons best known to them, the state government had decided to leave Chinny and Dubem out of their financial magnanimity.

Do I ask for another advance at work? Would that not be ridiculous? Maybe I should talk to Lancelot. No, no, that would reek of taking advantage of a privilege. Should I approach Chief Utah when he gets back? No... it would seem presumptuous. Deep in thought, Dede did not realise that Dubem's steps had faltered and that he no longer walked beside him. He turned back to beckon on his son to find glazed eyes and an ashen face. He followed Dubem's eyeline and for a moment, his heart ceased to beat. Dede's legs became like jelly and holding his chest, he crouched. Dede opened his mouth to speak but no words came. He straightened and took a good look at the carcass he once called home, for before him lay one of his four blessings – burnt to the ground. Rapid breathing, profuse sweat, dry mouth and his son's strong arms holding him up served as Dede's last memories before he floated into oblivion.

Confused and unsure of his location, Dede tried to get up from the uncomfortable eight-spring bed but Kika's arms restrained him. Recollecting, Dede choked, "My house… my house… fire… how? Oh God!!" Uncontrollable tears coursed down his face. He wailed like a baby as the full impact of the situation hit him. Violet and Adaiba rushed in and tried unsuccessfully to comfort him. Kika could feel his brother's distress and did his best to soothe his aching heart.

Not making any headway with consolations, he resorted to encouragement and ended with, "Brace up my brother. You are a man. One way or another everything will work out. Be a man."

Outside and sitting in despondency, Dubem listened to his father being comforted and wondered if his mother would find or take any comfort when she heard the news. He thought it was normal to go through rough patches in life, but was now convinced that even the most resilient of people would crash while navigating the unique terrain he and his family had travelled for as long as he could remember. Certain that her heart would break into fragments, Dubem wished for a part of his mother's pain when it came to her, for there at the hospital she sat, expecting their early return. He made to go into the house, but his father's soliloquy stopped him at the door.

"All my life, I was told that being a man solved the problems of humanity. That as a man, fate was on your side. It is a man's world, they say. Time has taught me that fate is no respecter of gender. Male or female, calamity, anguish and misfortune will befall you if fate so desires. Male or female, love, fortune and success through hard work can decide to pick you as a candidate. Yes. Indeed, male or female, you are not absolved from taking responsibility for your choices, actions or the lack of them. Hmmmm. We are but mere participants in this board game called life, striving hard to reach our various mapped out destinies. I am a grieving man, lost and hopeless. Let me grieve. If that is all I can do. Let me grieve."

Adaiba almost bumped into Dubem on her way out to hide her tears. "Dubem, come," she whispered, pulling him further away from earshot. "What happened? What is going on? The fire happened three days ago. We called everybody, but all the phones were either not reachable or switched off. Nobody knew your whereabouts. My father made up his mind to report to the police station this morning, only to learn everything from the 7:00 am news. Mama rushed to the market to buy some condiments and was just cooking lunch to bring to the hospital when someone came to tell us that Uncle passed out."

Dubem told his cousin that the media said it all. "So, you mean Chinny is still unconscious?" Adaiba asked, distressed at Chinny's state. "They say the fire must have started from the kitchen. Hmmmm. Dubem, it was horrible. You need to have seen how people tried to save the house. Especially Ejiofor – your neighbour. That boy is something else. After we heard the news this morning, we went to his house to find out if he knew about the villa saga, only for him to tell me that he witnessed the whole thing and that he feigned ignorance of the whereabouts of your family because he did not want the horrible news of the fire to be dumped on you just yet. Not with Chinny's condition." Dubem shook his head in regret at the paradigm shift as he realised that not every shadow gave the reflection of the true height or width of its original figure. It all depended on the time of day. Ejiofor's behaviour as relayed to him by his father now made perfect sense.

For the first time, Ama had a genuine smile when she saw Violet and her husband. Unlike her parents, Adaiba was always a delight to see. "I cooked rice and *susuu*," Violet said, handing the flask to Ama. Home-cooked food never looked more appealing as Ama, holding in a chuckle at how Violet pronounced 'sauce', began to dish the food. Dede declined, saying he had lunch with Kika. So, forgetting for a moment the beep from the machine attached to her daughter's chest and arms, Ama sat back to enjoy her lunch. As she chewed on her smoked fish, Ama apologised to

Kika and his wife for the way they ran off to Item town without informing anyone, explaining that the delicacy of the circumstance caused them to act in haste and without thinking. Ama tried to fill in the blanks in the account they heard from the media, Dede and Dubem, saying that the media enjoyed being sensational with news, while men had never been detailed in storytelling. *They could not have done better than her at recounting the incident at the villa*, she thought.

At ease and with no sense of the steady rise in tension within the room, Ama chatted away. Adaiba fixed her eyes on Chinny, willing her to sit up and ease her mother's imminent pain. When Dede brought himself to tell his wife about the fire, he thought he saw her eyes dilate and drown in unison. The almost-empty plate of food went crashing loudly to the ground.

On cue, Kika and his wife began to move in on Ama who Dede already held down with one hand. "Wait, wait... wait," she breathed in a pain-laden voice. She continued as she withdrew from her husband's grip, "Nobody should touch me. I need to understand what you are saying." Still sitting, but turning fully to face her husband, she asked, "Dede, are you saying that as at this moment, we have no house?" Dede died a little as his fragile wife crumbled into pieces before his eyes. She made to stand, but her legs failed to support her, so she let the weight of her pain push her back down. Ama began to sob. She clasped her mouth with both hands for fear of attracting the attention of the already forbearing hospital management. "How?" she asked looking from Dede to Kika. "What happened to my home?" she asked again, turning to Ejiofor, Violet and Adaiba, her voice the sound of her just-broken plate. There was a curt knock on the door and the doctor on duty came in with two nurses.

14

THE MEDICAL STAFF BLINKED AT THE NUMBER OF PEOPLE IN THE room but recovered soon enough, responding with measured calmness to the chorused "good evening". The male nurse busied himself with aerating the room and admitting more of the natural evening light by drawing the curtains and opening the windows. The medical doctor, a middle-aged man, read the screen of the beeping monitor, prised open Chinny's eyes, felt for a pulse on her wrist and took notes, while the female nurse propped up Chinny's head, puffed her side pillows and adjusted her to make her more comfortable. She took her temperature and began to note the reading when the doctor asked Dede and Ama to join him in his office. As the staff filed out, Dede followed them. Standing, Ama wiped her tear-stained face to also do the doctor's bidding.

Once the door closed behind Ama, Kika and Violet scampered to Chinny's side, alarm and worry in their eyes. Kika peered into the monitor. His stance drew a smile from Dubem's face as he wondered what his uncle hoped to find on the screen. "It is just checking her heartbeat... to make sure she is fine. They made her sleep to reduce the pain in her head," Dubem said in answer to his uncle's unasked questions.

"Oh. Okay," husband and wife chorused and returned to the other end of the room. Quiet and morose, Ejiofor suffered a different and more intense pain compared to everyone else. Leaning against the wall beside Chinny's bed, Adaiba's eyes rested on her cousin – willing her to wake up.

The doctor's office, a room one-and-a-half times the size of Chinny's hospital room, had two chairs on the other side of the desk from where the doctor sat. With furrowed brows, the doctor asked them to sit down as he pored over some files. After what felt like a lifetime, he looked up and informed Dede and Ama that based on the scans and X-ray reports which had come back to him, besides her head injury following her fall, Chinny did not suffer further injuries. The swelling in her brain was contracting but not as fast as anyone hoped for. He informed them of the need to change her medication from Thiopental to Midazolam. However, the challenge with the new drug which had been established to be the best for a clinically induced coma and known to promote the healing process was its economic factor – it cost almost seventy per cent more than any of its counterparts. More worrisome was the mono-directional nature of the drug since it could not be substituted once administered. In summary, the doctor required payments for previously dispensed treatments as well as the inevitable further treatments. The name of the medications alone sent shivers down the Onas' spines.

"Although we have received the sum of 85,000 Naira from one ehm... ehm," the doctor fished around his desk for something. Dede and Ama looked at each other in puzzlement, wondering what he meant. "Yes. Found it!" the doctor continued. He informed them that the payment came from one Mr Kenneth but that it would only suffice for so much and hoped there would not be any need to continue with the medication beyond seven days. Dede and Ama thanked the doctor and left for their daughter's room, their hearts spilling with gratitude for Kenneth's kindness.

Now closer to the reception area, raised voices floated towards them. "There are too many people there. *Oga,* you have to wait," shrieked a nurse.

"I understood you the first time. I am neither deaf nor daft. All I ask is for you to go and fetch me either the mother or father. That's all," the man hissed. Dede's eyebrows took a rise.

"I know that voice," he told his wife. Ama did not recognise the voice. Her thoughts were in a faraway place. "It sounds like Oliseh. I'll check. You go on," said Dede as they approached the reception entrance. Ama walked on, taking a right bend to the wards, her heart, grateful for the unexpected financial aid, but heavy with the thoughts of homelessness and looming disgrace – how would the remaining hospital bill be paid?

The two friends exchanged a warm embrace as Dede cast an apologetic glance at the nurse who gave him a professional smile. "How did you hear? Who told you where we were?" Dede asked. Oliseh chuckled as he told Dede that his fame had gone ahead of him.

"The story is all over the news. My friend, the media is having a big party with the story about how a young lady in search of her abducted brother uncovered a kidnapping and human trafficking ring." Dede tried his best to fill his friend in on the other details, including the fire. Short of words, Oliseh hung his head in empathy and after a few moments, placed his hand on his friend's shoulder in consolation. Kika, Violet, Ama and Adaiba met them at the reception area and after Ama greeted Oliseh and went off with their visitors to the gate, Oliseh asked if he could see the children. Dede explained that he may only be able to speak to Dubem since Chinny still lay unconscious. Amused at his friend's awful attempt at masking his worry, Dede obliged Oliseh and took him to the hospital room.

Oliseh would have sworn that the young man who sat on the hospital bed at Chinny's feet was a statue till Ejiofor raised his head and let out a low "Good evening sir". Dubem's incandescent happiness at seeing his benefactor and friend received equal reaction from an overjoyed Oliseh. Ama came back into the room and they all talked for a bit, but not long afterwards, each drifted off in their own thoughts. A while later when it became obvious that the only sound to be heard in the room was the beep from the electrocardiogram attached to Chinny, Oliseh announced his departure. At the reception door, he declined Dede's offer to walk him to the hospital gate and took out two envelopes from his bag.

He handed Dede the first envelope saying, "This is not much but it would solve a need. Please my friend, do not refuse it. This other envelope contains proceeds from the sale of two out of Dubem's four kilns. Please hand it to him and apologise on my behalf for the liberty I took in making the sale." Dede thanked his friend, but as he returned to the room, his creased forehead expressed puzzlement at the meaning of a kiln, why his son had it and why it fetched such a heavy bundle. In the room, as Dubem started to explain the use of the contraption he built, Ejiofor excused himself.

"I must begin to head back home," he said. The Onas could not agree more as the young man looked as though he would burst into tears in no time. As soon as they were alone, Dede examined the contents of the envelopes he had just received. The smaller envelope contained 45,000 Naira while the larger envelope had a sum of 130,000 Naira.

Dubem shoved the envelope back to his father saying, "Father, I did it all to help us… our family." Overcome with gratitude, Ama and Dede's guilt grew limitless. It was not their children's place to cater for them – not at their young ages.

The rest of the evening slid by with an easy air. Dubem said he would go back to Uncle Kika's house for the night but intended to push it until as late as when Adaiba brought dinner. He went back to the house with her, promising to come early with breakfast the next morning.

With a troubled night and a mind battered by a plethora of questions regarding renting a house, funds with which to pay off the mortgage and hospital bills, a groggy-eyed Dubem, accompanied by Ejiofor, came in carrying a breakfast of moimoi with milk and sugar-laced pap. Everyone ate in silence as Dubem stared at his still-unconscious sister. Contrary to the common saying, Google was not Dubem's friend on this occasion. Nothing he read on the internet did anything to encourage him about how soon Chinny would become well.

The hospital had been quiet since the discharge of the sixteen girls, who now underwent rehabilitation in a centre situated in Enugu, and did not have as much bustle as it did a few days ago. A little bird whispered that there would be a formal handover of the girls by the state government to their respective parents who were still being interrogated. And the hospital management hoped to feature in the headlines… again.

Not long after the dishes were put away, the doctor came in holding a big envelope. The result of the scan taken last night came back with great news. The swelling had shrunk remarkably and a steady reduction in the dosage of Midazolam could begin. Several minutes after the doctor left, Dede, Dubem, Ejiofor and Ama still floated in the euphoria of the welcome news but the reception nurse informed them of Chief Utah's arrival, cutting short their victory party.

As soon as he entered the room, everyone stood uneasily, muttering, "Good morning sir". Chief Utah apologised for not checking in on them these past few days. He explained that he had to travel to Abuja regarding his obvious involvement in the sordid case. It only made sense, since his property served as the collection and dispatch point for the trafficking ring. Though happy to hear about Chinny's improvement, he warned Dubem not to take his apparent bounce for granted, emphasising his need to take his days one at a time. He glanced at Chinny, muttered that she would be just fine before taking his leave. At the door, he beckoned on Dede who swiftly followed him out.

Chief Utah began, "On returning from Abuja, I reported at the police headquarters as is required of me and learnt of the fire incident." There could not have been a better cue as Dede confirmed the fire, describing how it razed his entire house to the ground. Awash with sympathy, Chief Utah asked if they had any family to stay with while they thought of ways to pick up their pieces and Dede answered in the affirmative. The chief's car disappeared in the distance and Dede almost kicked himself. The opportunity to ask for a loan sat on his lap and he let it slip away. How would he face Ama with no answer to their homelessness and mounting debts? The question of whether they were now in the blue or still in the red with the hospital accounts department hung around unanswered. Dede also feared Kika and his family may soon crack under the weight of the burden he suspected they had become.

In the quiet hospital room, Ama busied herself reading the little blue Gideon Bible while Dubem and Ejiofor stared at Chinny's monitor. Glancing at Dubem, Ejiofor sliced through the silence.

"A kobo for your thoughts?"

The two men never exchanged much in terms of conversation. Dubem let out a dry laugh and told Ejiofor that he would come out badly bruised if he ventured into his head. To that, Ejiofor offered no response. The minute Dede returned, Ejiofor made to take his leave, but his mobile phone began to ring. It was his father. Ejiofor listened to the voice on the other end of the line before offering that he was at the hospital. Afterwards, he handed his phone to a surprised Dede. Lancelot had been trying to reach Dede and had to resort to contacting him through Mr Clarke. He wanted Dede to concentrate on his family and promised that his job waited for his return to the office. Dede expressed his gratitude but decided to follow through with his previous plan to go to the office the following day.

$$\sim$$

Day six after OPS VOID and Ama sat alone in the hospital room since Dede had gone to the office to give a formal report of the reason behind his unplanned absence. He thought it to be the responsible thing to do, his finding good grace with the company Chief Executive Officer notwithstanding. As she wondered when and to where they would leave the hospital, Ama stared at her ever-boisterous daughter lying unconscious in bed, her heart heavy with worry. The doctor said she should be on the way to consciousness. She touched Chinny's forehead and shook off the fearful thoughts that crowded her mind. Exerting needless energy as she pushed the curtains aside to let in more sunlight, which was no match for her gloom, Ama's tears began to fall. She concluded they were mapped out to remain at the base of the tower of happiness. Ama had just finished with Chinny's routine bed-bath when a knock robbed her of the luxury of an extension of her pity party. Chief Utah walked in.

The uneasiness which Chief Utah's presence emitted filled the room but as was always the case, it dissipated as soon as he flashed his ever-genial smile. "How is she today?" he asked. Ama told him that the machine beep remained the same and that she had still not blinked, even though the doctors had stopped the coma medication, as she referred to it. Chief Utah's brows creased in worry. And telling Ama that he would be back in a moment, he left the room.

On returning, Chief Utah met Ejiofor and Adaiba in the hospital room. Eating the breakfast they brought did not make Ama's list of things to do, as she sat brooding. Chief Utah asked to see Dede but on learning that he had left for the office, asked to talk to Ama instead. They stepped out of the room with two pairs of curious eyes boring into the back of their heads. A while after, Ama returned to the room alone. The mask on her face threatened to crack from its tautness. Ejiofor and Adaiba were not sure if the looming crack was due to excitement or agitation. Moments later, Ejiofor left for home. His folks would be back today, and he wanted to be there to welcome them. Adaiba informed her auntie that returning with lunch would be pointless since she adamantly refused to eat any breakfast. Before Adaiba left for home to prepare the dinner her mother was to bring back for Ama later in the evening, she told her that it would also be her mother who would bring breakfast and lunch the next day. Suspecting at once that Adaiba smarted from the rejection of her breakfast, Ama took a few mouthfuls as she asked her why she would not come to brighten her day as usual and sensed a clamming uncharacteristic of her niece. She probed further, and the jolly lady buckled. Adaiba could not tell a lie to save her life. She was grateful nobody ever asked her about her so-called sewing classes. More so, she had deep affections for Ama who nobody assumed served as a major pivot in her aspiration to succeed. She noted in admiration, the difference between her mother and Ama. A difference she realised stemmed from one of them having the will to ride above life's cruel shenanigans. This difference, as she came to know, was what put the 'extra' in the ordinary life of her sweet cousin Chinny.

Petrified at the real reason behind Dubem's unusual absence this morning and the planned absence of Adaiba and Dubem for the better part of the next day, Ama blamed herself for allowing the flurry of all the events around them to make her forget that the long-awaited GCE interview was scheduled to be held the next day. She listened with growing alarm as Adaiba told her of how Dubem, Ejiofor and herself beseeched the GCE officials to either postpone the interview date or reschedule Chinny's since she still lay unconscious in hospital. With a small voice, Adaiba told Ama that all their pleas fell like water on the back of a lizard. She confided in Ama about their planned rally, to peacefully demonstrate their position on the proposed day of the interview. Adaiba and a few others planned to boycott the interview in the hope that it would make the GCE officials change their stance.

Though thankful for how much they were sacrificing for Chinny, Ama feared that it may all go wrong. "What if the police get involved? You know, like the other time when the youth demonstrated over the death of that woman and her two children," Ama said in agitation. As Adaiba assured her that they intended to go quietly and let their placards do the talking, Dede walked in. He responded to Ama and Adaiba's greetings, dropped the nylon bag he came in with and went straight to Chinny's side. He touched her forehead, asking Ama if she noticed any change. The slow and resigned shake of his wife's head sent Dede's passably happy mood southbound. He stood by the window, silently sipping the bottled water he held and barely looked in Adaiba's direction when he bade the young lady goodbye as she left for home. He threw the now empty bottle into the trash can and made to return to his unseeing gaze out the window when his eyes caught something. In an instant, he strode to the bedside, his eyes poring over Chinny. Scampering to his side, Ama asked him what the matter was, and Dede swore he thought he saw their child's eyelids flicker.

It took almost twenty minutes for Dede and Ama to quit peering into Chinny's face. Their daughter was still unconscious. Dede tried to lighten Ama's mood by showing her the few items he bought from the market on his way back. Some tops and bottoms for himself, Ama, Dubem and Chinny. As much as they appreciated the clothes Kika and his family provided, Dede figured that they would be more comfortable in their own clothes. There was also a pair of rubber flip-flops for each of them and a multicoloured hairband for Chinny. Somewhere in the corner of Ama's mind, she was certain that the hairband would either end up at the bottom of Chinny's box or as a gift to someone, most likely Adaiba. Her daughter preferred less dramatic colours.

The early hours of Friday found Dede and Ama talking about what next to do. Optimistic that his new job would provide a level of succour, Dede's only looming cloud was that Chinny's unconsciousness lingered. Ama began slipping into despondency when she remembered her grand plans to help their financial status. Her farm lay in ruins and hopes of leasing her property to another telecommunications outfit seemed like a mirage. When she told Dede about the GCE interview and the planned rally, Dede became troubled. He thought Dubem should have confided in them. Ama lit up suddenly. She had forgotten all about Chief Utah's visit yesterday.

"Chief Utah came here yesterday morning. I forgot to tell you. He said he would be leaving town again soon," Ama began. "He wanted to see you but when I told him you went to the office, he decided to talk to me. He said he would have preferred to talk directly to you but that considering the urgency and delicacy of the issue, he thought it best to convey his proposal to you through me." Alarm bells went off in Dede's head at the word 'proposal'.

"What is it? What proposal again? Honestly, I am tired of these rich people always seeking to trample on the less privileged few. I do not want—"

An at once puzzled and agitated Ama interrupted her husband with the voice of an angry school teacher. "Allow me to land Dede!!! Since when did you use a one-size-fits-all bag for the entire world? The man said he found out that the hospital management, in their frenzy, misunderstood his instructions before he hurriedly left for Abuja. He told them he would be responsible for Dubem and Chinny's hospital bills. As we speak, a cheque refund of all the payments we have made so far is sitting with the accounts department."

15

E NGULFED BY PENITENCE FOR THINKING THE WORST OF CHIEF
Utah, Dede wondered if he would catch him at the villa before
he left for his intended trip. Ama knocked her husband's socks off
when she told him the other part of the discussion. "He asked us
to move into one of his guest chalets, pending when we can sort
ourselves out, if we do not mind. He said that because of the incident
at the villa, he now has only one cook, one cleaner, one driver and
one security guard. The villa is bare and too quiet for his liking. This
is like a dream Dede!!! I could not contain myself… But, I thanked
him and told him I would check with you," Ama finished, the look
of uncertainty etched on her face as she searched Dede's star-struck
eyes.

Unable to contain the bubble any longer, Dede began to do something
between a foxtrot and *atilogwu* – a traditional spirited dance from his
ethnic group. Overwhelmed with gratitude, he stopped momentarily,
took Ama in his arms and began to sway in rhythm to the beep of the
machine attached to their daughter. From the warm wetness on his left
shoulder, Dede sensed Ama crying but did not fret because he knew
she cried for joy. Life had dealt them a few ruthless blows. Blows that
almost robbed him of his reasoning and Ama of her sweet soul. Blows
that made them almost lose their son, that still threatened to steal their
priceless jewel from them. Yes, there have been blows. There were still
blows but surely, they were being handed cushions so plush that they
made the pain of the blows begin to feel more like mere shoves. In a
surge of overwhelming gratitude, Dede stopped dancing and clasping
his eyes shut, prayed.

I do not deserve this... I do not. I know I do not. I asked for a twig, but you gave me a boat. I am sorry for not living up to your expectations of me, but I am thankful. Thank you God for forgiving our sin of bitterness, of thinking life consisted only of what we could do on our own in the way we thought best... Thank you for the signposts you keep giving us to show that you can change our drumbeats to any tempo you like. Thank you because now more than ever, we know that Chinny will be well and that...

Dede paused for a heartbeat but continued,

and... and that everything will be fine. Help us to always remember that you are the one who beats our drum... the one who dictates the tune. In Jesus' name.

Dede and Ama chorused Amen.

At half-past seven in the morning, a nurse knocked to inform Ama and Dede of the medical director's request to see them. Sensing their worry at leaving Chinny alone in the room, the nurse offered to stay with her till they returned.

"There is some news," the medical director informed them. All their medical bills had been paid.

"We are aware that Chief Utah cleared the bills in excess of 150,000 Naira, but we prefer to wait till our daughter is discharged to confirm exactly where we are with the accounts department," Dede said. The director shook his head smiling as he informed them of the Federal Government's interest in the case and of how in a twist of events, they decided to take over their hospital bills. He continued, his voice shaking with excitement, "We informed Chief Utah at once and asked him to come for a reimbursement, but he said the refund should be made to you. So, Mr and Mrs Ona, there is a sum of 355,000 Naira as a refund with our accounts department, waiting to be claimed. But of course, we can arrange something if you decide to subscribe to our medical insurance..." The director's proposition received a good-natured decline even as Ama and her husband expressed their unabashed gratitude to who? The Federal Government? The director? Chief Utah? Divine providence? Or God? Quite frankly, the medical director did not care who their gratitude went out to. He had an idea of how they felt. The joy stamped on their faces was infectious.

Dede, who before now thought that all he had to his name after he withdrew the part payment for the hospital bill came to some hundreds shy of 50,000 Naira, could not keep his excitement on a leash. They left the doctor's office walking on clouds. Still bubbling with excitement when they got back to the room, they thanked the nurse who stayed with their daughter while they met with the medical director. As the nurse left the room, a doctor and a different duty nurse breezed in to wheel Chinny away for another batch of tests.

With the GCE result defence interview scheduled for today, Ama picked at her breakfast of milk and bread, thinking about the planned rally. Dede doubted that the demonstration would yield much and prayed the children came to no harm. But he, unlike his wife, dug into his mini loaf with gusto. Ama suspected that the funds injection they had just received was the cause of his unmistakably good appetite. Gusto or not, Dede did not miss the faraway look in his wife's eyes and asked what troubled her. She blurted, "What if all this is a ruse?"

Lost, Dede asked, "All what a ruse?"

Ama continued, her eyes brimming, "A trick, a ploy to get us prepared for the worst. What if all the blessing thrown our way through this entire experience is a ploy to reduce the pain of the biggest blow? What if Chinny does not pull through this and—" Dede cut her off with the sharpness of a newly crafted blade. He warned her to continue being double-minded and risk receiving nothing further. Pulling his frayed nerves together, Dede tried for encouragement.

"Ama, do not allow your mind to fight you. It is man's greatest known enemy. Our child will be fine. I choose to see this cup as half full. She will pull through this," he ended, feeling a tad sorry for his now tear-stained and subdued-looking wife.

The scuttling outside drew Dede's curious legs and opening the door, he peered out to find two nurses running off in the opposite direction. They stopped to speak to a male nurse who screeched, "Are you sure? Okay," and ran off while the two nurses returned to where they were coming from. Dede recognised one of them as the duty nurse who wheeled Chinny out for her test and told Ama so over his shoulder. As they made to pass by, he asked for his daughter. The two nurses looked at one another in uncertainty, shook their heads, mumbling as they scurried past. Something looked wrong and by now, Ama stood next to her husband, looking anything but comfortable.

Urgent steps carried them towards the test room that held their child. It had been over an hour and a half since Chinny had gone in. Dede knocked, demanding to see his daughter but a doctor said they were yet to conclude the tests and Ama began to wail. Something did not sit right. Another doctor came out of the test room and respectfully asked them to go back into the hospital room to wait. After what seemed like a truck load of appeal-garnished coercion, Ama agreed to be ushered back to Chinny's room but Dede remained obstinate in his refusal to move away from the locked doors.

Heavy in heart, Ama knelt on the floor of Chinny's hospital room, plunging face down on the bed that once accommodated her daughter. Her sobs could be heard down the hall. She restrained herself from heading back to Dede as she pulled at the sheets in anguish and let out primitive torture-cloaked groans. "God, I begged you. I begged you ooo. I begged you. Hei, hei, after everything. Oh oh! Oo! My child, Chinny!!! God, I begged. I begged…" Her heart threatened to rip out of her chest. Twenty minutes later, Ama still lay sprawled on her daughter's bed crying but the sound of the door creaking open made her turn around.

Dede bounced in with stars in his eyes. "She is awake, she is awake, Chinny… she is up!!!" Dede screamed at his confused wife. Ama opened her mouth to ask if Dede saw her with his own eyes as a nurse came in behind him with a wheelchair-bound and weak but conscious Chinny.

Ama wanted to run to her child's side but she faltered in her steps and stood rooted to the spot. Chinny's eyes looked terribly weak. Her head felt as cold to Dede's touch as the sound of her voice when she said, "Nne'm, I am fine. Why are you crying?" It was all Ama needed as she flung her arms over Chinny, who flinched in pain. Dede managed to fight off the tears threatening to spill from his eyes.

Overjoyed for the Onas, the entire hospital staff on duty did their best to make Chinny as comfortable as possible and by 4:00 pm, after having sipped only on water, which she could swear was at least a gallon, Chinny received a reward of a warm bowl of custard, laced with honey and milk. Nobody had brought any lunch for Dede and Ama, but they did not mind as they appeared content gazing at their sweet daughter. They answered with enthusiasm all the questions Chinny threw at them save for the one regarding when they would leave for home. "The doctor has to discharge you first," came Dede's clipped reply. Violet arrived with pounded yam and bitter-leaf soup for lunch and made no effort to hold back her tears on seeing a conscious Chinny, almost in her usual happy mood. She called Kika instantly to tell him the good news. Further adding to the happy mood, Violet told the Onas that Dubem and Adaiba called her mobile phone earlier to say they were fine and on their way back.

At about 5:45 pm, Chief Utah breezed into the room. He came as soon as he learnt from the hospital when he called as usual to find out how Chinny fared. Due to leave for Abuja on a flight at 7:10 pm and Nigeria at 10:30 pm, he had a couple of minutes to spare at the hospital. His smile almost ripped his face as he chided Chinny for holding the whole country to ransom.

"It feels good to be famous," responded a now-sated Chinny with a giggle. Amidst casual chatter, Chinny greedily gobbled the mildly spiced fish pepper soup from the hospital kitchen.

Chief Utah had to go, but was interrupted from taking his leave when the door flung open and Dubem, Ejiofor and Adaiba ran in squealing. A happy Ama cautioned them to lower their voices but the hospital staff she bothered about did not appear to mind one bit. Another ten minutes encroached on Chief Utah's already choked time, so he turned to leave, promising to return in a few days. Dede started to thank him for all his support and care, but Chief Utah waved it off, saying they had done more for him than they could imagine. At the door, he told them that he had left the keys to the chalet in the care of Rufus his security guard, and that they were free to move in as soon as Chinny was discharged. Without another word, he left in a hurry for the airport. Chinny looked from her father to her mother, then to Dubem before asking why Chief Utah offered them his house.

"What is wrong with our own house?" she asked no one in particular.

Deciding that if there was ever going to be the feared event of a relapse, the hospital was the best place to have one, Dede told his daughter that Chief Utah magnanimously offered to accommodate them for a while because they had a fire incident in the house. Everyone exhaled when in a calm voice she asked what started the fire and how much of the house it destroyed. Rushed chorused explanations of an electrical fault and repairable damage rolled over one another. Chinny seemed to take the news well because she only shook her head in resignation and finished her soup. It had been one exhausting ordeal for her, and she was drained of energy – even for worry.

No tantrum, appeal or coercion from Chinny could change the doctor's decision to observe her till the next day at the very least. So, she settled back to endure her hospital bed for at least one more night. Somewhere within her, though crushed at the uncertainty the fire caused, the prospect of camping out in one of Chief Utah's three guest chalets was something to look forward to. The evening grey fast turned to the night's black so Kika, Violet, Ejiofor, Dubem and Adaiba got up to begin their journey home. But Dede asked his son to accompany him to the villa. If his family received shelter on a gold platter, he thought it responsible to at least take a look beforehand and make it warm for them on their arrival. So, Ama and Chinny were left by themselves but this time, the light in Ama's eyes filled the room as she called out after her husband, "Okay, don't be long!"

⟿

A dizzy spell hit Chinny when she stepped out to board the car kindly provided by the hospital and she leaned into the hook of her father's right arm. For the first time, she did not shake her head in resignation at the sight and smell of spilling refuse bins mixed with water and dust. Both of which featured in the plethora of reasons for her mounting dissatisfaction with living in any country without snow and people who spoke through their noses – Uncle Kika's colourful description of the Caucasian missionaries who almost succeeded in convincing his father to send him to school. Deliberate in her action, she drew a lungful of

167

the humid air outside, appreciating the puddle-filled potholes of varying dimensions, splashed through without a care by tricycles, bikes and cars as they sped along the strip of untarred road beside the hospital. Thinking, *You never know what you have until you lose it*, her face broke into a guilty smile. Everything seemed surreal to the Onas as they got into the vehicle and waved at Safe Trust Hospital's chief medical director and staff. In Chinny's opinion, this treatment, fit for only royals, and all the financial assistance and goodwill they received during their stay in the hospital, could not for one minute be put down to luck. Certain that a superior force chose them as a show screen, she settled in her seat and closed her eyes to enjoy the ride to her new home... temporary or not.

Rufus walked on cloud puffs as he ushered the Onas into their new home. It was bigger and sat further from the gate than the chalet where Chinny had met with Chief Utah. Though grateful that Dede and Dubem did all the cleaning required for a long-abandoned house, Ama noticed the absence of a few items and drafted a conservative list of essentials, from pots, matchsticks and spoons to food stuff, drinkable water and spices. Shortly after they settled in, Dede put on his shoes again. Duty called; he had some shopping to do.

At 8:15 am, the sun stood high in striking splendour, but the Onas sunk deeper in absolute slumber. Who would not after spending so long on hard chairs and a cramped hospital bed? Besides their dinner of fried yams, plantains and fish which Dede bought from a well-sought-after food vendor, the cool air from the air-conditioning unit and the king-sized beds in every room made certain their slumber dug even deeper.

It was a taste of heaven for Ama as her back hit a bed that still had room even after fully stretching her arms. Her eyes slid open, but she refused to give up the softness that still caressed her back. "Hmm! This luxury will need some getting used to," she sighed with a self-indulgent smile. The doorbell chimed and Ama jumped. Running with the speed of greased lightning, she unlocked the door to see a man in a white baker's cap, holding out a wicker basket.

With a huge smile, his cheerful voice rang, "Good morning, madam. Breakfast from Chief Utah. He thought it would be too early for you to have settled in to cook anything and left orders to give you a soft landing. I am so sorry, his order came in very late last night so I could not make anything available for your dinner." Ama did a poor job at concealing her enthusiasm as she gushed her gratitude. Beyond exhausted, Ama had given breakfast not even one fleeting thought.

The need for lunch was successfully given a rear seat after the delicious breakfast. None of the warm croissants, baked beans, perfectly scrambled eggs, steamed green peas, milk and sugar-laced oats or fruit salad stood a chance as they received the full venom of the Onas' exhaustion and stark excitement. Listening to their animated chatter, it was difficult to associate them with the level of pain, uncertainty and utter hopelessness they found themselves grappling with for a stretched number of years.

Dubem cleared the dining table and practically ran his mother off when she attempted to do the dishes. Besides the occasional anxious glances cast Chinny's way, fearing she would scream in pain and slip back into unconsciousness, the chalet exuded relaxed warmth. But Chinny neither screamed out in pain nor slipped back into coma. She just missed her phone and so did not chat much.

Near frustrated, Dubem stood for almost ten minutes, trying to turn on the television set. The remote control sent out signals when he tapped the power button – as shown by the red light on it – but the TV did not come on. The power button on the TV set did not do much to help either. More annoying was that nobody could locate the power cable or switch. Ama thought the set may be running on batteries, but Dede disagreed. He thought it would not make any economic sense to manufacture such television sets.

"Moreover, the power-providing companies would be greatly disturbed at the prospect of becoming redundant and would fight the manufacturers or distributors of such a product with the ferocity of a wounded lion," he argued. Only at the point of frustration and near-resignation did Dubem look behind the television to find the power cable carefully knotted and plugged into a socket discreetly screwed high on the wall behind the TV. Letting out a sigh, he clicked the switch and turned it on using the remote control. Halfway into the morning breakfast show, Ama joked about how Chinny's birthday stole past them on Thursday and how today, Easter Sunday almost did the same!

They agreed that all church services would have ended and wondered if Chief Utah went for Easter service. Did he belong to any church denomination or community? Was he a Christian? It dawned on the Onas that they knew next to nothing about their kind-hearted host.

Chinny needed to rest and went into her room for a siesta. Yes, her room. The guest chalet had four bedrooms with individual toilets and bathrooms. The sitting room was big and well laid out with an impressive dining area opening into an equally large kitchen area.

Not long after Chinny's head touched the pillow, there was a knock, a pause and then the bell chimed. It was Adaiba and Ejiofor. Violet sent a cooler of white rice with palm fruit sauce and goat meat for lunch. She and Kika planned to visit later in the evening. Ejiofor took a seat while Adaiba asked to be pointed to Chinny's room. She skipped off to her cousin before Ama's warning to keep her animated self in check reached her ears.

Adaiba whistled, snapping her thumb and middle fingers in open-mouthed appreciation of the sheer luxury around her. "Chi, so this man just gave you guys this house... for free?" Chinny quickly corrected her cousin. She told her that the house only served as a place to 'camp out', pending when they pulled themselves back up. Adaiba's excitement suffered no dampening. She simply thought they were in paradise and secretly blessed the ill fate that brought them this good luck. "Hei! From no home to mini palace... from no home to mini palace! From no home to mini palace..." Chinny found it impossible to stop herself from laughing at her cousin's chant.

When Adaiba brought herself back on planet Earth, she started in a tentative whisper, "Chi, err... Ejiofor is here oo." At Chinny's raised eyebrows, she added that he was in the sitting room but that his parents and sister stayed back in their car a few metres away from the villa. Immediately heading for the sitting room, Chinny asked why they refused to come into the house. Adaiba told her it could very well be an uncertainty of the reception awaiting them, given the now non-existent friendship between the two families. Chinny held her friend in a bear hug and she, together with Ama, Adaiba and Dubem, went out to usher the Clarkes into the house. Try as the Onas did to hold on to their hurt, the realisation that all their south-bound journeys found a way to turn northwards expanded their hearts, making it impossible to stay bitter at the Clarkes.

Chiaka came along with a cooler of spaghetti and fried chicken, while Mr Clarke carried a cool box, filled with bottles of soda and packs of juice. He did not speak, save for his muffled and tentative "Good afternoon and Happy Easter" to Ama and Dede. Ama suspected he regretted what he did and tried to ease him into their happy ambience, but it did not help much that Dede did not feel at all chatty.

While everybody other than Dede and Mr Clarke chatted away, it struck Chinny that her birthday and Easter Sunday were not the only dates to elude them. So she asked, "How about the GCE interview? Did it hold?" Adaiba stuttered for a bit before bracing for the worst. She recounted how the several appeals she, Dubem and Ejiofor made to the officials for the interview to be postponed or at least for Chinny to be given a separate date fell on rocky ground. Chinny's eyes lit up when Ejiofor mentioned the rally but dimmed when Dubem told her that when it mattered the most, the few intending participants pulled out. In the end, only Dubem, Adaiba, Ejiofor and two others participated in the rally with Adaiba being the only one with an interview at stake. To lighten the fast-dipping mood, Ama and Zara, Ejiofor's sister, began serving the rice, spaghetti and drinks. It was almost too late for lunch and too early for dinner, but they enjoyed the meal regardless. By the end of the day, the Onas had more food than they needed since added to all the food they received from Violet and Chiaka, Chief Utah's standing order at his kitchen remained valid. Thankfully, the huge refrigerator in the kitchen more than matched the task. In spite of all the madness, this Easter Sunday was one of the best the Onas had experienced in a very long time.

16

FIVE DAYS IN THE VILLA AND ANYONE WOULD THINK DUBEM HAD lived there since forever. He was the only one not taking a siesta – a battle Ama had long conceded for her sanity's sake. Her son's aversion to sleeping in the day defied every reason. *This is the life*, Dubem thought as he plugged his phone to charge in a corner. Dede had retrieved their SIM cards and bought cheap and cheery but functional phones for everybody. He plopped down on the longest sofa in the living room to enjoy a match between Barcelona FC and Arsenal.

Grumbling, Dubem tore his eyes away from the football match and hurried to the door to find Rufus grinning as usual. "*Where is small Miss?*" he asked. When Dubem told him that his sister was having a nap, he went on, "*No problem, tell am Chief don come back! E just come back now now!*" Promising to inform Chinny of Chief Utah's return as soon as she woke up, Dubem smiled at the guard's enthusiasm about his job, but did not wonder why, since his employment conditions told the reasons out loud.

At about seven forty-five in the evening, Dede stood at the entrance to the main building, thirty-five feet away from their chalet. He wanted to know if he could speak with the chief. The steward led him into the anteroom and a while later, Chief Utah asked Dede to join him in the sitting room.

Once inside, Dede almost whistled at the luxury before him, but clutched onto his composure. Although not cluttered with furniture, the seemingly endless space of a sitting room had in its centre a rug piece, wide enough to accommodate eight able-bodied men, the depth of which could not be less than two inches. Dede longed to touch the black fur of the rug. The chief's hair, wet from a shower, glistened under the soft spotlights in the higher than usual POP ceiling as he offered Dede a seat and asked if they had been comfortable so far.

"We could not wish for anything better, even if we tried," said Dede as he thanked him and sat, holding out a cheque with the hospital bill refund. "Here is the refund from the hospital sir... we cannot..." But Chief Utah stopped Dede. He wanted nothing to do with the refund.

"Your daughter... Errr, Chinny rescued me. Before I met her, I was a husk of a man, aloof in my cocoon. My chance encounter with her pulled away the shutters over my eyes. For as long as forever, I drowned myself in my pain, not having any desire to see beyond myself. Yes, I did a sprinkle of good works, attempting to fill my void, but nothing I did emerged from selflessness. When I met your daughter, everything changed. Meeting her was heaven's response to my silent call." Chief Utah stopped for a moment and went on. "Your child handed me a second chance at life after the death of my wife. And please, it is light years away from what you think. I gather you have a budding career and will therefore not fiddle with your ego. Please tell your wife to submit a proposal for anything she wants to get busy with and I will make it happen."

Dede's fingers tapped on the arm of the deep-grey leather seat he sat in, distracted for a moment by its rich oak trimming and the low hanging crystal chandeliers, one each in the sitting room and dining area. The curtains travelled from the ceiling all the way down to the black-splotched grey marble floor. Each copiously garnered curtain set comprised a rich grey piece between two bright white pieces. Bringing himself back to the present, Dede began to shake his head, muttering his refusal of any more kindness from Chief Utah who smiled with that self-satisfaction inexorably associated with the rich and said, "You have no idea, do you Mr Ona? I am repulsively rich and before now, it would have meant absolutely nothing to me whether you accepted my offer or not. But as it stands, I owe you and your family for a lifetime and back. And I hate to be a debtor." He paused for air and resumed talking. "Please, this is your home for as long as you want. Do not hold back from accepting my hand because, it is only a reciprocation of the help your child inadvertently brought my way. You may wonder at the improbability of being able to do anything for someone who seemingly lacks nothing. But one day soon, I will tell you my story."

Unable to grasp the real reason behind Chief Utah's intensity, Dede managed to convey his gratitude to him in not many words. He had an almost irrepressible urge to fling his arms around his host, but not wanting his masculinity to come under a cloud, he shook him with both hands instead. Long after Dede left, Chief Utah sank further in his chair, with the smile of a sated infant, the warmth, slow in its spread from his heart through his entire being.

⌒ↄ

The date for the formal handing over of the rescued girls had just been announced. Everyone was talking animatedly about the evening news and the details of Dede's chat with Chief Utah when Chinny's phone rang. Ejiofor's voice reverberated with excitement. He wanted to know if she had listened to the evening news. In his opinion, the handover ceremony was fast becoming an event everybody would want to attend but Chinny expressed her indifference. While everyone chatted away in the chalet, Chief Utah received a call and an accompanying electronic mail from the governor's office, inviting him to the handover ceremony, slated to be held in exactly one week's time. He graciously accepted the invite and began to consider a plausible excuse not to attend, when an adjoining mail asking him to prepare a five-minute speech hit his mailbox. He realised the futility in planning to evade the ceremony.

The next morning, Adaiba called to ask if Chinny had heard about the handover and proudly informed her that a few friends in different dance troops told her they would be making presentations at the ceremony and were now having rehearsals. With an all-important tone, Adaiba informed her cousin that someone whispered something about the attendance of not only the president of Nigeria, but the president of the Dominican Republic. "Famous musicians will perform live. And I also learnt there will be so much to eat and drink," she said.

Chinny laughed at her cousin's ignorance, which she found both amusing and refreshing on most occasions. Frustrated at Chinny's phlegmatic disposition at most fun things, Adaiba cried, "Chinny! Are you not thrilled? It is a big deal com'mon!" But when it became clear to Adaiba that her beloved cousin did not and would never share her

174

enthusiasm at things she considered trivialities, she let out an angry grunt saying, "It seems you do not want to attend. Anyway, as for me, I will go there and soak up as much fun as is humanly possible. If and when you decide to become as human as the rest of us, let me know."

Deciding to put her cousin out of her misery, Chinny pacified her between chuckles. "All right, I am sorry Ada. No more laughter. To be honest, I heard everything you said and more in the news. Like err... the name of the president of the Dominican Republic which by the way, I think you should look up," Chinny said, unable to resist the jab. Adaiba clicked her tongue in defiant protest but Chinny continued, "I also know something else." In answer to Adaiba's surprised "Oh?", she went on with a mischief-drenched smirk, "Entrance to the venue would be strictly by invitation!" And pop! went Adaiba's balloon. Angry at Chinny for allowing her to go on about an event she knew she would attend only in her dreams, Adaiba said an out-of-character "Good night" and hung up.

Amused at her cousin's enthusiasm for anything in the least associated with fun, Chinny shook her head at her phone in absolute fascination and went to the kitchen for a glass of orange juice. Although happy with the twist in the near-fatal events, Chinny did not share in even one tenth of her darling cousin's excitement. A cold blast of air hit Chinny as she held the fridge's door ajar for longer than necessary, soaking up the sight of the well-stocked shelves. *So, this is what it feels like to have a fridge*, she thought, pouring herself a glass of cold orange juice, thankful she did not have to freeze and thaw to enjoy a glass of cold drink. Glass in hand, and heading for the sitting room to join everyone else, Chinny wondered about Kenneth and if he had been following the news. She regarded Dubem, feigning annoyance at him for dipping his head and slurping almost a quarter of the full glass of juice she held. *He is different now. Playful maybe*, she thought before blurting, "Has anybody seen or spoken to Kenneth since last Saturday?" When her mother shook her head with down-turned lips, she continued, "Hmm, I hope he is all right wherever he is. Nne, I think we should find a way to at least thank him for his cash aid." Ama told her that her father mentioned refunding Kenneth's cash support since the government already paid their bills.

Forty-eight hours before the official handover of the rescued girls, word went out confirming the attendance of not only the president of Nigeria but also that of the Dominican Republic, who saw this as the perfect opportunity to make his country's stance on human trafficking and girl-child repression clear.

Considering the budding ties between Nigeria and the United States of America, President Hugo Dolores did not second-guess himself on his decision to pay Nigeria a courtesy visit. The Dominican Republic desperately needed an ally in the United States of America, a country dedicated in her fight against female repression. Bad publicity and being portrayed as a proponent of depravity did not quite fit into his box of strategies on forming alliances.

As soon as the authorities of the Dominican Republic learnt about the sordid event, they engaged in a massively publicised sweep across the country and as many illegal immigrants as they were able to identify were taken back to their home countries. A handful of the former victims of the trafficking ring now enjoyed the flamboyant lifestyle their 'jobs' afforded and could not be bothered with going back home, while others, cowering under the looming stigma, went into hiding.

Adaiba called Chinny to ask if she could drop by after work. Yes, she still scrubbed walls and floors and had since doubled her efforts following her inevitable need to re-sit the general certificate examinations. And even though Chinny had still not talked about it, Adaiba did not doubt that her purpose-driven cousin also thought along those lines. Chinny told her that the villa gates were always open to her. As she headed to the kitchen, Chinny paused, looking pointedly at Ama who sat engrossed in her new art of writing, crumpling and throwing paper all over the floor. "Nne'm, what have you been writing and discarding all morning?" she asked.

Determined to own her project from start to finish and everything in between, Ama refused any help from Dubem with putting her proposal together. She was bent on stretching herself to perfection or dying trying. Kneading her nape, Ama answered, "It is a proposal. I will write it myself and take it to a business centre for typing before allowing anybody to see it. After that, I will send it to Chief Utah." Chinny said nothing, but within, her heart expanded with pride at the woman she called mother.

Peeping through the kitchen door, Dubem asked his mother what to do with the beans on the burner and without lifting her head from her stack of papers, she told him to turn it into pottage with diced plantains and vegetables. Chinny took a sheet of paper from her mother's stack and sat down to do some writing of her own. Hoping her diced beef clientele had not given up on her, she thought the time had come to return to the pedal.

Staplers, nylon wrapping packs, deep-pan fryer, big pot, strainer… Pausing for a moment to think of the other items she needed, Chinny resumed writing her list… gas burner, vegetable oil, spices… She looked up as her father walked into the sitting room, smiling wryly at his wife. Ama had been on her proposal-writing mission for almost two hours and remained adamant in her refusal of help from anyone. Though impressed at her grit, Dede thought her obstinance at stretching herself thin on something in which she lacked experience, now rested on the line where resilience verged on thick-headedness. Looking at his daughter who also sat on the dining table, Dede asked in feigned disbelief, "You too?" Chinny giggled as she explained the less complicated nature of her assignment in comparison to her mother's.

"I am only drafting a list to resume my meat business. It is time to resume saving towards school." Dede stared at his daughter as though she just grew an extra head. Ama's head shot up from her work and Dubem came out from the kitchen. Everyone began to talk at once, telling her in different phrases that she must be sleepwalking to think anyone would let her drown herself in any more stress. Dede for one told her that he now possessed the ability to provide the basic needs of his family.

"I have been handed an opportunity and it will suffice my child, by God, it will." Chinny weighed everyone's reasoning for a moment but shook them off as fast as they came. She reminded them that even though Chief Utah refused his refund, nobody knew if Kenneth and Mr Oliseh would do the same.

"Education costs so much these days. And do not forget our house renovations and the mortgage loan," she said.

Dede announced that Oliseh asked him to tuck his own refund away. "He intends to use it for Dubem's wedding gift," Ama chipped in, attempting to lighten the mood. Dubem's eyes grew wide in mock surprise, saying he did not realise he had a bride. The previously tense atmosphere began to ease, but adamant about putting that phase of their lives behind them, Dede still held on with his teeth and claws. No way would he allow his daughter to go back to the grind. Outnumbered, Chinny rested her case. Or did she?

Adaiba poured out her frustrations over the phone. She finished rather late and would not be able to visit as planned. "Some of these rich people eeh! The state of their houses each week would make anyone think they are cleaned only once in three years. Imagine having to first fold clothes, then arrange shoes strewn all over the room and depending on the type of paint, scrub or wipe children's scribbling off the wall before starting the actual cleaning." Chinny consoled her cousin, suggesting that the following day being a Sunday may be a better day for a visit.

⌒つ

It turned out that Chief Utah belonged to a denomination and attended a church after all. Although it had been years since he last attended a church service, his enthusiasm shone through his eyes as he and the Onas rode in his car to church on Sunday morning.

After the short but interesting service, the Onas thanked their host for the ride and had begun their short walk to the chalet when Chief Utah requested to speak with Dubem at his earliest convenience. Nobody knew what to think when it came to Chief Utah, so the afternoon wore on with a dash of unease.

As you would have guessed, Adaiba came visiting a little after lunchtime. Ama suspected the young lady may not mind relocating to Item town, and that her reasons would not rest solely on her fondness for Chinny with whom she chatted away in the bedroom. Ama broke up their party, calling her daughter to the living room.

"Chief is here. He wants to talk to us," her mother said in an uncertain but excited whisper, wondering why their benefactor decided to bring 'the party' to them. It was short and simple. Chief Utah decided to pay Dubem the sum his staff owed him. He took responsibility for the rot that he, as a result of his self-centered unwillingness to look beyond his immediate pain, had allowed to be perpetrated on his watch.

"I will pay you three times what they…. I owe you. I should in truth do more considering all I gained from everything you went through," he said, adding that he would follow up on their burnt house, to find out if an insurance policy existed and what effect such a policy would have. Turning to Chinny and Dubem, he told them to spread their wings in applying to any institution of higher learning of their choice and that he would make sure they studied whatever and wherever they pleased.

The Onas were awestruck, but each thought the same thing; *Here we go again, what does he want in return?* They had no words in response to Chief Utah, who with laughter in his eyes said, "Now this is the point where you gush… Oh, aaah, thank you very much, God bless you, we appreciate your kindness." But nobody appeared to understand his joke.

Their chorused but strained "Thank you sir" sounded like the reverberating clang of a steel plate on the stone floor of an empty room. They stared at him, suspicion seeping through every pore on their skin. Unable to stand the choking discomfort any longer, he got up to leave. Chinny spoke up as his hand touched the door handle, his back to them.

"Why sir?" she asked, not sure of whose voice rang in her ears.

Chief Utah turned and readily answered, "Because I can!" But the steel in the young lady's eyes and the unsmiling faces staring at him told him it was 'truth or dare' time. So, he took two steps back towards the family, huddled together in a united protective stance, and in a rushed voice, began.

"Many years ago, I lost part of my early memories after a near-fatal accident. Months after, my parents sent me to England to undergo reconstructive surgery, but I fell in love with the English and stayed back to study. There I met the one I called my soulmate. After dating for four years, she still made the butterflies flutter in my stomach. I loved her with every cell in me and she felt undoubtedly the same. On graduation,

Mel followed me back to Nigeria, turning her back on everything she held dear. We hoped to get married and live happily ever after. But that, as I discovered, was wishful thinking. My folks would not hear of it because she did not belong to 'kindred spirit' – she was British and a white one at that. It took another three years of unsuccessful appeal to my parents for us to realise that our marriage would never happen.

"Broken, I stood by and watched Mel crumble to micro-pieces. After many years of clutching at threads, I went to pay her a visit, to tell her I preferred to run away with her, to face the consequences rather than to live one more day without her as my wife, but only met a note from her. She could not stand the rejection and pain any longer and had left for Australia. We had to go our separate ways and find alternative happiness. Some things were just never meant to be, she said. I mean, Australia? The other side of the world?! Besides, she did not have any family or friends there. At least none that I was aware of. She carefully handpicked her refuge and robbed me of one last fighting chance."

Four people and one hiding behind the door were held in rapt attention. Chief Utah continued after pausing for an infinite number of heartbeats. "I lost it. I tried. God knows I tried but I could not find her. So, shattered, hollow and lost, I began a long, dark and winding journey to self-destruction, in defiance of culture and mindless prejudice until I met my late wife. During my dark journey, I earned myself the nickname 'Don Kay' and picked up a chieftaincy title, utterly beyond belief in its needlessness. My full name is Donald Kanayo Utah. My late wife was an angel. Believe me, sometimes, I thought she had actual wings. She saved me and gave me a reason to rein in. An exposure to some toxic gas in her perfumery snatched her from me. Only then did I realise I was not scheduled for happiness. On the day I met your daughter, I had a meeting with my lawyer, to sign off all I possessed to various charity organisations. It is with deep shame that I say this, but I planned to take my own life. The money in the stolen briefcase would have been payment for the 'intruder' who was to break into my house – on a day my key security officials were going to be conveniently off duty. The 'intruder's' job was to shoot me. I did not want to exit like the loser I had become. It had to look like murder. Chinny's act of bravery on that day at the car park made me stare hard at my own cowardice. After the event following Chinny's quest for her lost brother, I was summoned to the Federal Capital Territory for further statements, and on my way back, I ran into Mel. She never left Nigeria and wait for it... she never got married. While I expended resources searching for her abroad, she crouched under my nose, refusing to move on."

Chief Utah looked at Chinny square in the eyes. "Now do you see why? I do not have the resources to show you my appreciation. You gave me my life back." And with that, Chief Utah hurried away, leaving a stupefied audience behind.

17

EVERYONE TALKED IN HUSHED TONES LONG AFTER CHIEF UTAH left, cringing at how much they misjudged this broken man. It all now made perfect sense – his feeling of indebtedness.

On her way to get her cousin the next available tricycle, Chinny almost bumped into Rufus. He was coming to inform them that a visitor waited at the gate. Out of town at the time of their discharge from the hospital, Mr Oliseh returned from his trip only two days ago. After exchanging pleasantries, Chinny went on her way, questioning how this gentle-hearted man almost always managed to find his way to them.

Minutes of warm chatter and sharing good food slid into hours and Mr Oliseh forced himself to bid the Onas goodbye at the onset of twilight. "Remember, my home is open to you. The resources available to me are at your disposal. Please come in anytime and make this old man quake with laughter once more," he said to Dubem, the fondness in his eyes unequivocal.

Twenty minutes into the seven o'clock evening news, the door knocker rattled the easy calm of the chalet. Nowhere near as calm and unperturbed about life as he always looked, Rufus told Ama about some unwanted guests. Two siren-blaring vehicles forcefully gained entrance into the villa and bright headlamps now flooded the compound. Out jumped four broad-chested men in black trousers, shirts and jackets, their eyes shielded with dark spectacles. *Who wears sunglasses in the evening?* Ama thought. Dede rushed out and placed a protective arm around his wife. Rufus offered in his usual diction, *"Them say them want to see small Miss."* Mother and children shrunk further into the house.

One decisively bold step after another, Dede went to the men who now stood side-by-side in one straight line, legs at ease and arms folded across their chests. In the most confident voice he could muster, he asked them who they were and what they wanted with his daughter. One of the men responded in a surprisingly genial voice. They came from the Government House, with a letter that must be hand-delivered to Miss Chinny Ona. Dede asked Rufus to fetch Chinny. She managed to overpower her reluctant feet and came out to identify herself and receive her letter. The men had instructions to, on identifying Chinny Ona, deliver the governor's seal-embossed envelope and stand by until she confirmed complete understanding of the contents of the letter.

Chinny had been invited to the formal handover ceremony of the rescued girls. Her invite admitted any ten guests of her choice. The men allowed Chinny, her mouth slightly agape, to admire the ostentatious design of the envelope for a while before asking if she needed clarification on any part of the invite. "Ehm, yes. Was Chief Utah invited? Must I come with all my guests or can they come on their own? If there are not up to ten guests, will I be disqualified? Is there a dress code? Are there penalties if we arrive late?" Chinny's questions flowed unending, but the men smiled with knowing looks as they patiently answered all her questions.

Yes, Chief Utah was invited a few days ago. For ease of accountability and access, it would be best if she arrived at the venue with her guests. They would all be conveyed from her house tomorrow. No, there was no dress code. Any nice outfit would do. A second man, who sounded even kinder, chipped in with a smile, "Just look good, bearing in mind that you will be meeting with two presidents and the state governor." Chinny and her father thanked the men as they drove off, with a promise to see them the next day.

As soon as the vehicles disappeared, Ama and Dubem jumped out of the house, whistling and squealing when they heard Chinny shout, "We are invited! We are invited! Tomorrow… the handover!" Rufus was not left out in the excitement as they huddled around for the details.

Thankful that Chief Utah was not there to witness a first-hand display of their most primitive expression of excitement, the Onas almost went deaf and out of breath from their own exhilaration. Then came a torrent of questions; who should they invite, how would everyone convene in the villa before 10:00 am and what could be considered as 'acceptable' attire?

Tinkering on the edge of hysteria, Chinny drew a list of her prospective guests. Father, Mother, Dubem, Adaiba, Uncle Kika, Auntie Violet… She paused, not sure if her ten guests included herself. Deciding it did, she realised she had three slots left. Had Ejiofor not left after Easter, she would have been glad to invite him. But Mr Oliseh's name made the list after Dede confirmed he would be available. A myriad of thoughts filtered through Chinny's head as she fiddled with giving the last two slots to Eniola and her mother. But without a mobile number she could call, Chinny realised the futility in expecting them at the villa by 10:00 am the following day. But her list would not be complete without one person. Chinny decided to ask Rufus for a favour.

The night sped past as nobody in the Onas' home slept before 1:00 am. Their apprehension mixed with excitement caused dizzy spells and at first light, everyone scampered out of their not-so-warm beds, bubbling about ironing clothes and polishing shoes. Frantic demands of "Why did you not pick up my call? Did you see my text message?" "Have you left yet?" and "Where are you now?" were made from different mobile phones.

The handover ceremony fast turned into a fanfare. On learning about the event, lobbying for invites by various individuals of influence seeking relevance hit the government house at all levels. A last-minute adjustment in the initial venue by the event planners became inevitable as the Government House grounds, formerly planned to be the venue, could no longer accommodate the expected number of guests.

Almost bursting with people, Bay Events Centre blazed and buzzed with lights and activities. Representatives from both national and international television stations darted in a flurry of activities. One look at the hall setting, and Chinny's bravado received a blow after she realised how grossly underdressed she and her guests looked. They took a table in a corner, close to obscurity but that did not appease the god in one of the ushers, who relocated them to the table closest to the exit. She wanted an apparently more affluent group to take their original table. Chinny and her guests did not appear to mind as they cheerfully obeyed the usher, grateful they received an invite in the first place.

They soaked up all the entertainment from dance troops, poets, musicians, comedians, stage plays and choirs. Ejiofor implored, so Chinny took as many snapshots and videos as her phone memory could handle. Though good-natured and grateful, it was hard for Chinny and her guests to pretend not to notice how the different coloured and delicious-looking drinks in glasses, arrays of exotic snacks and other appetite-stimulating finger foods showcased masterful creativity in circumventing their table. Added to not being catered for, they were constantly bumped into and stepped on as the ushers carried on with their duties in skewed enthusiasm.

Chinny's phone began to vibrate. Unable to recognise the number, she picked up the call and strained to hear the caller. "Kenneth?" she shrieked. She could barely hear him and made to step outside, but the entrance was now choked by two bodyguards in white shirts and dark suits, cautious in their attempt to disperse a crop of guests, who judging by their shiny shoes, wristwatches and jewellery, gave the impression of being the crème of the society. They wanted a glimpse of the two new guests who had just arrived at the venue.

The crowd refused to budge but the men in dark suits, now desperate, began to body-shove them. Scanning for an exit door, Chinny made to step back, but caught a glimpse of the six-inch long shining silver steel in the gaping jacket of one of the bodyguards and everywhere started to twirl before her. Last night's dinner attempted a sneak peek through Chinny's mouth and shutting her eyes tight, she charged out of the venue with the strength of an angry bull. Strong arms caught her as she fell head-long screaming, "Chimooooo Chimooooo!!!"

Four bodyguards succeeded in barring guests from rushing out while one extricated Chinny from the arms of one of the new guests who just arrived. After a quick scan, he certified Chinny unarmed and harmless. The light-skinned man in whose arms she fell, chuckled with a strange accent, "Young lady, I am also delighted to see you, but I must look a lot like your Chinese friend 'chee-mooo'. My name is Hugo Dolores, President of the Dominican Republic. What is your name?"

A bodyguard who Chinny now recognised as one of the men who delivered her invite the day before asked, "Chinny Ona?" Still dry-mouthed, Chinny bobbed her head up and down in quick succession.

He muttered to his colleague who whispered to the President of the Dominican Republic and another security official. Whatever information being passed filtered through the security officials until it reached the President of the Federal Republic of Nigeria.

Chinny was a bundle of nerves as she stepped aside for the entourage to file in. The President of Nigeria stopped by her and whispered, "You are one brave young lady and I consider it a privilege to meet you." He continued with the procession, leaving a thoroughly unsettled and open-mouthed Chinny. All the guests got on their feet at the announcement of their arrival. And as soon as the entrance cleared out, everyone on the Onas' table ran out to find Chinny still rooted to the ground. They understood what happened to Chinny and assured her that in time, the sight of a gun would cease to evoke the kind of fear she just exhibited.

At the end of the national anthem, the most remarkable thing happened. The moderator's voice rang through the public address system. "Chinny Ona and her guests are to please come up to the table reserved for them. Chinny Ona, please, where are you? You and your guests have a reservation. Kindly indicate and you would be ushered to your table." Their chatter took a nose-dive as alarmed bright eyes stared at confused bright eyes. Taking unsure steps to their new table, Chinny saw Mr Peters. His countenance reflected looming implosion and in one moment of sudden triumphant discovery, she not only saw, but heard the void in his heart scream in frustration and silent desperation. A soothing freshness coursed through Chinny's once-battered mind, as she, with a smile borne out of unalloyed pity spreading across her face, sashayed past him to take her table.

The rest of the events went on in rapid succession. The state governor gave his speech where he almost beat to death the stance of the Federal Republic of Nigeria on human trafficking in any form, and vowed not to relent in the development of systems geared towards promoting deterrence-oriented consequences. Soon after, Chief Utah gave his speech, asserting his position on human trafficking. He ended with profound apologies for not paying enough attention to those he entrusted with his property and promised to spend his lifetime making right the wrong he unwittingly caused.

Afterwards, the visiting president reiterated his country's disposition towards child labour, human trafficking and female repression. He thanked his host country for giving the Dominican Republic the benefit of the doubt and vigorously working with his government to annihilate the racket.

Gripped with fear at how close by crime lived, everyone watched a playlet illustrating the sordid episode at the villa, as presented by a group of secondary school students. After the playlet, more background music in the company of even more food, drinks and snack bites flowed through the hall. This was an interlude thought by most guests to be a welcome reprieve from the several lengthy and thought-provoking speeches.

President Bennett C. Okofeli of the Federal Republic of Nigeria inhaled the charged air and nodded in appreciation, waiting for the eardrum-popping applause that heralded him to the podium to fade. He thanked the government of the Dominican Republic and all the guests who took time out to celebrate the safe return of the girls. Recalling how far the human race had come since the eradication of the legal slave trade, he stated that the discovered ring and countless others yet to be exposed, ran nothing short of slave camps and urged everyone to shun them in their entirety. A further charge to parents, to not only care for their children, but pay particular attention to their female children and wards, met with vigorous nods and exclamations of "Exactly, true talk and tell them!" from the testosterone-rich crop of guests.

At the end of his speech, the president recognised the young lady, whose quest to find her missing brother led to the exposure of the callous and criminal web. Amidst thunderous applause, Chinny and all sixteen girls responded to the president's invitation to join him on the platform. Scholarship grants, up to university graduate level, were given to those of the girls interested in formal education. For those who didn't care much about following the academic path, opportunities to train for any vocation of their choice were given. On graduation, they would be set up as caterers, bakers, fashion designers, make-up artists or the like. Wild with excitement, more applause reverberated through the hall as they filed out, most of them running into the waiting arms of their emotion-bashed folks.

With the glee on Adaiba's face as she munched on the large onion rings from her plate of what resembled peppered snails in tomato sauce, Chinny could tell she was missing out on all the sumptuousness being served at her new table and made to return to it at once. But the president motioned for her to stay behind. His next words made her almost swoon.

"I believe any lady with such courage and resilience would have a word of inspiration or two." Cameras zoomed in on Chinny and the air in the room became too heavy for her to inhale. A speech?! She had not prepared for any speech. Dry-mouthed with a distinct awareness of the fast-forming sweat in her underarms, Chinny's eyes flipped to her folks. Ama's forehead, furrowed with a single line, threatening to splice the bridge of her nose in two, Adaiba's smile, unsure as the waves and Dede's bland face did nothing to tell her everything would be fine. Then she saw him… Chief Utah gave Chinny the double-thumbed 'okay' sign and the biggest smile she saw in all eighteen years of her existence. Rubbery legs floating on unending applause and blinding camera flashes carried Chinny towards Nigeria's number-one citizen, to stand before the microphone he had been talking into a little while before.

Once she stood before the microphone, the silence became as deafening as the just settled applause. This had to be one bubbly dream. None of this was real. And in a voice she hardly recognised as hers, Chinny began.

18

"GOOD AFTERNOON DISTINGUISHED LADIES AND GENTLEMEN. This has come to me as a huge surprise, but how dare I refuse my president's request?" Light applause and laughter rang through the hall. She continued, the initial tremor in her voice ebbing. Thanking the government for inviting her and her guests, she talked briefly about her family background, mentioning their slog up the mountain of life and the values they live by – love, friendship and mutual respect. Factors responsible for making her strong even when she had no reason to be.

At the end of her speech, questions were granted. The state television correspondent went first.

"How were you certain of your brother's detention in Chief Utah's villa?"

In response, Chinny said, "The security guard to the villa happened to be a good friend of mine. He mentioned some troubling events happening in the villa and also told me that Chief Utah was not nearly as terrible as he had been made out to be. This gave me the courage to press on with my quest. More so, my initial chance meeting with the chief helped me put the final bounce on my courage." Mild laughter bubbled through the hall.

A radio station representative asked her to talk about her encounter with Chief Utah at the car park and in as few words as she could manage, Chinny narrated the botched theft which was to set the tone for all that happened afterwards. Next was the national television correspondent.

"We gather that you do not have a secondary education. How did you come to sound this well-read and impressively exposed?"

Chinny paused for a heartbeat before she responded, "For as long as I can remember, life has not been an amusement park for my family. So, an education for two children in the same family, a concept taken for granted by many, became a luxury fit for only the more fortunate. But, my childhood friend Ejiofor, handed down all his used books to me, with which I home-schooled myself, prepared for and sat for the private general certificate examinations. So, on the contrary, but for the unfortunate cancellation of my results, I am almost certain that I would have been a secondary school certificate holder." A round of thunderous applause rang through the hall.

The moderator granted one last question, and a lady took the opportunity. Her cameraman had the inscription 'CNN' on his shirt and camera.

"Being a female yourself, what do you propose would put an end to human trafficking of females in particular?" she asked.

Chinny's eyes sparkled when they rested on Mrs Johnson, her former principal. Rufus kept his promise and left at first light to deliver the hand-written invitation to her. Chinny's many years of self-doubt, punctuated by her school principal's sedulous words of inspiration, "You can be anything you want to be, Chinny, never forget that!" hurled at her even when they met at her mother's vegetable stall, crystallised into one precise truth... regardless of what life flung her way, history would make her important today. She began to tap the pad of her right foot, and with her voice as crisp as new bank notes, she responded:

> *"The popular opinion would be to educate the girls, but I say, educate the girls and especially the boys. My rather young but eventful life still teaches me that the concept called education is not limited to how well one can reproduce what has been taught in class. Education is developing mutual respect for individuals – male or female. It is religious, cultural and ethnic tolerance. Education means cultivating a lifestyle relentless in its quest to rise above mediocrity, both when abounding and when abased. It creates in everyone a receptacle large enough to contain whatever surprises life throws your way. The male child*

is the lever sitting on the fulcrum of human existence. He must be taught from an early age that enslavement, debasement or repression of the female is not a prerequisite for attaining a good life, influence or respect. A man with such values inculcated in him would never represent the decadence we so furiously fight today. Instead, he would be a true reflection of an angel, casting illumination in every dark crevice of human existence. I should know – I am surrounded by a plethora of them. My best friend Ejiofor – he made my journey seem like a walk in the cool evening breeze. My Uncle Kika brought to earth my adorable and supportive cousin, Adaiba. My friend Kenneth who I once suspected to be an actual angel. There is Mr Oliseh, a man with a heart large enough to contain everyone in this hall, and my brother Dubem who I secretly call my sacrificial lamb – a fine gentleman, always happy to make a bridge of himself over a pool of mud for the women in his life. Chief Utah, a man of uncommon honour. There is also my maternal grandfather who made a strong, resourceful and resilient woman out of my mother. And my father, Mr Dede Ona who not only allowed me cross paths with Mrs Johnson; my inspiration, but also showed me the true meaning of humility, reflected in the courage he applied in facing and dealing with his mistakes. He is a man who loves his two children – male and female – unconditionally and who fought the financial pressures and cultural expectations that sought to rob him of his role as a father. So, my proposal is this – illuminate the boys to grow into men who would someday head homes poised to serve as enabling environments to raise completely rounded individuals – male and female alike. Thank you.”

Chinny received a standing ovation. The tears in Ama's eyes refused to stop flowing. Dede looked like the cat that lapped the last bowl of warm milk; her brother, cousin, uncle and auntie just applauded; Mrs Johnson fought back her tears, while Chief Utah and Mr Oliseh smiled in admiration of the enigma called Chinny Ona.

191

Clips of the official handover aired on the 7 o'clock news of the same day and many days after. The Cable News Network tagged their interview with Chinny – "Illuminate the boys – the solution to female repression, through the eyes of a Nigerian teenage girl". And as is known to be typical, CNN aired it four times a day, over four days.

Countless calls and text messages from Kenneth literally overwhelmed Chinny's phone memory. After a sizable volume of her giddiness diffused, she returned his calls. Kenneth explained that shortly after her admission and following certain events he would rather not rehash, he went into his usual solitary confinement and by the time he came back to civilisation, she had been discharged from the hospital. On reaching Chinny's home in search of her, he learnt about the fire and would have called her but lost his mobile phone and it took an unusual stretch of time to retrieve his contacts. Now in Greece for a short medical course, he promised to visit as soon as he returned. Beyond pleased to hear her friend was all right, Chinny attempted to thank him for all his help and also broach the subject of the hospital bill refund but met with the stiff rebuff she now learnt would remain a radiant feature in their interactions.

Proud to be remotely associated with Chinny, Ejiofor could barely cap his excitement and did not stop telling everyone who cared to listen that she has been his best friend since he said his first words… Though Chinny thought his claims may be adding an extra three years to the lifespan of their friendship.

Events following the handover ceremony were surreal. Adaiba received a re-invitation for her GCE result defence and right after the ten-minute interview, skipped away with a printed copy of her results. Chinny's results arrived at the villa by courier with a note of apology, saying that her interview with CNN was enough defence.

Weeks down the line, after Donald introduced Mel to the Onas as his soon-to-be bride and informed them of his intention to relocate to Abuja immediately after the wedding, Ama submitted her business proposal. She wanted to start up a domestic staff servicing company and hoped to begin her career by staffing Donald Utah's new villa in Abuja. Ama almost floated away on cloud puffs when he said, "Consider your proposal accepted and all your terms and more met." Without thinking to evaluate, Ama threw her arms around her host as happy tears coursed down her face. Now she could really do something gratifyingly filled with purpose. Drifting into sleep that night, Ama thought Donald Utah held a vague familiarity to someone she could not quite remember but waved it off at once as a fall-out of her appreciation of his unusual munificence.

⌒⌒

One fine afternoon, Rufus alerted Chinny of a courier asking to see her. Her hands shook as she accepted and signed for the mail. Global Women's Network Worldwide (GWNW), a non-governmental organisation in partnership with the First Lady of the United States of America, had invited Chinny to not only attend a seminar, but tell her story to other ladies aspiring to rise above constraining factors like poverty, early marriage, rape, neglect and low self-worth. If she accepted the invite and informed them via her electronic mailing address, the visa, tickets and itinerary would be arranged.

Awake in bed and reflecting on the events of the past couple of months, Chinny Ona shuddered at how far she and her family had come. Though not deluded into thinking about life as one big tea party, since there were still issues to surmount, her heartfelt gratitude to Donald Utah as he now insisted on being addressed, remained undiluted. She and Dubem now actively researched schools and were also taking relevant examinations to aid their admission into the university. Life seemed to have finally lifted the sledgehammer off the Onas – or was it merely time and chance at play?

EPILOGUE

The calm November breeze played with the sand and trees on the Burj Al Arab beach, Jumeirah. Holidaymakers idled in the evening sun, enjoying the natural luxury which Dubai's iconic hotel offered.

"Phone call for you Dr Clarke," the waiter's voice rang through the cool ambience. It was 4:30 pm and the conference convener called to confirm that the event would begin in two hours. It was a good thing the meeting would be held in one of the hotel's many auditoriums. Taking the last sip of the decadently delicious fruit cocktail, Dr Clarke settled for a quick nap. The alarm tone of the mobile phone could rouse anyone out of slumber, however unwilling.

At 5:35 pm, the alarm went off and an unconscious arm stretched out to hit the snooze button. Ten minutes later an even more annoying ring-tone blared from the phone and Dr Chinny Clarke gave up.

Many years ago, as a little girl, Chinny dreamt of a day when she would be able to sleep for as long as she liked without a zealous cock crowing or her father clearing his throat in warning for her to wake up or else... Today, the cock was her infinitely annoying alarm clock and her husband's adamant phone call now served as her father's warning.

"Hello Eji," Chinny purred.

"Hi wife. Get your lazy bones up. There are thousands of ladies waiting for you to breathe life on their dying dreams", Ejiofor jabbed her in that way only he knew how. With eyes crinkling at the sides in soundless giggle, Chinny got up from her cabana and sauntered towards the hotel block, wondering if or when her dream to sleep for as long as she liked would ever become a reality.

It was not the first time and held no promise of being the last time that Chinny would receive a standing ovation after a presentation. As she stood on the podium amidst loud applause, she closed her eyes briefly to savour another one of her humbling moments, knowing that the eyes of the grand master of this orchestra called Life remained wide open, and would always align her waves for a perfect sail.